SUTPHIN BOULEVARD

SANTINO HASSELL

DREAMSPINNER PRESS

Published by
DREAMSPINNER PRESS

5032 Capital Circle SW, Suite 2, PMB# 279, Tallahassee, FL 32305-7886 USA
http://www.dreamspinnerpress.com/

Sutphin Boulevard
© 2015 Santino Hassell.

Cover Photo
© 2015 Mel Seser, http://www.melseser.com.
Cover Model
© 2015 Juan Forgia.
Cover Design
© 2015 Natasha Snow Designs.
Cover content is for illustrative purposes only and any person depicted on the cover is a model.

ISBN: 978-1-63476-325-7
Digital ISBN: 978-1-63476-326-4
Library of Congress Control Number: 2015905045
First Edition July 2015

Printed in the United States of America
∞
This paper meets the requirements of
ANSI/NISO Z39.48-1992 (Permanence of Paper).

For all members of ACA.

Acknowledgments

An extremely large and heartfelt thank you to my beta readers for helping through the first several drafts. Without their in-depth comments and suggestions, this may have turned out to be a very different book.

I also want to thank Adriana for providing translations! She and my beta readers were a huge help in terms of verifying that my portrayal of Puerto Rican culture was accurate and realistic. It's always been important to me to not only write diverse books but to have them be authentic.

Susan Spann was my guiding light when it came to getting through my first publication. With her help, I learned a lot, and that knowledge will be invaluable to me for years to come.

Most of all, I'd like to thank Lenore DiTrani for her editing help and continued encouragement while I was writing this book.

Lastly, I have to give a big shout out to everyone I've met in NA and AA, my pops for giving me my first copy of the ACA big red book, and of course to my first and only true love—NYC.

Chapter One

July

"YOU SHOULD be glad he cheated on you, Michael."

"That's one of the stupidest things you've said to me."

I looked up at the sound of clinking glass. Nunzio was pulling bottles of liquor from a black plastic bag and lining them up on his chest of drawers.

"My point is, Clive was a dick and you were never going to end it. He gave you a way out."

"Whatever you say."

Nunzio finished emptying the bag and balled it up. "Stop moping. It's Friday. We're young... ish, in the gayest neighborhood in New York, and now we're both single. The possibilities are endless."

"The possibilities are annoying."

A few weeks ago, I would have been the first one out the door, but now I couldn't muster a single thread of enthusiasm. I couldn't pinpoint the exact reason why the charm of going to the club every weekend had faded, but it'd likely had something to do with my now ex-boyfriend's endless litany of disapproving complaints.

We'd been together for nearly two years, but Clive had gotten over me at record-breaking speed. In a span of five minutes, he'd called to tell me that we were finished, changed his status on Facebook, and blocked me. Social media made relationships less private and more shallow, and Clive's burning desire to flip me off in front of our mutual friends had led to me deleting my account.

If I wanted to be honest with myself, I should have expected it. There had been red flags from the start. If I had never watched *Closer* and developed an infatuation for Clive Owen, I would have never dated the fuckhead. The name had hooked me, and his body had drawn me in, even though he had been smug about everything from his appearance to his law career. I'd let those minor niggles slide until his aggressive insecurity caused me to consider jumping back into the sea without a life jacket. But he'd decided to end it before I'd found the courage to do it first.

"You look so damn miserable, Mikey. It's making me want to smack you around a few times."

"What do you want me to say? It was brutal, and I'm in a bad mood."

"How brutal?"

"Humiliating."

Nunzio's pale blue eyes flashed the way they did when he was ready to light the fire on his Sicilian temper and go explosive on someone who had pushed him—or someone he cared about—a little too far.

"What did that motherfucker say to you?"

"The usual. I'm just a broke-ass teacher with a bum-ass family, and I drink too much and spend too much time with you. Us going to Italy together this summer was his breaking point, so he took the liberty of banging other dudes for the past few months until he found a suitable replacement."

"Want me to fuck him up?"

"Oh please. I could fuck him up if I wanted to, pendejo. But we're thirty-two, not eighteen, and it doesn't work that way anymore. Just forget it."

Nunzio was still looking like he wouldn't mind imprinting his knuckles on Clive's fine-boned face, and the sight of him all bent out of shape was enough to make me smile for the first time all day.

I stood. "Cógelo suave. I'll be fine."

"You sure? Because—"

"I said I'm fine. I'm more pissed off than hurt. It's okay. I'll go out."

It wasn't really okay, but I didn't want to be responsible for Nunzio's pretty-boy face going all mean mug, or the way his shoulders built up with tension. We'd known each other since we were twelve, and he'd been protective of me since then, even though I'd grown up taller and broader.

I rubbed Nunzio's shoulder. "Seriously. Relax."

"Fine." Nunzio gestured to the bottles he'd lined up. "Pick your poison. It's time to get faded."

I nodded at the tequila, and he measured out the shots. I watched the amber liquid pool in miniature glasses from different vacation destinations around the world and tried to rally myself for the night. Nunzio and I had stumbled our way into adulthood drunk and oversexed, and we'd always had a good time doing it. Even if I was tired of the club scene, I knew we would ultimately have fun.

We did two shots together before Nunzio assessed my outfit.

"I hope you know you're not going out like that."

"Why not?"

He scoffed, not dignifying the question with an answer. Tall, well-built, and lankier than I was, Nunzio looked sharp in dark jeans and a button-down. He didn't try very hard, but he didn't have to—his piercing eyes, olive skin, and tousled black hair ensured that he always looked gorgeous. My tendency to forget to shave and my love for time-beaten T-shirts and broken-down jeans put me into the hot mess category more often than not.

"I don't look that bad."

"You look like you're about to start doing jazz hands for change on the subway. Did you even shower?"

"I brushed my teeth."

Nunzio gave me a look of disgust. "Look, I know you're upset, and I don't blame you, but we can't go have rebound fucks if your ass isn't even washed. It's inconsiderate and unhygienic."

"Christ. It's not like I skipped out on my annual bathing."

"Go, you filthy animal. I actually have clean towels this time."

He blasted music while I showered, but my enthusiasm was still nil despite his efforts. I finished up, left the stubble spreading across my jaw, and didn't bother styling my hair. By the time I left the bathroom, Nunzio had found me an outfit more appropriate for hunting down a rebound lay.

"We could just stay here and drink."

"No, dude. When you get dumped, you have revenge fun."

"You sound like a fucking rom-com." I approached the dresser and downed two more shots in quick succession.

"Whoa, whoa, whoa." Nunzio held up his hands. "Put on the brakes, big boy. It's called pregame, not introduction to sloppy drunkenness before we even get to the damned club. Slow that freight train of intoxication down."

"I'm good." I loosened the towel wrapped around my waist and dried myself in front of him, shaking my head at the theatrical leer he aimed at my dick.

"I can't believe that idiot cheated on you. You're almost as hot as me."

I didn't answer. I jerked on the slim-cut jeans and the random black polo he'd decided I should wear. Everything felt too tight on my broader frame, but he walked around me as if assessing whether or not I'd get him any good offers on the auction block.

"Your ass looks good in those jeans."

"Great."

Nunzio stopped in front of me and crossed his arms over his chest. "Your bulge looks good too. Damn. I dunno if I like you being my competition for meat."

"Get over it, Medici," I said with a half grin. Nunzio got competitive over everything from teaching practices to how much ass we got at a club. "If you want me to get into party mode, you better get used to it. Just wait until we leave for Italy. It will be no-holds-barred."

"Give me a break. Even before your boring-ass boyfriend was in the picture, it wasn't no-holds-barred."

Nunzio bumped me out of the way of the mirror and adjusted his own collar, popping it up before smoothing it back down with a grimace, and then angled himself sideways to check out his profile. He adjusted his dick, stared harder, then gave a decisive nod.

I stifled a laugh.

"Let's do this."

I WAS starting to hate nightclubs almost as much as I hated Top Forty, and even Nunzio could not change that. Between the endless stream of either heckling or harassment from strangers with you-better-fuck-me smiles, and the depressing spectacle of at least a dozen fading gays yearning for approval as they watched the dance floor from the bar, only Nunzio's energy kept me in the game. That being said, I did like to dance. As much as rhythmic grinding could be called dancing.

We'd only been at the club for an hour, and I was already three sheets to the wind and writhing against the nearest hard bodies. Sandwiched between my best friend and a tattooed guy in a sideways baseball cap, life could have been worse.

I gasped in Nunzio's ear that I was thirsty, and he shoved me in the direction of the bar.

Clive popped into my head, uninvited. I scowled at the bartender, demanding water, and banishing the mental image of my ex. Who cared if he'd always taken care of me when I drank too much? He'd been lining up backup generators in case the power in our two-year relationship fizzled.

"Come on," I muttered, glaring at the bartender's back. "I just want some water!"

The bartender turned, scathing in his spike-covered vest, and gave me a glass of water the size of a thimble.

"Fuck you too."

The aggressive beat of the music almost drowned out my voice.

"What do you expect? You snapped at him as soon as you got here, and I've been waiting ten minutes for a beer."

I looked to my left, prepared to unleash the full extent of my rage on the poor bastard who'd dared to speak, but the words shriveled up before I could get them out of my mouth.

The guy was lovely.

I noticed the smile first—too big, drunken, but bright enough to light up a funeral parlor. He had a great face—big dark eyes that stood out like coals in a pale face, wide mouth, and platinum hair. He was several inches shorter than I was, and his body looked slim beneath a T-shirt emblazoned with the periodic table.

"Nice shirt you have there. Nerd."

"What's nerdier? Me wearing it or you knowing what it is?"

"What idiot wouldn't recognize the periodic table?"

The guy raised his hand and twirled his finger to indicate the people around us. "Mostly everyone who's tried to shove their hand up it."

"Big tally?"

"Could be if I'd thought to keep one. Keeping track of the number of morons in the world didn't seem like a useful way to spend my time."

I wanted to have sex with him.

"Who's this?" Nunzio slung an arm around my shoulders and sloppily kissed my cheek. He squinted down at T-shirt Guy. "Whoa, the periodic table! That's awesome!"

I wanted Nunzio to piss off. Instead of saying so, I shoved him away and wiped my face.

"It would figure that the only two smart people in this establishment are together."

"We're not toge—"

"It's because we're teachers," Nunzio interrupted. "Teachers are supposed to be smart or the world turns out stupid."

I willed a sinkhole to open under Nunzio's feet.

"I'm Nunzio and this fine as fuck Puerto Rican piece of man-meat is my best friend Michael."

"I'm David."

"Hello there, David." Nunzio grabbed the front of the shirt and tugged David closer. "So, check it. Michael just broke up with his boyfriend. You should suck his dick to make him feel better."

I hated Nunzio less. Especially when David looked up at me with a 100 percent interested smile.

WE CRASH-LANDED into a cab at five in the morning. Nunzio swiped his credit card at nothing, missing the card reader twice before managing to pay, because he had one hand down David's pants while David tried to figure out how my tonsils tasted. The cabbie watched us in the rearview mirror, unmoved.

"No mess," he said when David let out a low moan.

"You got it," Nunzio gasped.

The card machine beeped, and I opened my eyes just enough to see Nunzio kick open the door and stagger out. I hauled David out with me, nearly breaking my neck when the guy shoved me backward in an attempt to grind up against my dick. My back met air, and I crashed down to the stoop.

"Jesus, you horny little freaks, get your asses inside," Nunzio said with a husky laugh.

"You taste good," David panted into my mouth.

"You taste gorgeous."

My words were nonsensical and so slurred they barely sounded like English, but David didn't seem to mind. He licked the side of my face with a hot, wet swipe of his tongue and followed it up by biting down on my lower lip. The ability to move was fading fast, but Nunzio grabbed my shoulder and hauled me up.

My desire to get David in bed was so urgent, the four flights of stairs seemed more like four hundred. He ripped my shirt off the moment we entered the apartment, and I heard Nunzio flip the locks as we stumbled to the bedroom. Nunzio was close behind, but I almost forgot he was a participant until his breath ghosted along the ridge of my ear.

"Get his pants down."

I nodded and he pressed his face against my neck. I could feel the filthy smile tipping up the corners of Nunzio's mouth as his hands got busy with my belt. When my pants were gaping open, he helped me get David shirtless and worked off his jeans and shoes.

David lay splayed out on the bed beneath us. His heavy-lidded eyes moved between me and Nunzio. He smiled.

I grabbed the band of his briefs and tugged without bothering to be gentle. His dick aligned with his taut stomach and smeared precome on his pale skin.

Nunzio's breath was hot on the back of my neck. "Damn, that slut wants it."

I shuddered at the words and stretched my body along David's, sprinkling kisses along his throat and smiling when I felt the vibrations from his answering moan. I trailed down, dragging wet patches across David's warm, sweaty flesh, and occasionally nipping at it to leave little red marks.

David writhed on the bed, making breathless noises that were eventually muffled—by Nunzio, I assumed, because his presence disappeared from my back. I looked up, and my dick pulsed in response to seeing my best friend balls-deep in David's mouth.

It was hot—intensely, incredibly, mind-blowingly so. Before I'd drenched myself in shots and beer chasers I hadn't wanted to share, but now it didn't matter. Without Nunzio orchestrating this little porn opera, I wouldn't have even been able to skin David out of his pants. And being this close to Nunzio while he used the guy's mouth was more of a turn-on than I'd expected. In fact, I couldn't stop staring at his cock—slick with saliva and so hard the veins protruded.

"Jesus, his mouth is sweet."

My hands went still, and David was temporarily forgotten. I lost my fucking mind at the sound of Nunzio's voice scraping out low and throaty, his eyes closed and head tilted back just so. I only stopped staring when Nunzio bucked his hips forward hard enough for David to jolt.

I exhaled and knelt between David's thighs again, tracing my tongue up the side of his dick before wrapping my fingers around the root. I sucked on the head, flicking my tongue along the slit, and started working his girth with my hand as I took him deeper into my mouth.

David's hips gave a stutter before flexing into a full-on, brutal face pounding, and I pumped and sucked to help edge him along.

My own erection was agonizingly hard. The feeling intensified every time I looked up to find Nunzio staring. He seemed transfixed, and that ratcheted up my pulse further.

"Shit, Michael, you suck dick like a pro." Nunzio pulled back, his cock stiff and damp with spit. "I want to watch you fuck him," he said.

I sat up on my knees, fly hanging open and jeans sliding down my hips like the request had been a command. My belt buckle hit bare flesh, and the cold scrape of it snapped me out of my daze.

"You want it?" I asked David.

I caressed his smooth, pale thighs, gliding up and down, before brushing his balls with my thumbs. I could hear things being knocked around in the side table that was still littered with empty shot glasses.

"Yeah," David whispered. "We could take turns."

The square of a condom smacked me in the chest.

Nunzio chuckled. "Nah. Sorry, champ. We're not about that life. A little touchy, some huggy, but no fucky when it comes to Michael and me. Unless he's feeling adventurous...."

"Shut up." I ripped open the condom and rolled it onto my dick.

"Too bad," David said. "You look good together." He bent his legs at the knees, spreading them, and my balls tightened at the sight of his hole waiting and wanting.

"Too many clothes, Mikey."

Nunzio's voice came from behind me again. His hands hooked into the belt loops of my jeans and tugged them down all the way. He wrestled them off and forced me to relinquish my hold on David to free myself of shoes and pants. Nunzio squeezed my cheek to illustrate the a-little-touchy rule, and muttered something about my ass having been wasted on the ex. Then he reached around and slathered my dick with lube, teasing me with two pumps of his hand.

"Fuck," I gasped.

"You want this little twink's ass, not my hand. Right?"

A faint, pathetic noise escaped me. I realized that I wanted both.

"He talks a lot," David slurred.

"It's part of the charm." Nunzio gave the cheek he'd just squeezed a firm smack. The head of his own dick crested along my ass. "Rail this motherfucker while I jerk off on you."

The abused curve of David's mouth curled up into a dirty smile. I grabbed one of his hips, guided him up, and I slammed in with one smooth thrust.

"Oh shit," David gasped. His back bowed, and his fingers clawed in the wreckage of Nunzio's bed.

He was so tight that I released a sharp cry. It was too high, too desperate, and too close to a needy whine to belong to me. Nunzio made an appreciative noise in my ear, bit it, and rutted up against my ass like maybe he wanted to get in it after all. I pushed back on him and reached behind to grab his hamstring.

"Don't tempt me, Michael," Nunzio whispered. "Don't fucking do it unless you want it."

I ground back on him again, drunk and mindless, knowing only sensations and no logic as he humped my ass with more intent. My mind supplied images of him drilling into me, using me as I used David, and I pushed back harder.

"Oh fuck, maybe this was a bad idea."

"Shh," I breathed in a way that was likely not reassuring at all, and started a slow, rocking rhythm as David stared right up at me.

Between him and the surprising way Nunzio was turning me inside out with lust, this was a hell of a rebound.

I dipped my head forward, and slid my tongue between David's parted lips while my hips went to work. We tongued each other until my breath caught in my chest, and I pulled away to lick a trickle of sweat from his temple. Everything about him felt so good that I couldn't get enough, or so I thought until Nunzio yanked me back by a fistful of hair and I had to fight a sudden urge to kiss him too.

I turned my face as I slammed my hips forward, and Nunzio's mouth latched onto my neck. He sucked lightly, and I knew his eyes were glued to the way my dick was stretching out David's hole. I couldn't rip my gaze from Nunzio's rapt expression until David started getting loud enough to disturb the neighbors. I took it as a sign to give it to him harder.

It was a rough ride, but David took it all in, wrapping his hands under his knees and holding them up and back so I could angle deep. The pleading noises falling from his mouth should have been enough to enrapture me, but I really just wanted to encourage Nunzio to keep his hands on me. At one point he cupped my balls and my heart stopped, jump-starting only when he pulled away. Every touch of Nunzio's hands on my body was a tease, and I wished I could see him jerking off.

"So hot," he panted. I could feel the head of his dick gliding against my ass with each of his strokes. His free hand grasped my jaw as he spoke directly into my ear again, deep voice reverberating. "Give him that big dick, Michael, and make him fucking come."

"*Fuck.*"

Heat sluiced through me, and when Nunzio's fingers brushed my lips, I sucked them into my mouth in a fit of delirium. I blew the long digits like I'd have blown his cock.

"Jesus Christ."

Nunzio's voice broke on the last syllable, and his hips shifted, angling up with a low groan. The sudden burn of my ass being breached swept through my nerves. I shouted in surprise.

His cock slid home deep inside me, but the pain didn't override my hunger for him. I lost my grip on David when Nunzio speared into me with two more delicious strokes. I wanted—needed—more, but he came on the next thrust, and the hot rush of his semen filled me.

David arched up, planting his hands on the mattress, and kissed me again. I tensed, bowstring tight, and fucked myself back on Nunzio before shoving my hips forward to impale David on my dick. Nunzio was still stiff and rooted in my ass, his breath guttering out when he reached around to jerk David with erratic twists of his wrist. Things got messy and tangled, hands and mouths everywhere and a cluster of three deep voices encouraging and groaning, until David came all over Nunzio's hand and I busted so hard I lost the ability to breathe.

I listed forward, but a sticky hand held me in place.

"Sorry," Nunzio muttered.

"'S okay."

I pulled away and collapsed on the bed next to David. He rolled on his side, exhausted and sweat-covered, and curled against me like the spot under my chin was made just for him.

"Adorable."

Despite the sarcasm oozing from his voice, Nunzio cozied up behind me and wrapped an arm around my waist. He buried his nose in the nape of my neck, muttering another abashed apology, and I dozed off sandwiched by them both.

Chapter Two

THE ROOM was burning hot. Why wasn't the air conditioner on? I tried to shift on the sweat-soaked bed, but someone was crammed against my back and drooling down my neck. I knew the offender was Nunzio even with a timpani drum banging inside my head.

I slammed my elbow into his sternum with pissed-off, hungover lack of care that he might be in a similar state.

"Get offa me."

He grunted and detached himself with an incomprehensible slurry of Italian swearwords. He rolled over, splayed out, and continued to take up the majority of the space.

Nunzio was definitely not cut out for sharing a bed.

The thought brought a realization to mind, and I jerked up too fast for the state of my stomach. I lunged for the side of the bed and crashed to the floor in a heap of limbs, just managing to grab the wastebasket before upchucking.

Nunzio peered down at me. "Ugh. You couldn't make it to the toilet, bro?"

"Shut up." When I stopped heaving, I leaned on the wall and shuddered.

Nunzio moved to the edge of the bed with the sheets pooled in his lap. The memory of him fucking into my ass while I sucked on his fingers wanted to leap to the forefront of my discombobulated brain, but I wouldn't let it.

"Where's that guy?"

"Made tracks as soon as the sun came up." Nunzio stretched, yawning and arching his back with a ripple of flexing muscles. "He woke me up to lock the door behind him and wouldn't look me in the eye. I think he was embarrassed that he got used. Or else he had morning-after shame because of a boyfriend."

"So I'm guessing he didn't leave a number."

"No." Nunzio stared at me like I'd sprouted another head. "What the fuck, did you think that was a date?"

"No, but I wouldn't mind railing his sweet ass again." I groaned. "Help me up."

Nunzio grasped my hands and pulled me to my feet, allowing me to slump against him.

"Oh God. Just kill me."

"Nah. I think I'll keep you around for a while."

"No, seriously, just fucking kill me."

Nunzio guided me to the bathroom and turned on the shower, then nudged me under the spray. I couldn't even shoot him a grateful smile because I was too busy sliding down the tile and sprawling on the floor with the water beating down on me. I fumbled for the knob to reduce the temperature. The steam didn't help the building pressure in my skull, but having the sweat washed off my body was worth it.

The night before returned unbidden. It had been like something out of a porno and easily the hottest sexual encounter of my adult life. It was weird that Nunzio had been part of it. Even though we're both gay, we had never done anything beyond an awkward kiss in middle school. But there was no awkwardness now. He was treating me the same as always, despite me having invited his dick into my ass by grinding all up on him while sucking on his fingers like a whore.

I went from flaccid to semihard, but I didn't make a move to touch myself. Ejaculating while half-dead and passing out in the shower wasn't going to improve my situation at all. Even so, it took a lot of willpower to ignore—especially the mental images of him combined with David.

There was always the possibility that someone had only been attractive through a filter of alcohol and lust, but I distinctly recalled a tight, fit body, a fat ass, and the kind of mouth that had been engineered solely for giving head.

I wished I'd been awake to demand a number. Or for threesome round two. Maybe with Nunzio in me for longer.

"You all right?"

"Uh, yeah."

Nunzio slid back the shower door and poked his head in. "Have you even moved? It's been like twenty minutes."

"If I stand up, I'll die."

"Oh Jesus. You act like we ain't never drunk before. I don't know how you're going to survive the summer partying with me in Italy if this is the best you got."

"Suck my dick."

He smiled wide, and I flipped him off. Nunzio just laughed.

TWO HOURS after Nunzio had dumped me back into the bed and left me in his apartment to go be a functional human being, my brother showed up. He nearly kicked down the door after I ignored the first few knocks, and he pounded until I finally dragged my ass out of bed.

"What's taking you so long, son? Unlock the damn door."

"Pérate, pendejo," I growled loud enough for him to hear.

I hesitated, glancing over my shoulder to check for obvious signs of gay sex before undoing the chain. Raymond barged in without a greeting and shoved past me.

Raymond was seven years younger than me, but we were the same height. That was where the similarities ended. His build was leaner, skin a few shades lighter, and he'd come out a lot prettier, despite his perpetual mean mug. I found myself continuously suppressing the urge to take a pair of scissors to the glossy black hair he wore in a long ponytail or ragged knot beneath his baseball cap.

"You realize this is not even my house, right?"

"It might as well be, as much as your ass be over here." Raymond looked around. "Where the fuck is Zio?"

"Don't know. I was hungover, so he didn't wake me up."

Raymond swung his hooded gaze back to me. "Look, you gotta come home."

I glanced at the red numbers on the cable box. It was already four in the afternoon, and I had just begun to kick my headache.

"I don't know about all that. I have a bunch of stuff to do before I leave for vacation in a couple of weeks."

"What vacation? You didn't even tell me."

"I did—you were probably high and playing Xbox." I rubbed my head and willed Nunzio to appear so he could run interference on this developing argument. "I told you I'm going to Italy with Nunzio for a few weeks. I told you this when I bought the ticket back in February."

He still looked at me like I was playing a trick on him.

I heaved an exasperated sigh. "Ray, just tell me what you want."

"We got family shit."

Raymond had this amazing ability to annoy the hell out of me with just one sentence and very little information. We used to be close enough to be friends as well as brothers, but that had changed after I'd moved back to our childhood home in Queens to help take care of our mother. After her death, Raymond had started copping an attitude that reminded me a little too much of my most defiant students.

More often than not I wanted to return to the city and get the hell away from him, but I couldn't bring myself to move out of our mother's house again. I knew it would be condemned if I left it in his care, even though it had been more his home than mine for the past decade. Raymond seemed hell-bent on doing as little as possible until the money our mother left him was gone.

"What are you talking about?" I slid off the arm of the couch and sank down onto one of the cushions.

"I told you—we got family shit."

"Ray, I'm hungover. I don't have patience for fifty questions."

"That's your problem. I got the car. Get your shit on so we can go." Raymond looked at his watch. Perhaps he didn't have room in his busy schedule of Xbox, weed, and random fuck buddies to squeeze in my demands for clarity. When I just stared up at him, he kicked my foot. "¡Vete!"

"Vete p'al carajo." I kicked him back. "What the hell is your problem?"

"Look, Dad showed up, and I don't got the patience for him. He and Titi Aida came by all of a sudden, claiming he needs cash and a place to stay."

My stomach twisted in a way that had nothing to do with my hangover. "No thanks, I'll pass."

"You gotta be kidding me."

"I have to go to the mall, the pharmacy, the cleaners, and I have to figure out what reliable person is going to pay bills at the house while I'm gone. I also have to make sure I'm all planned out for school in September since I won't be back until August. When I say I don't have the time, I really don't have the fucking time. Even if our father decided to pop back up because he's out of beer money."

Raymond didn't respond, and that indicated trouble. When I looked up, his eyes flashed in the way he reserved for fistfights. He reminded me too much of our father when he was angry—how his expression darkened before a coming beatdown. I was inching away when he grabbed my shoulder, but all he did was haul me to my feet.

"If you leave him to me, I guarantee one of us will be in jail before the night is over. Now get your shit on and let's go."

I SLID into the passenger's seat of Raymond's Altima and secured the seat belt to prevent flying through the windshield when he rear-ended someone like an asshole. Raymond's driving was a summation of him as a human being: reckless and much too fast. That, combined with the queasy feeling in my stomach and the reggaeton he insisted on blasting, landed me in a shitty mood by the time we emerged from the heavy traffic on the Queensboro Bridge.

I still knew nothing other than that our father had appeared after months of radio silence and he was being more of a dick than usual. Raymond was so vague and edgy that worst-case scenarios had begun to heighten my tension.

I hadn't seen my father since the day we'd all met with my mother's attorney. Dear old dad had stormed out after realizing he was not a life insurance beneficiary and that the other half of the house was now in my and Raymond's names. It had been an ugly scene, but I'd spent the past six months bracing myself for a reappearance. He always returned once he needed something he couldn't scam from anyone else.

I peered out the window through a pair of aviators and kept my forehead tilted against the glass until we turned into the driveway of the tan clapboard house we'd grown up in.

Raymond shut off the engine and got out of the car, but I remained sitting and stared at the park across the street.

As a teenager I'd cut school in Kings Park on a daily basis to play handball with older guys. I'd picked off the gay or curious ones to take up to the rooftop of one of the nearby apartment buildings to indulge in the kind of casual, reckless sex that would have made my health teacher cringe. I cringed just thinking back on it.

The sound of my aunt Aida's voice floating out from the house prompted me to drag myself out of the car. Unlike my father, she checked in with Raymond and me on a regular basis, but her pleading the old man's case was a totally new development. I wondered what was wrong.

Nothing looked out of place besides the fading paint on the house's vinyl siding and the lawn that was looking increasingly shabby since our mother's death in March. Merengue was playing through the dented screens in the windows, and when I stepped inside, I caught a whiff of my aunt's arroz con gandules.

I'd made it three feet before Aida swept in with a big smile.

"Hey, Titi." I kissed her cheek. "¿Bendición?"

"Dios te bendiga." She pulled away and nodded at the rack by the door. "Take your shoes off."

I complied, even though I was only wearing flip-flops. She made rules for us even when she was in our house.

"What's going on? Where's my father?"

She returned to the bright yellow kitchen, where my father stood by the counter, cracking open a can of beer with a fierce glare on his face. Joseph Rodriguez looked the same as always—lean and tall, salt-and-pepper hair falling in waves down his neck, and wearing a torn-up jean jacket. After her cancer diagnosis, my mother had aged rapidly, but it seemed like Joseph always stayed the same.

His presence unfurled a sense of loathing deep inside me, but along with it came a vexing reminder of the promise I'd made to my mother as she wasted away in the hospice. She'd wanted me to give my father another chance. Until the end, she'd worried more about him than her own well-being.

"Nice to see you too," I said flatly.

He took a gulp of beer and jerked his chin at Raymond, who was glowering by the back door. "Your brother has been talking shit since I got here. Acting like this is his house."

"This is my house." Raymond looked coiled to spring, fingers tucked into his palms and malformed knuckles ready to fight. "You ain't staying here."

"Raymond." Aida slapped her hand against the counter. "Cállate."

"No, fuck that. This piece of shit thinks he can come waltzing up in here like king of the castle every time he needs some dough, but it ain't like that no more. Mami ain't here no more, Joseph. It's a wrap."

My dad looked ready to toss the beer at my brother's head, but Aida intervened. "Raymond, go outside so I can talk to your brother."

Raymond muttered something inaudible and pushed away from the counter. The screen door slammed shut behind him when he stormed out into the backyard. Even covered in tattoos and drenched in bad attitude, Raymond fit in more with the family than I ever had. I was oddly adrift without him in the room.

The sense of not belonging had set in the moment I'd hit puberty, but had grown more pronounced with each year I'd spent living away from my mother and the house, not seeing the rest of my family as I'd created my own life away from them all. I was an outsider, disconnected from the family and off living some foreign lifestyle in Manhattan while Raymond stayed at home like a good son. He'd never worked a real job or bothered with school, but still… he was the one who had been deemed loyal.

I rubbed the back of my neck and looked at the stove instead of the simmering rage brewing inside my father. The makings of a large dinner were in the works, even though it was the middle of the week, and Aida didn't look like she planned on staying the night.

"What's going on?" I asked finally.

"I'm coming home."

"Home," I repeated.

"Yes. I'm moving back in."

Joseph said it like it was the most natural thing in the world, even though he hadn't lived in the house for years. After middle school, he had only dropped in for a few weeks at a time. My mother's continued acceptance of his presence in our lives had always been a complete mystery to me. Especially since he'd always shown up reeking of booze and ready for a fight. He'd only been beaten in the mean department by Nunzio's asshole parents.

The black eye Joseph had given me on my thirteenth birthday had acted as a catalyst for me bonding with Nunzio in the seventh grade. We'd sat next to the chain-link gate during recess, comparing bruises and battle scars. My dad hadn't been around all the time, but Nunzio didn't have the same lucky break. His own parents were awful.

After realizing that Nunzio lived across the park from us, my mother had practically adopted him.

"You can't be serious."

"I don't have to ask you for permission. This is my goddamned house."

I didn't raise my voice, but I did stare at Joseph like he'd lost his mind somewhere in the last six-pack.

"How the hell is this your house? Half is in your name, but you've lived here for a grand total of four months if I put all the days together in the past two decades. Just because Mami let you come in and stay the night every time someone kicked you out doesn't mean you're entitled to anything."

"Michael, stop it. He's your father."

"The hell he is." I shouldn't have been surprised that Aida was taking his side, but I still was. She'd always agreed that he was an absentee bastard who hadn't even bothered to take care of my mother toward the end, but he was her younger brother. Not that their oldest brother was any better. "He didn't take care of us. All he did was show up and try to convince my mother to give him the money for our Christmas presents."

"That was one year—"

"No, it fucking wasn't. All you ever did was use my mother and treat me and Raymond like crap. If you think I'm going to fall for whatever sob story you have now, you're bugging."

Aida put a hand on my father's arm and nodded, giving him the signal to unleash his complete load of bullshit on me.

Except, it wasn't bullshit.

Joseph spoke for the next twenty minutes without interruption. He told me all about needing a stable place to live while battling the aggressive nature of his cirrhosis. He also told me about the effect it was having on his body, and all the ways he was starting to fall apart. At times his voice was unsteady and thick enough to wring an ounce of compassion from my heart before my eyes settled on the beer still clutched in his hand.

He didn't want a place to stay while trying to get healthy. He wanted a peaceful place to drink himself to death. He didn't want help with getting treatment or rehab, he wanted a dark hole to retreat into, even if that meant asking his children to watch another parent slowly die. It was so apparent, and so unbelievably selfish, I couldn't find the words to express how disgusted I was with the entire display. I wondered if, on top of everything else, he really had come to beg for money but knew better than to ask at this point.

By the time Raymond returned to the kitchen, I was staring down at the table and thinking about that last conversation with my mother.

Give him another chance, she had insisted. *Promise me you won't shut him out of your life forever.* And I had fucking promised.

"Listen, mijo, I just want us all to try to be a family again," Joseph said after several minutes had gone by without a word from me. I was picking at the plastic tablemat, trying my damnedest to peel the little coquí frogs from the center. "Your Tío John is coming by tonight to eat with us. Aida cooked and everything."

"She always cooks." Raymond pointed at me. "And I bet he's going back to Manhattan. He don't wanna be here. He has to prepare for his big Italy trip with Nunzio and leave me here to deal with your stupid ass."

"What Italy trip?" Dollar signs were likely popping up in Joseph's head. "You have the money for something like that?"

Raymond had the decency to look regretful for spilling my business. I didn't even bitch at him. The chair scraped along the floor when I stood.

"I'll take the train."

"You haven't seen me in months and you're leaving?" For a moment I thought I saw a glimpse of dejection in Joseph's eyes, but then he took another long drink.

"What does it matter? You're staying, right? Going to fill the refrigerator with beer and cheap vodka and ask me to make you comfortable while you wait to die."

"Michael, stop," Aida said again, tone getting sharper and more impatient. "Have you no shame? If Vanessa was here—"

"Titi, no. Please don't bring up my mother." I blew out a slow breath and tried to keep the heat from my voice. "And to answer your question, I don't have any shame. Not when it comes to this fucked-up situation. Give John my love."

The last part came out heavy with sarcasm, but it was no secret that I despised their older brother. The guy was a homophobic douche bag who'd started with the gay jokes as soon as Nunzio jumped out of the closet with a bullhorn after high school. No one in my family knew that I'd been sucking dick longer than my Sicilian best friend.

Raymond followed me when I strode out of the room, cursing under his breath and sounding just as disgusted as I was. I slid my feet back into my flip-flops, relieved when neither my aunt nor my father followed us.

"I'm canceling the trip. I have to go tell Nunzio."

"For what? I was just fucking with you, man. You should go."

I pushed the door open and stepped outside. My body was tight with building anger that I wanted to unleash on everything around me. "And trust you to pay the mortgage and the utilities? Right. And even if I did, now that he's here, he'll wreck the place and have his lowlife friends over. Maybe a couple of whores he'll pick up on Sutphin Boulevard. And you'll get so pissed off that you'll either try to kill him or spend the whole time getting high in your room while he takes over. Sounds fucking brilliant, Raymond. Do you have any other stunning ideas?"

"Don't be a dick about it. Ain't no one telling you to not go on your little trip. Don't put that shit on me."

"I have insurance on the ticket."

A keen urge built in me, making my fingers itch and my hands sweat. I pictured the respectable number of bottles I'd accumulated over time to fashion myself a minibar. Grey Goose, Johnnie Walker, Jack Daniels—one of them would quell the surge of tension and frustration, but I wasn't about to go back up to my room so Aida could spend hours lecturing me.

"Look, do you want a ride?" Raymond pressed. "I wasn't trying to come down on you. I'm just stressed."

I stopped halfway down the driveway. The commute back to Nunzio's apartment would take me an hour, and I was still hungover enough to flip out on the first person who shoulder checked me too hard on a subway platform.

"C'mon, bro. It's the least I can do."

Raymond looked so determined that I acquiesced. He gave me a tight-lipped grin in response.

"It's for the best, though," Raymond said as he peeled out of the driveway, tires squealing. "Because you're right. I'm a fuck-up, and I'll take that motherfucker out if he says the wrong thing. I hate that dude so much. I'll never forget the way he acted after she died. You got no idea."

I had an idea, more of one than he did. Raymond had been too young to remember the details of the explosive arguments between my parents that had finally gone nuclear the day she kicked him out. The memory was burned into my mind, and I saw it every time I saw Joseph.

Him reeking of booze and slurring curses at my mother, and her threatening to take his head off with a cast-iron pan. How I'd feared it would become physical even if it never had. I'd reminded our mother of those things several times in the years that followed, but it had never made a difference. She would just look at me and say I wouldn't understand until I was older.

Twenty years later, and I still couldn't figure out what it was about him that she'd loved. All I felt was resentment for being trapped in a promise I never should have made. Deep down, I'd hoped to never see him again so I wouldn't have to make the attempt.

Raymond was white-knuckling the steering wheel, and the car was void of the music he normally flicked on with a Pavlovian reflex. "You're all dependable," he continued, likely trying to reassure himself more than he was trying to compliment me. "And what if that bastard is actually sick? I won't know what to do. You're the smart one. You knew what to do for Mami."

I looked out at the park again.

"Anyway, do you want to make sure Nunzio is home before I drive all the way over there?"

"It doesn't matter. I have keys."

Raymond gave me a too-knowing look, and I wondered if he was finally seeing through my permanent-bachelor act. It was only a matter of time. But instead of commenting, Raymond silently guided the car back to the bridge.

Chapter Three

I GOT out of the car with a muttered good-bye. Raymond cast me a side-eye full of suspicion but didn't voice any concerns. He never did if he thought he would be rebuffed.

Raymond and I bickered more than 50 percent of the time, but he could read me as well as Nunzio. Even when I thought I was being discreet about my stress level, the kid sniffed it out.

I dragged my feet up to Nunzio's apartment. The hangover had dulled to a faint source of discomfort, but gritting my teeth for the past hour had initiated another throbbing headache. It worsened with every step I climbed.

Sweaty and aggravated, I used the keys Nunzio had given me when he'd first moved in. Nunzio still wasn't home—I didn't know if I was relieved or disappointed. No one could comfort me the way he could, but before the day was over, I would be letting him down.

Less than five minutes later, I had helped myself to an already open bottle of vodka. I sat in an armchair by the window and didn't move until the burn of the alcohol set all thoughts ablaze. Memories of my mother, frail and sunken in a hospital bed, intensified along with my fear that Joseph would soon share her fate.

I didn't want to be concerned. I'd cursed him for most of my life. More than once I'd said I wouldn't even attend his funeral when he died. But now the reality of him being gone was a lot different than me making claims about a future that seemed far away.

Setting down the glass, I tried to shift gears. I turned my thoughts away from my family, away from the hell that would now be my summer, and redirected them to Nunzio.

I got up and paced around, straightening the apartment as I waited for his keys to jingle in the door. I changed the sheets on his bed and threw out empty bottles and a condom wrapper before moving to the living room. I didn't have much to do, but I was jittery with nerves and couldn't keep still. If I sat down, I would end up working through

Nunzio's collection of alcohol, leaving myself a mess by the time I had to break the news that he would be flying to Italy on his own.

He'd been excited for months, planning our itinerary and plotting out a road trip down the eastern coast before ending our trip in Palermo. Just picturing the disappointment on his face when I would have to tell him months of planning were down the drain made my stomach churn.

With no other ways to distract myself, my restlessness tripled, and I left his apartment to go to my favorite bar on Tenth Avenue. I shot Nunzio a text message to meet me there, and hoped the public venue would make this conversation less difficult.

I felt grungy in my jeans and an old T-shirt, but the bar was enough of a dive for no one to care. With the exception of the after-work crowd and a few college kids sitting at a table in the corner, it was empty. The place attracted a mixed clientele during the day because of the cheap food and drinks. It was the one spot in the neighborhood that still reminded me of old school Hell's Kitchen, even if the patrons were now predominately gay yuppies.

I made a beeline for the bar and managed a small grin when I saw a familiar face behind the counter.

"Hey, Miranda."

"Hey, Rodriguez. I haven't seen you around in a while."

I sat at the corner, leaving several stools between me and the small group of guys in suits and ties at the other end. "Yeah, I made the mistake of trying to change my ways because of some asshole's judgment."

Miranda grabbed a wide mug. Without having to ask, she filled it from the tap with Shiner Bock. "That boyfriend of yours?"

"You got it."

"The one that Nunzio bitched about?"

"Maybe. What was the nature of the bitching?"

She set the foam-topped mug in front of me. "A couple of times I asked him where you were and he mentioned how your boy didn't want you going out anymore. Poor bastard. I suggested maybe it's time for him to cut the cord."

I scoffed. "Never."

"That's what he said." She leaned over the counter and clapped my shoulder. "Let me know if you need anything. I've been ignoring the suits for a while now."

Miranda walked to the other side of the bar with a plastered-on smile. I watched her pretend to be interested in their lives without really listening to anything they said. Their voices blended with those of the loud college kids in the corner and the afternoon news playing on the television. The din of noise washed over me, distracting me from my spinning thoughts and the lance of tension that had jabbed at me in the silence of Nunzio's apartment.

Sighing, I stopped examining my mug and looked up at the news. On the TV, a reporter with a chiseled face and earnest eyes was standing at a busy intersection and gesturing to a cluster of police cars behind him. I couldn't hear what he was saying, but I recognized the street. It was only a ten-minute walk from my house.

The banner at the bottom of the screen proclaimed that a teenager had been shot on a city bus. I shook my head. Home sweet home.

I understood why Raymond continued living in South Jamaica, but sometimes I wished he'd let go and move on. He had accepted the crime and neglected public spaces because it meant staying close to our mother, and those family values were ingrained in him deep enough to leave visible marks. She had attempted to instill that same sense of loyalty in me, but her success had been limited. Not wanting to become trapped in the dysfunction of my family in my adulthood, I'd maintained as much distance from them as I could, without going so far that they would implode.

My old neighborhood wasn't all bad, but even my fondest memories didn't make me want to stay in a place that gave the broken-windows theory any kind of validity. Jamaica wasn't the worst, but it was definitely not where I'd pictured living as an adult.

Yet I'd returned and didn't see a way out in the foreseeable future.

"The guy in the striped shirt wants to buy you a shot."

Miranda's voice jerked me out of my reverie. I hadn't even noticed her approach.

"I already have a drink."

She nodded at the other end of the bar. "He thinks you look sad."

I didn't pick myself up from my slouch against the bar, face still braced in one open palm. I peered past her—the guy in question was giving me an appreciative grin. He was good-looking, but I wasn't in the mood to hear anything a buttoned-up yuppie had to say, especially not when I was unkempt, unshaved, and sweating in a torn-up T-shirt. Misery might love company, but Rodriguez men historically liked to suffer in silence—preferably with a bottle of rum while listening to Héctor Lavoe.

"He looks like a banker."

"Close. He's an accountant."

"Sounds thrilling." I turned away again, lifting my mug. "Tell him I'm straight."

Miranda stifled a laugh and returned to the other end of the bar. I didn't watch the exchange. I wondered how transparent my unhappiness was to everyone around me. Ever since my mother's death, I'd had random strangers encourage me to smile. Both men and women liked using the you-look-upset line to spark up a conversation. The logic of harassing a pissed-off or sad person was lost on me. When someone looked like they were in a bad mood, I took that as a sign to leave them the hell alone.

My phone chirped. A message from Nunzio said he was five minutes away.

I made more of an effort to sit up straight and wipe the angst off my face, but the attempt was in vain. He knew something was off as soon as he strode into the bar and took a seat by my side.

"Hey."

"What's going on?"

I resumed my slouch. "We'll talk. Get a drink first."

"Christ. Is it so bad I need to be plied with alcohol first?" Nunzio nodded at Miranda. "Can I get a beer, sweetheart?"

The use of the endearment earned him a lethal glare, but she snorted when he only smiled in response.

"That guy down there is staring at you." Nunzio spun on the barstool so he was facing me, his knees brushing my thigh. "He looks mad, though."

"He tried to buy me a drink. I got Miranda to tell him I'm straight."

"Maybe that's why he's grilling me now. He knows you're full of shit."

Nunzio wiggled his fingers at my admirer in a sarcastic wave. I shoved his hand down to the counter.

"Don't be a dick."

"You're the one who turned down a free drink. The poor guy just wanted an excuse to look into those pretty brown eyes of yours."

"I'm not in the mood. Especially not when his suave way of hooking me was to point out how sad I am."

"You do look like one miserable fuck." Nunzio picked up my beer and gulped it. "So what's going on, Mikey?"

Miranda saved me from answering right away by returning with his beer. They bantered back and forth for a few minutes. To an onlooker, it would have seemed like they were flirting. Nunzio's smile was infectious, and he couldn't stop himself from casually touching people when he talked, not that anyone ever minded.

Nunzio had always been the charming one of our duo. The one who could get an allegedly straight frat boy to drop his pants with no more than a suggestive comment and a raised brow. It was a talent that had kept him away from long-term relationships for most of our adult life. I envied him that, but I couldn't aspire to it, even though all of my attempts at serious dating had failed.

If it wasn't the jealousy at my closeness with Nunzio causing a problem with men I had been with, it was the fact that I wasn't out to my family. Apparently after thirty, people were a lot less compassionate about a grown-ass man being in the closet.

I couldn't deny that continuing to hide it was pathetic, but I didn't see the point in coming out until I was in it for the long haul with someone. My gayness would only sprinkle hot oil on the fire that already blazed between me and the rest of my family. Especially my father.

Nunzio snapped his fingers in front of my face. "What the hell is going on? Is it about last night?"

My train of thought screeched to a halt. "What? No! Why would I be upset about that?"

"Gee, I don't know. Maybe the part where I ad-libbed the porn script and shoved my dick in your ass?"

"Ay Dios…." I glanced around. "Keep your damned voice down."

"Fuck these people."

I elbowed him. "Calm yourself. It's not about that. We were drunk. It happened. It wasn't a big deal."

The corners of his mouth curved down. "That so?"

"That's not what I meant and you know it."

I rubbed my thumb through the gathered condensation on the bar around my mug. Trying to describe the previous night brought up a slew of things that I wasn't in the mindset to deal with. The sight of David shared between us, Nunzio's eyes trained on me in the darkness, and the salty taste of his fingers between my lips right before his thick cock had rammed into me. Bareback.

My mouth went dry, and I shifted on the barstool. That discussion would either have to wait, or never happen at all.

I nursed my beer and glanced over at Nunzio. He was still watching me, clearly expecting a response.

"It was insane," I said finally. "I've never done anything like that before."

"You had fun, though?"

"Yeah, I did."

He nodded, still too serious for the nature of the conversation. "Would you do it again?"

My head filled with a chorus of resounding *yeses*. That morning, stone-cold sober and sick as a dog, I'd thought about having a replay. Hours later, the events of the night before were much further away and an affirmative just seemed awkward.

I rubbed a hand over my face as if that would wipe away the dirty thoughts, along with their effect on me. "Look, I don't know. I can't even think about that now. I'm in a terrible mood thanks to my family, and we need to talk about something real."

"Okay. Sorry. I just wanted to make sure—" Nunzio cut off the sentence with a shake of his head. "Doesn't matter. What's the deal? Is Raymond being a pain in the ass?"

"I wish it were that easy. My father is back and wants to live in the house."

Nunzio's eyebrows disappeared into the unruly mess of his black hair. The grim set of his mouth made it clear he already understood the gravity of the situation. Nunzio had been there for most of the trouble with my father, and had even had some of his own. Joseph was one of those polite homophobes who waited until the offending gay was out of earshot to mutter about their life choices being a shame. Like that made it better.

"Damn. Where did that come from? He hasn't been around in months."

"Not since the reading of the will. He and my aunt showed up and announced that he's moving back in. Since he owns half of the house, there isn't much I can do about it. If I try to throw him out, it will get ugly. My aunt and uncle would for sure fight me on it and probably even take my ass to court."

"What did Raymond say?"

"Looked a few seconds away from throwing his fists up and forcing my father out."

"Sounds like Ray."

"Yeah, exactly. The two of them locked in the house together with nothing to do but be unemployed and ornery is going to make my life really fucking fantastic."

Nunzio winced.

"Your face is my thoughts. I'm so done with all of this shit."

"So be done with it for real. Just move out."

"I can't."

"You did before, and that was when your mother was still living."

We'd had this argument in the past, and it wasn't the first time I felt myself getting defensive in response to the pointed questions. I rolled my shoulders and looked up at the television again.

"Mikey, you gotta stop this shit. I know you feel like it's your responsibility, but at some point you have to live your own life. I've told you so many times before, bro. Move out, save what's left of your sanity, stay with me until you find a new place, and be done with it once and for all."

"And trust Raymond and my father to take care of the house? You know that won't happen."

"Then convince them to sell the house! I'm pretty sure your pops will not argue with the chance to get half of the money you'd earn on it. It's worth twice as much as it was when they bought it."

"No."

"Why? Just explain to me why you want to keep making yourself miserable."

"Because my mother worked herself to the fucking bone to get that house, and I'm not going to get rid of it." My voice rose enough to carry over everything else in the bar. The din of noise quieted. I felt people staring. My face warmed, and I grabbed my beer.

Nunzio spread his hands in surrender. "I just want you to be happy. Okay? Sorry."

"I know that, but you need to understand that it's not as simple as you make it sound. It's complicated. I have to worry about Raymond—"

"Because you and your mother both babied him," he interrupted. "I love Ray like my own brother, but he's twenty-five going on sixteen because no one ever expects him to be anything else."

"Regardless, the damage is done. I can't rely on him, and I definitely can't rely on my father, especially now that he's claiming to be sick."

I launched into the whole explanation, repeating Joseph's story about his short and failed stint in rehab, and the discovery that he had advanced liver disease. I tried and failed to omit the parts about the promise I'd made to my mother and how my resentment over the situation still didn't smother my fear that Joseph was not exaggerating. By the time I stopped talking my voice had a ragged edge and Nunzio was rubbing my back, his strong hand an anchor that kept me from sliding off the barstool and succumbing to weariness and resignation. I wished I'd just waited for Nunzio in his apartment where I could bask in his affection without an audience.

I pillowed my head on my folded arms, sighing when he squeezed my shoulder. He could unwind me with very little effort, but it wouldn't last. It couldn't.

I looked up. "Nunzio, I can't go."

"Can't go where?"

I fought the urge to bury my face in my arms again. "I can't go to Italy. Not with all of this going on."

He stared at me, wide-eyed.

"I'm sorry."

"Michael, we're leaving in like a week."

"I know. You have no idea how sorry I am."

Nunzio dropped his arm, expression disbelieving. "Are you fucking kidding me right now?"

"I wish I were, niño." I covered his hand with my own, squeezing it. "Leaving them in this situation is a bad idea. I can't do it. It would be on my mind the whole time we're over there, and I won't be able to commun—"

"You don't even have insurance on your fucking ticket. There's no way in hell we're canceling this trip because your pops decided now is a good time to make an appearance."

"We're not canceling anything. You're still going."

"Michael…."

The storm brewing on his face was so evident that my stomach started to do backflips. "Nunzio, I'm not going to change my mind. I can't do it. Not like this. Just go and have fun."

"I don't want to go by myself. I want to go with *you*! What part of that is—" Nunzio's barstool scraped the floor with a screech. "What's the point of me going without you?" He clenched both hands in his hair.

"Now who's being ridiculous? What kind of question is that?"

"Ridiculous? Really? You fucking—you really have no idea what the hell—" He broke off, his jaw clenching. We stared at each other as everyone in the bar likely stared at us. Nunzio broke the standoff by taking out his phone. "Fuck this, I'm calling Raymond."

I slid off the stool and grabbed his wrist. "Stop."

"I think he should know you're going to eat fifteen hundred bucks because you completely lack faith in his ability to function."

"Because he has no ability to function." I twisted the phone out of his hand. "Do you think this is easy for me, man? Do you think I'm happy?"

"I think you're an idiot!"

Miranda cleared her throat. I shot her a wild-eyed look.

"Maybe take it outside, gentlemen?"

I opened my mouth to apologize, but Nunzio was already storming out the door. I swore under my breath and fumbled for my wallet, but Miranda shooed me away, telling me to come back to pay later. I tried to force a grateful smile, failed, and hurried out the door after Nunzio. He was pacing the sidewalk outside the bar but spun on his heel and jabbed a finger into my chest as soon as I stepped out of the door.

"It's not your responsibility to take care of them. They're grown people, and you don't always have to fix everything. When are you going to get that through your head?"

"I don't know, but it's not a decision I'm going to make on the fly with my brother threatening to kill my father, and him supposedly on the verge of death. Ay Dios mío, Nunzio, what do you want from me? To just turn my back on them all of a sudden?"

He shrugged, mouth tight. "I did."

"Yeah, but that's different!" I stepped forward, grabbing his shoulder and drawing him closer to me. "Your family was straight-up evil, and my family is just... they're just fucked-up and broken! They didn't ignore me and beat the shit out of me just for the hell of it like your parents did. I can't just say fuck it and go to Italy while Raymond and my father are at each other's throats. I have to be sure my brother will be okay before I take off for a different continent. They're a pain in the ass, but they're still my family."

"So what am I?"

I looked at him through the hazy filter of heat and my throbbing headache. "What do you mean?"

"Nothing. Forget it."

"No, what do you mean?"

Nunzio shrugged, cutting his gaze away from mine to focus on the pavement. "Never mind. I meant nothing."

"Nunzio, please."

When he refused to look at me, I pulled him closer until he had no choice but to meet my eyes. The full weight of his disappointment made the knot of guilt gnaw at me with sharper teeth. His whole demeanor had changed—shoulders sagging and hands balled up like they did when he was forcing himself to stay calm.

I hugged him until he responded to the embrace.

The sun was beating down on my back and my damp T-shirt was sticking to his, but the feel of Nunzio pulling me to him instead of pushing me away made up for all of those petty discomforts.

Suddenly I wanted nothing more than to go back to his apartment and hold him for the rest of the day. We would be separated for the entire summer. I hadn't considered how distressing that reality would be until he'd accepted it. I started to say just that, but Nunzio's shoulders shook and the sound of his laugh shattered the moment.

"What?"

"That dude in the suit just walked out and gave me the only bitch face."

I barked out a laugh and glanced down the street. Sure enough, the accountant was walking away from us. Poor guy.

"Damn."

"Who cares?"

Nunzio pulled away. His face was flushed, and he was still wilted from the news, but the anger had drained from his posture.

"Are we good?" I asked, touching his cheek.

"Yeah." Nunzio shrugged. "But I can't even explain how much this sucks. Every plan I had is fucked."

"That's not true."

He laughed again, but this time the sound was harsh and sardonic. "It really, really is. But it doesn't matter. I understand."

"Are you sure?"

Nunzio chucked me under the chin. "Don't worry about me. You got enough on your plate."

"Okay…." Unconvinced, I forged ahead. "And if something was wrong with you, I'd drop everything to fix it just like I'm doing for them.

The difference is, I'm stuck with those motherfuckers, and I chose you for myself."

Again Nunzio stared at me. He didn't respond, and our conversation stalled, words replaced by the honking of a taxi and the exuberant laughter of some teenagers at the far end of the block.

I scowled. "Thank you for making that really awkward."

"Sorry." He looked down. "You just make things harder than they already are by saying mushy shit at random."

"Oh, shut up. I take it back."

"No, you don't. I need to go home and start packing."

"All right."

"Call me later?"

I nodded, but I was confused by the abrupt end to the conversation. He gave me a strained smiled and walked away. I watched until his lean form disappeared from view.

I didn't feel satisfied about him understanding. I was simply hit with despair.

Something had shifted radically in the last ten minutes, and I couldn't pinpoint what it was. All I knew was that I'd let him down. I'd bailed on a trip we'd been planning for two years, and I was spending the next several weeks of my summer vacation in the trenches of the Rodriguez family home.

My body tightened with anxiety as I replayed every furious word Nunzio had said. I agreed with each one.

Defeated, I reentered the bar. I paid for Nunzio's drink and asked Miranda to open a tab. If I was going to get through the night—and the summer—with my sanity intact, it was going to take a lot of amber liquid, suds, and eventually something with a higher proof.

Chapter Four

September

A PIERCING beep jolted me out of sleep, and on reflex, I groped for the offending device to hurl it across the room. I lay there taking deep breaths, trying to will the room to stop spinning. After several minutes I couldn't tell if the dizziness had receded or if I'd just acclimated myself to the sensation after several weeks of waking up in a similar state.

My phone chimed from across the room, and I stumbled to my feet to find it. I was pantless but still in a faux-military shirt that was now missing several buttons—not that I remembered how they'd been ripped off. I bent to retrieve my phone, and my foot caught in the comforter that was hanging off the bed. I stumbled and looked down at the screen.

The alert flashed *6:45—Work,* but that was impossible. At least, I convinced myself it was until I saw the date in the corner of the screen.

September 2.

I was due back in the school building at 8:40 a.m.

"Hijo de la gran puta—"

I fumbled with the phone, trying to solve the kindergarten-level mathematics that my alarm app required to shut it off. If I couldn't handle two plus two, I had no idea how I was going to survive the day of professional development on school safety and inquiry-based strategies to the Common Core while getting screwed dry by the Regents. Jesus Christ, how had I forgotten the date?

I managed to mash the right number into the keypad and sat on the edge of my bed, strongly debating calling out. It wasn't even a matter of being late; I just lacked the mental preparedness to return to teacher mode. There was a Bloody Mary at an outdoor café somewhere on Broadway with my name on it. Going to work sounded like a nightmare.

I took a deep breath, but the phone exploded with sound before I could find any kind of Zen.

Nunzio.

Somehow that surprised me, even though it made perfect sense. He'd returned from Italy in mid-August, but we hadn't seen each other since our argument in front of the bar. Our communication had been nonexistent while he'd been away, which was more my fault than his.

I chewed on my lower lip and let the phone ring four times before picking up. "Hey."

"Rise and shine, rock star!"

I lay back on the bed with a groan, squeezing my eyes shut. "You're so fucking loud."

"As always," he said, still sounding entirely too chipper. "Want me to meet you in Midtown? I wanna get to school by 8:00 so I can check out the state of my classroom. I don't know what those morons did over the summer, and you know damn well we won't have much time to set up today or tomorrow."

"I'm not even alive yet. I'll get there at 8:39."

"C'mon, Mikey. Don't leave me hanging. I'll even get the good bagels."

Bread sounded like a good idea, but I rolled over and shoved my face into the mattress. "You think Price will be pissed if I call out?"

"Is that a trick question?"

"Ugh."

A rustling sounded and then the squeak of his shower turning on. I wondered if he'd been talking to me while having his morning piss.

"Get up, Michael. Don't mess around and start the school year like this. You know how they got with us last year."

Did I ever. Angela Price—our principal—had caught on to the fact that Nunzio and I were coming in late and calling out on the same days, and had thrown a shit fit about professionalism. It had only been a handful of times, and I hadn't even chipped a dent into my cache of fifty-plus sick days, but our dynamic duo was starting to bug her in general.

"All right, all right. I'm getting up."

"That's my man. I expect to see your ass at the station in forty-five minutes."

"IS IT necessary for you to look that attractive on the first day back?"

Nunzio was tanned five shades darker, and somehow looked fitter than he had been before leaving.

I was lucky to have shaved and showered without cracking my head open or accidentally slitting my own throat. Considering I had spent half the summer in a slovenly daze, it was a miracle that I'd found clothing suitable enough for the mix of yuppies and hipsters that taught at McCleary High School. As usual, Nunzio looked 100 percent better than I did.

I was irritated and sweating after having walked the eight thousand miles across the Times Square station in order to transfer to the train we took together into Brooklyn. McCleary was too far for me to commute every morning now that I'd moved back to Queens, but I was willing to deal with the extra thirty minutes of traveling, since switching schools was more of a pain in the ass. And I was still holding on to a thread of hope that one day I'd return to Manhattan.

Nunzio ignored my pseudo compliment and frowned when I stopped next to him by the inside of the turnstile. A toddler was screaming nearby and a cluster of police officers was standing in front of a discount T-shirt shop as their radios crackled obnoxiously.

"Are you sick?"

I dodged the question by heading for the staircase leading to the N train, walking around a slew of shocked-looking tourists.

"Why are you all pale and skinny?" Nunzio persisted, following close behind.

"Why do you ask so many questions?"

He slapped a brown paper bag to my chest and jogged down the stairs of the platform.

"Everything bagel with butter and jelly, bitch. Now tell me what's up."

"How was Italy?"

Nunzio sneered. "Funny you should ask, Mikey. I called you every day I was in Europe, and I got the phone bill to prove it. Ninety-nine cents a minute just to leave your sorry ass some voice mails that you never replied to."

"I know."

I bumped my shoulder against his, flashing a tired smile. He scowled and shoved his aviators up on his forehead. His hair was everywhere and longer than it had been in July. I widened my smile until he made a face and grinned back.

"So what the hell have you been up to? I was worried you wallowed in misery all summer, which was pretty much confirmed by Raymond."

"You spoke to Raymond?"

"Yes. He picks up his fucking phone."

I felt like a jerk. We began to walk down the platform, navigating the throngs of waiting straphangers to get to the end.

"I wasn't avoiding you. I was avoiding reality."

"Uh-huh." Nunzio's brow creased. "Did you just get drunk for the past month? Because that's what it looks like."

"Pretty much. I had a steady diet of booze and benzos."

"Dude...."

"Don't start lecturing me," I said. "If you had to deal with my ridiculous family, you would want to put yourself into a coma too."

"I understand that, but—" Something in my expression must have warded him off, because Nunzio didn't finish the sentence.

The train rumbled into the tunnel and screeched to a halt as we strode a bit faster to get to the last car. It was too packed to move deeper inside, so I stood with my back to the door and Nunzio facing me.

The motion of the train made my nausea rise, and I fought my intensifying dizziness. I held on to his shoulder to support myself and realized he was analyzing every inch of my face, searching for hints about what I'd done while he was away, and why I'd avoided his calls.

"How's your pops?"

I shrugged and looked at the people around us. Everyone was on their phone or wearing headphones, completely disconnected from the reality of the morning commute.

"A mess."

"Like father, like son."

"Ha-ha. Cute."

Nunzio smiled and cuffed my shoulder. "Really, though. You haven't told me anything. Is he still being a pain in the ass?"

"Yes, but it turns out he wasn't bullshitting about his liver being shot. He's barely functioning, but that doesn't stop him from being a dickhead most of the time. He also keeps drinking like a fish. If Raymond doesn't kill him, the next six-pack will. He doesn't even go to the doctor like he's supposed to. We argued about it, but it got so heated I had to give up. I can't force him to care about himself."

"I don't get him. At all."

"You and me both." The train stopped at the next station, and I winced, wishing I'd popped a few aspirin. "Look, I don't want to talk about this. I can't focus as it is."

The crush of people in the car intensified, and Nunzio moved closer until we were squished against the door. He didn't hesitate to align our bodies until we were chest to chest, his mouth brushing my ear. I let him lean into me and didn't pull away like I normally did when he showed these public displays of affection.

Nunzio was oblivious to the curious stares his touchy-feely nature garnered, but homophobes were generally reluctant to mess with two guys over six feet, no matter how much he cuddled me. And I couldn't deny that I'd missed it.

"I wish I'd been here with you. I shouldn't have gone."

"I wouldn't have let you stay."

"Like you could have stopped me?" Nunzio snorted. "I know how you get when you're all stressed out and depressed, Mikey. I could have at least distracted you so you didn't feel the need to knock yourself out every night."

"You distracted me plenty before you left."

When Nunzio tilted his head back in confusion, I wiggled my eyebrows and smiled at his startled expression.

"I thought you'd forgotten about that."

"Yeah, right. The one time we fuc—had fun."

"You never mentioned it again, and then ignored my fucking calls. What did you expect me to think?" Someone bumped Nunzio, and his coffee slopped over the edge of the tiny opening of the cup. "Besides, you could have forgotten about it while you were partying it up. How often did you get laid?"

I'd gotten laid quite a bit if I counted fucking my hand, but interaction with other human beings had been limited to a couple of perverted Grindr chats. Not that he needed that information.

"Enough."

"Clive come crawling back yet?"

"I saw him out once, but we haven't spoken. I heard he goes to some swinger club now."

Nunzio's brows flew up. "That's... random."

I shrugged, uncaring. "I haven't thought about him much, to be honest. I had enough going on."

"Yeah, I bet. Did Raymond and your dad ever stop…." Nunzio trailed off when I shook my head. "Damn, still? Why?"

"Because they're both hardheaded and hot-tempered, and neither wants to back down. Typical tough-guy bullshit."

"Isn't Joseph a little old for that?"

"Ha. Tell him that." The train jolted and rocked so hard that half the people in the car staggered to the side. My head thumped the door and I hissed. "And now I really don't want to talk about it anymore. If school is good for anything, it's a distraction from my horrible home life."

"You said that same shit when *we* were in high school."

"I'm sure I did. And after all that effort, I ended up right back where I started." Nunzio opened his mouth to reply, but I waved him off. "No—forget it. Change the subject. Tell me about Italy."

"You sure, man? If you need to vent…."

"I'm positive. Take my mind off that bullshit for a while."

He smiled. "I'll try."

MCCLEARY HIGH School was what happened when a principal got a brand-new school with a brand-new building and had the opportunity to handpick staff from the ground up. Most of the teachers were in their midtwenties or even younger, and transplants from an out-of-state school—sometimes an Ivy. Everyone thought they were saving the world, or the poor inner-city kids, and being around them made me want to throw myself from the rooftop.

This feeling hit me as we entered the building for the first time since June. I was immediately summoned to Price's office. Apparently I was the only one with a one-on-one meeting on the first day back, because the main office was a ghost town, with the exception of a neat stack of agendas by the sign-in log.

I sipped Nunzio's coffee while reading the planned activities. It was a lineup of the exact same fun-filled shit we'd done on the first day last year, which meant the day would turn into me reviewing old lesson plans and following pundits on Twitter.

"Michael, you can come in."

Wishing I'd worn something less casual now that I was being graced with Her Majesty Principal's presence, I gripped the coffee cup and went inside. It looked the same as it always did, and I was briefly struck by how much it felt like no time had passed at all. A lot had changed since June, but there was no sense that I'd been out of the building for longer than a week.

"How was your summer?"

I sat across from her. "It was okay. You?"

Price made a so-so gesture, and I got a load of the diamond-covered bracelet on her wrist. She looked different. Shorter hair, deeper tan, and she wasn't wearing her usual tweed ensembles, which made her look a lot younger.

"I went on vacation with my kids, so they had a great time."

I couldn't help but smile. "What did you want to see me about?"

Price leaned back in her chair. "There are two things we need to discuss, only one of which you will be glad about."

"Okay...."

"I'm replacing you as team leader for the tenth grade."

I nodded slowly, face frozen in a mask of neutrality. Being grade team leader amounted to nothing more than organizing meetings and delivering information to the rest of the tenth grade teachers, but it had sucked up an additional couple of hours a week that I'd been reluctant to spare. Not having the extra responsibility would be a load off my mind, but I didn't really see her making the executive decision to remove me as being a positive.

"Any reason why?"

"I heard you weren't happy."

Fucking rats. I tried to remember to whom I'd complained who would have repeated my words, but months of drinking had cleansed my memory of anything related to work.

"I see."

"Are you displeased with my decision?"

"Not as long as it didn't come from you deciding I'm suddenly not up to par."

She flipped a ballpoint pen between her fingers. "There were some comments made about you from the leadership team."

Oh brother. Here comes the bochinche....

"It was stated that you weren't being as much of a team player last year as in previous years, and that you were being contrary about several decisions being made on the third floor." Price didn't seem to be expecting a response from me, because she flicked her fingers dismissively and moved on. "In any case, you won't have to worry about that this year."

"That's fine." And it was, but now the possibility of people whispering behind my back during summer school would nag at me. "Who's replacing me? Nunzio? He's been teaching the longest besides me."

"No. That's the other change I needed to discuss with you."

"Regarding Nunzio?"

"Yes. I'm moving him from the tenth grade team."

The statement sent a shard of outrage through me in a way that my own demotion had not. I didn't try to maintain the facade of apathetic professionalism. "Why? We've all been together for the past four years. Our team is solid."

"Your team was solid until last year when there were issues with professionalism."

"Ms. Price, we called out simultaneously two times in four years."

"Two times in the same year on a Monday, as well as showing up late at the same time three times, and there were accusations of cliquish behavior on your floor. Apparently some people felt there was an unwelcoming vibe created by your inner circle."

I kept my mouth shut and looked out the window. In the park behind the school, three kids shared a joint and watched an old Chinese lady stretching in the basketball court while a hipster chick wearing a long denim skirt used a hula hoop nearby. This neighborhood was my constant reminder that somewhere out in the world, weirder things were happening than the batshit teacher drama that went down at McCleary.

"You're switching him to a different floor?"

"He can either teach Earth Science downstairs or teach using his special education license on the eleventh grade team up here. I'll let him choose before I discuss the change with a few new hires."

"I'm sure he will appreciate that."

Price gave me one of her sideways stares. "Let's make this a good year, Michael. I don't want there to be more changes than there have to be, but we need to maintain the culture of the school and keep this a welcoming environment."

"Of course." I could tell my lack of ass-kissing wasn't flying with her, but I also didn't care. "Should I go downstairs?"

She nodded and looked down at the folders in front of her, the usual signal for dismissal.

NUNZIO WAS flushed, pacing his former classroom and digging his hands in his hair. His face was set in hard, angry lines as the clock ticked and we missed the staff breakfast and opening announcements for the day.

"I should walk out right now," he said, pointing at the door. "She had all fucking summer and last spring to tell me, but she tells me now? I have nothing prepared to switch curriculums. I should tell that old bitch some shit about herself."

I put a hand on his arm. "Cálmate, Nunzio. Just take a deep breath."

He jerked his arm away but stopped his cagey movements around the room. Although it had been cleaned for the summer, there were still traces of his bulletin boards and items he'd taped to the wall near his— or what had been his—desk. His eyes settled on a collage of former students who had now graduated.

"This sucks."

"It does, but there's nothing you can do about it now except decide where you want to go."

"Why didn't she switch *you*?"

"I'm assuming it's because you have two licenses and two possible openings whereas I only have my license in Social Studies."

"Yeah. I guess."

His expression drifted from angry to despairing, and I could practically hear the questions populating his mind—whether or not this job was worth it, what else he could be doing with his life. We asked each other those questions every year, but this was the first time it seemed like he would follow through and walk out.

I wanted to argue that he was overreacting—this happened to teachers all the time. But on the other hand, it was difficult to argue that years of experience teaching a subject and building a curriculum being ripped away over a few instances of lateness was justifiable.

"You'd be with the kids from last year if you taught SpEd on this floor." I sounded pathetic. "That wouldn't be so bad, would it?"

"I don't know."

"Come on. You loved those kids. It's better than going downstairs with the Stepford clones who think they're Michelle Pfeiffer in *Dangerous Minds*."

Nunzio's lips twitched, and I swooped in on the crack in his dead-eyed mask. I put an arm around him, and his strong body melted against me. I dropped a kiss on his forehead.

"You'll be okay. I'll help."

"Nah."

"Yeah, I will. You'll be the co-teacher for humanities classes, and that's my thing."

He shrugged again and turned his face into the crook of my neck. He inhaled deeply before releasing a noisy sigh, his breath ghosting over my skin. "Let's blow this place off and go get drunk."

"Don't tempt me, niño."

"I was kidding."

I pulled away. "If we leave this room, do you promise you won't do anything crazy?"

"Define crazy."

"Go curse out Price or quit."

Nunzio shrugged, still looking crestfallen. "I won't, but don't expect me to be fake, either."

"You wouldn't be my best friend if you were fake."

As I watched Nunzio stride to the office, I could sense a hint of fight left in the set of his shoulders. He'd be willing to hear what she had to say, and maybe even take the switch in schedule, but not without talking a lot of shit that was masked by educational acronyms and big words. Nunzio was good at making his defiance sound professional. I, on the other hand, just tended to shut down and stare at the wall, or get mad and lapse into sarcasm.

In the next few hours, everyone would adjourn to their grade team meetings. It made Nunzio's switch seem even more out of the blue. He would most definitely be using that in the case against Price and her rationale.

Unfortunately, after I caught the tail end of morning announcements and spent another hour in my social studies content team bickering about the school's refusal to order Scantron machines because they claimed it promoted a testing culture, there was no indication that Price's mind had changed.

When it was time for grade team meetings, I didn't rush. I stopped in the lounge to heat my uneaten bagel and stolen coffee, and texted Raymond.

He had promised to start looking for a job today, but I doubted he was even awake. I hadn't bothered inquiring about our father doing the same. The old man was applying for SSI, and I actually hoped he got approved. In my entire life, I hadn't heard about him working for more than a month or two at a time in a random place. Given his deteriorating health, who knew what would happen if he tried now.

Unsurprisingly Raymond didn't respond. I made it down the gleaming hallway to the location of the grade ten meeting, trying in vain to swallow the now-chewy bagel. After greeting one of the deans as he taped posters over the window on his office door, I approached the new science teacher's room.

It took some amount of skill to twist the handle and shoulder it open while balancing my food, clipboard, and coffee. I started to greet my coteachers with my usual blend of gloom and genuine happiness to see them, but the words clogged in my throat once I caught sight of our new Earth Science teacher/grade team leader.

It was David.

Chapter Five

DAVID HAD a deer-in-the-headlights expression, but he masked it faster than I did. I was caught in a moment of confusion where I couldn't figure out if this was real life or if I'd taken a couple of Xanax bars without remembering that morning and was now in some weird space-time continuum of illusions.

As ridiculous as it was, that explanation was a lot more likely than the third party in my first and only threesome finding his way to McCleary High School and landing a position as Nunzio's replacement. There had to be another reason for his presence.

Maybe he was a new educational coach or some expert on the new national standards and would be leading a PD for the next two days.

I searched my team's faces—Erica Larson (the English teacher), Danielle Kajowski (the Geometry teacher), and Kimberly Parker (the Special Education teacher)—for signs that David was an apparition, but there were none.

"Hey," I said belatedly. "I'm a disaster today. Alarm went off late, and I haven't recovered since then."

"You're always kind of a disaster." Erica shot me a good-natured grin and pointed to the spot next to her. "This is David Butler, the new science teacher."

I dropped in the chair next to her and placed my clipboard in front of me for lack of anything better to do. "Hi. I'm Rodriguez."

David's face flushed. With a clenched jaw, he stared down at his cute little MacBook. "Nice to meet you."

"Yeah, I just found out about Nunzio being replaced. You have a lot to live up to, my man."

David shot another glance at me, and there was no mistaking his surprise. I could almost see it in his eyes; the silent chant of *please don't say anything inappropriate, please don't humiliate me, please just shut the hell up.*

"I heard." David tried to smile, but his mouth crumbled under the effort. "I was originally going to teach downstairs, but they switched me."

"Why is that? Did Nunzio want to leave the team for some reason?" Danielle was giving me the side-eye, like she thought maybe it had something to do with some drama he and I had gotten into over the summer.

I'd almost forgotten that Danielle was bochincera number one on the third floor, but she was still one of my favorite people at the school. I'd lucked out and gotten a team that was a little more real than most of the others in the building. Until now, anyway.

"I'll tell you later."

"Got it."

Erica peered at me but didn't comment on my wayward best friend. "And Liz quit so we're short an ESL teacher since she chose to do it yesterday. They haven't hired anyone else yet."

"How are the kids going to get serviced?"

"I don't know. They'll get Maria or Karen to push in—"

David cleared his throat and sat up straighter. I took the opportunity to eyeball him. He was wearing a stiff button-down shirt and had a huge, shiny watch peeking out from the cuff. Apparently no one had told his green ass that the first two days of teacher time were for cleaning and setting up, not dressing for success.

"I made us an agenda," he said, unapologetically interrupting as he slid a little stack of half-sheet papers to the center of our cluster of student tables. "We only have this hour together for common planning today, so we need to make every moment count. After this, we break up for full staff meetings."

"Sounds good," Danielle replied, sounding not at all enthused as she held one of the sheets between two fingers.

With her dark hair pulled back in a tight bun and her all-black ensemble, she looked stern. The way she glared at the agenda didn't take away from that no-nonsense impression. She was the exact opposite of Erica, who was tiny, red-haired, and perky, and was already making little annotations all over the paper. Kimberly stared at David for a moment before following Erica's lead. A wrinkle appeared on her forehead, and she gnawed at her lower lip the way she did when she was confused. It tended to happen a lot.

Even though I'd been teaching with the three of them for a few years, they were still contained to the little box in my social circle meant for work friends, and I still couldn't tell whether they cared that Nunzio was gone from the team. It bothered me more than it should have. They were being professional, and I was being a baby. But I wanted Nunzio back.

I hadn't even glanced at the agenda before Erica looked up with a grin.

"I love warm-up games!"

Clearly she was not too broken-up over Nunzio's departure.

"We really have to play a game?" I glanced at David, but he was still avoiding direct eye contact.

"Yes. Even though you know each other, I'm new here. It's good for us to gain an understanding of how we can complement each other on a team, and what we consider our strengths and weaknesses."

Danielle looked like she wanted to kill herself, so I took one for our little duo of defiance and continued. "Can't we just share it verbally?"

All traces of embarrassment vanished from David's expression as he seemed to realize what he was dealing with—a pain-in-the-ass veteran teacher who was going to give him a hard time. It wasn't my intention, but I could see the unspoken accusation in his face.

"It won't take long."

With that, David pushed his chair back and stood up without asking Danielle's opinion.

It was going to be a long year.

BY THE end of the day, I'd played the same tired team-building games that I'd been playing for years. I was supposed to be professionally developed about the new evaluation system, but I couldn't say that I'd listened to the spiels. I'd spent the majority of the past several hours texting Nunzio and trying to drag him out of the funk he was entrenched in. He stopped responding and presumably disappeared with his new team while I stood in my classroom and evaluated how long it would take to set up. The prospect of decorating was about as appealing as wiping my ass with sandpaper.

A knock on the door took me out of my gloomy contemplation of barren bulletin boards and forward-facing desks.

David stood in the doorway, sleeves rolled up to his elbows and collar undone. He looked like a rumpled frat boy.

"'Sup?"

"I wondered if we could talk."

"How could I say no to my new grade team leader?"

David stepped into the room and shut the door behind him. His movements were quick and secretive even though he had every right to be in my classroom now that we were coworkers.

"Relax. No one else knows about that night."

"Nunzio does." David came to stand next to my desk, closer than I would have liked. His mussed hair and sweaty brow reminded me of more interesting things. "And I heard he likes to talk."

Any trace of admiration disappeared in a vortex of defensive rage. "Someone is talking shit about Nunzio already?"

"More like giving the new guy a heads-up."

"Why would anyone feel like they need to give you a heads-up about Nunzio? He isn't even on the fucking grade team anymore."

"Exactly." David waited for me to catch on while I stared at him like a dumbass and failed to see his point. After a beat of silence, David sighed. "Apparently he wasn't too happy that I replaced him. I don't know if he's taking it personally or if he's just mad in general."

"Of course he isn't happy," I snapped. "He was yanked off his grade team and made to switch subjects, and he is being replaced by some Teach for America or Ivy League baby."

David's cheeks reddened. He crossed his arms over his chest, averting his gaze, and I knew I had his number. I could sniff out his kind faster than I could sniff out a kid who'd just smoked a joint. The TFA or Ivy teachers usually had the same style, and they almost always came from a safe little town outside the city.

I smirked. "Don't get your panties in a twist, Butler. He isn't going to tell anyone that we all partied together."

"I surely hope not, since he would also have to admit to having sex with his former grade team leader."

"Former grade team leader?" I sat on the edge of my desk. "Papi, Nunzio and I have known each other for twenty years—since you were still watching Sesame Street and getting potty trained. I'm more than his former grade team leader."

David pointed at me, a triumphant look on his face. "I knew it! You *are* together!"

"No," I corrected. "We've been best friends for twenty years. We're not together the way you think. That was the first time we'd ever done something like that. You inspired us."

"Bullshit."

"How is that bullshit?"

David dropped his jutting finger. "The way he looked at you and the way you were all over him made it seem like you were lovers. Not to mention, he didn't even use a condom with you."

The kid sure as hell remembered a lot of details about that night.

"How the hell did you end up working here of all places?"

"I interviewed last spring. My previous school was horrible."

"Was last year your first year?"

"Yes."

Figured. I didn't understand by what logic my administration gave a second-year teacher any kind of supervisory role, but apparently I was too unprofessional to judge anyone about their decisions.

When I got quiet, David searched my face with his lower lip pushed out in a way he was likely unaware of. There was no way he was more than twenty-four or twenty-five.

"What about you? How long have you been teaching?"

"Eight years."

"What about Nunzio?"

"The same. Neither of us knew what the hell to do after high school and ended up taking the same accelerated Bachelor/Masters teaching program. We got our licenses the same year."

David wrinkled his nose. "And you decided to teach at the same school? Isn't that a little codependent?"

"No," I said, raising the pitch in my tone to mimic his voice. "We started at different schools, but both were failing and had no room to grow, so when this place was built, we both applied. We're not desperate to be together or something."

"People talk like you are."

Again with the bochinche. Did anyone ever shut the fuck up in this place?

"Most people also assume we've been sleeping together for years. They read into our every interaction to assign a deeper meaning because apparently two gay men can't be friends without touching each other's dicks. But these days, I think they'd be more interested in the fact that we had you begging for it in the middle."

The sound of laughter—likely Danielle's, since her room was across from mine—emanated from outside the door. David took a step closer to me so he was out of view.

"Listen." He lowered his voice. "I didn't intend to see you again. It was just a one-time thing. It shouldn't have even happened. I was just drunk and all of my friends left before me, so I got a little crazy. I don't do things like that."

"Didn't seem that way."

"You don't know me," he said sharply. "Because I don't."

I remembered the morning after the threesome and the way Nunzio had described our guest scampering away like a thief in the night. I'd dismissed it at the time, but now there was no mistaking the stench of guilt coming off this guy. He definitely had a boyfriend.

Just what I needed—to be the other dude when I'd just been dumped by a cheating asshole myself.

"What was that look?" David asked, a defensive edge in his voice.

"Did I give you a look?"

"Yeah. And it was full of judgment."

"Maybe you just have a guilty conscience." When David's face turned stony, I spread my hands. "Do you have a man?"

If he was taken aback, David didn't give it away. "It's complicated."

"Oh Jesus. How old are you?"

"What does that have to do with anything?"

"It's typical of your generation to answer questions with Facebook status updates."

"That's what it is." The defensive edge was back and stacked with attitude. "We're off and on. I don't have to explain myself to you."

"Then why are you?"

David didn't have a response for that, but he took a deep breath and stared over my shoulder at the busted projector screen. I tried not to look at him, but everything from the tanned column of his neck to his tapered torso reminded me of how I'd run my hands all over him. He'd been the perfect blend of smooth and hard, responsive and aggressive— and he'd milked my dick with the kind of talent that I loved in a bottom. So many dudes just thought it was enough to bend over and push back on it.

"Stop staring at me."

I laughed at his embarrassment.

"Can we just never talk about that again?" he pleaded. "Can we just be normal colleagues?"

"Maybe, but it will be hard not to think about."

"Try not to."

I leaned back slightly and his gaze swept over me in a way that I knew wasn't just interest in my lousy outfit.

"I know it's inappropriate," I said. "I'm not a total idiot. But I'm also not a saint."

"I'm not saying you have to be a saint, but we're colleagues now. I can't go around daydreaming about how I wanted to watch Nunzio fuck you all night."

Mental images flew back. Not that they were buried too deep. I'd jerked off thinking about that night multiple times. The description alone had my dick hard enough to strain against my fly.

But still, reality was far from what David had witnessed that night. We'd all been caught up in a fevered fit of drunken horniness. A Midsummer Night's Dream in Hell's Kitchen.

"I wouldn't say he fucked me."

David gave me a scathing once-over; it seemed to be his signature. "You rode back on his dick like you'd been wanting it for years while sucking on his fingers. At that point, my ass was a glory hole you used while the two of you got hot and heavy."

My fingers tightened around the edge of the desk. "Seems like you enjoyed the show."

"I did. You two looked amazing together."

I faltered, unable to find a suitable reply. He grinned at me, full of sass and self-satisfaction, and looked down at my crotch. I didn't even try to hide the bulge there. I had half a mind to tug him into the corner, way out of sight, and make him take it out just so I could feel his fingers on it. I'd blow my load from the contact alone.

"Goddamn, you're a nasty bastard, aren't you?"

"You're the one who wanted to keep bringing it up. Now you can't handle it?"

The challenge in his voice turned me on more, which defeated his purpose. "Are you sure you came to warn me? It seems like you came by to make me horny."

David shrugged and finally broke our standoff. He looked around my classroom as if he found it fascinating. Although he was standing ramrod straight, shoulders pushed back and still as a monument, there was no mistaking his heavier breathing.

I could hear it with every whisper of an exhalation, and I wanted to drag him closer. I didn't know if it was him I wanted, or if I was just desperate for *someone* after a month and a half of self-imposed celibacy, and a brain full of filthy thoughts starring him and my gorgeous best friend.

"Do you want to do something after you're finished up here?" I asked.

"Like what?"

I cocked an eyebrow. "Get a drink?"

"I can't."

"I can invite Nunzio."

"No!"

"So we go alone."

"Michael, I'm not going out with you." David unfolded his arms and swept one out in a dismissive gesture. "I'm attracted to you, but nothing else is going to happen. I don't care if you jerk off thinking about my ass, I don't care if I think about you blowing me, or have dreams of you and Nunzio going at it all night—it won't happen. So please, *please*, try to forget that anything ever did. Like it or not, I am your grade team leader now, and it has to be kept professional."

Jesus. What a cock-tease. My erection wilted at the sound of him reaffirming his fake-ass authority. I snorted and brushed past him.

The closet door stood open, so I stared inside, willing a distraction to magically appear in the packed confines. I didn't even remember why I'd unlocked the closet initially, but I grabbed a roll of bulletin board paper so it wasn't a total fail in front of my new faux supervisor.

"Will do, Papi. As long as you stop flirting with me like a hypocrite."

David didn't respond, but I heard the soles of his boat shoes heading for the door. I was hoping that was the end of it. David presented an anomaly that I couldn't wrap my mind around.

Desiring the same person who possessed every personality trait I loathed wasn't ideal, especially since he seemed like the type of dude to make a huge deal about it if I did continue with the insinuations and innuendos about our night in threesome heaven. Worse yet, I wondered if Nunzio could handle keeping his own mouth shut before this guy ran and reported us for some kind of harassment.

"I want to try to get along with you," he said before opening the door.

"So then do it. I don't see why you have to try."

"I just don't understand you. I don't know if you like me, if you resent me for being young and taking on your role as grade team leader and also replacing—"

"I don't resent you." I turned around. "And soon enough you'll figure out why I didn't want to be grade team leader in the first place. I know the new teaching programs prepare you kids to use all of your cute behavior management strategies, but none of that shit will ever prepare you for the bureaucracy or office politics of working in a school."

I almost added something reassuring after catching a flicker of uncertainty in David's eyes, but I didn't. Not with him already engaging in the kind of leadership tactics that typically resulted in throwing people under the bus and talking trash. I'd already had my fair share of people questioning my ability to be professional today.

"Watch your ass and don't become the type of *leader* that teachers hate. You're new here and maybe the administration loves you, but I guarantee your life will fucking suck if they're the only ones on your side."

"But isn't that what's important? I spent my first year teaching in a school that was more like a war zone," David said. "All I want is to not be on the principal's bad side."

"It's a fine line, and that's all I can tell you. Use your head and don't forget that you're still a teacher. Grade team leader is a supervisory role, but it doesn't give you any real authority. If you act like it does, your boat will sink fast."

I briefly thought he was considering my words, but then his face cleared. He half turned to the door and discarded my advice.

"I hope you give me a chance. I know you're upset about Nunzio, but maybe it was for the best. Maybe you're too close to each other to work effectively on a grade team."

It was quite an indictment for someone who had been in the building for less than a full day, but I didn't say anything more. I let my face default to my baseline work expression, complete with glazed fuck-your-whole-family eyes, and waited for David to leave.

He hesitated, looked back at me, and then hurried away with his hands shoved in his pockets.

At the back of my mind, I wondered if he'd relax a bit if I loosened up his ass.

Chapter Six

COME MEET me downtown. I have something interesting to tell you. Work related.

The text message was the most obvious kind of bait. The words "work related" were a lure I couldn't resist, especially given the way the school year had started.

"Who's that?" Nunzio asked.

"Danielle. She wants us to go to some gay club downtown."

"No thanks."

I looked up from my phone. "You're turning down a chance to cruise? This is a shocking turn of events."

Nunzio lifted a shoulder. "I'd rather stay here with you, my pizza, and Netflix like we planned. I want to relax before the kids are in school on Monday, not get turned up and hungover."

He had a point, and that was why I'd suggested our four-day weekend of movies and vegging out. With the school closed for Rosh Hashanah, it was a prime opportunity to get into teacher mode without the aggravation of drama or my family. Spending time with Nunzio for the first time in nearly two months had released the tension that had built inside me over the summer. As I lay tangled with him on the couch, I was finally able to breathe.

Not to mention, the seemingly unquenchable dryness in my throat had been absent for the two days I had spent in his apartment. Until now, anyway.

Now Danielle had planted the seed of doing shots and drinking whiskey in my head, and I couldn't push the idea away.

"Are you sure?"

"Pretty damn sure, Mikey. Let's watch another episode."

I eyeballed the message again and debated how much I wanted to know. The comments both Price and David had made continued to nag at me, and Danielle wasn't doing me any favors by dredging it up again, but I couldn't help myself.

"She said there's a ton of twinks."

"Don't care. Not getting up."

"She also said she wanted to tell me something about work."

Nunzio looked up. "Don't let her get you all riled up with gossip shit. She does it every time. She gets off on it."

"I know, but I still want to know what the hell she's talking about. I was uncomfortable with some of the things that came up with Price. I hate not knowing who at school is talking shit behind my back." I tapped my finger, considering. "This is why I used to keep to myself."

"You still keep to yourself," he pointed out. "All of our friends moved out of this bloodsucking city or got married."

"I mean at school. I got soft."

"Me too. I started expecting things to go well, which is always a stupid idea." Nunzio rubbed his eyes with the heels of his hands. "Seriously, though, I'm too fucking tired to go out. I feel like we haven't moved in like, a full forty-eight hours, and my ass is glued to this couch."

I nudged him again. "You're taking my position as lame hermit in this friendship."

He groaned theatrically. "Where is she even at?"

"I dunno. Some gay club in the Village."

"I'll never get why women dig going to gay clubs where no one is going to give them any play."

"Maybe they want to party without a bunch of guys thinking they want play."

"Where's the fun in that?"

I scoffed at him. "Just shut up and come with me."

When Nunzio released another pitiful groan, I turned on the sofa and straddled him. My lips parted so I could plead with him again, but his hands came up to rest on my hips and the words died before I could fully form them. A wicked glint shone in his eyes.

"Okay, then."

Nunzio slumped down farther, spreading his legs wide as a Cheshire smile curved his mouth up. "What?"

"Don't be looking at me like that, sucio."

He bucked up his hips, forcing me to bounce on his lap. I balanced myself so there was space between us, the position making my hamstrings burn. It would have been easy to slide forward and align our crotches at the critical point, but I wasn't ready to let him know I still fantasized about that night in July.

It was bad enough that I was now captivated by the way his full lower lip was caught between his teeth, the way his hands were gripping tighter, and the feel of his hard, muscular thighs beneath me. Unbidden, a voice in my head wondered how it would feel to ride him. My dick stirred, and I nearly leapt off his lap.

I cleared my throat after finding my footing once again. "If you come out to the club, you could pick up some hot twink and not have to spend your time leering at me."

"Can we have another threesome?" When I just stared, his smile wilted. "Relax, Mikey. Just joking."

"Uh-huh."

I rubbed the back of my neck. The implications of his sudden shift in behavior did not bode well, especially combined with my own gutter mind. If Nunzio started encouraging the idea of us getting horizontal, I wasn't sure how I would respond. My dick loved the idea, but my brain wasn't as certain. I kicked his bare foot.

"Come on. Get dressed."

Nunzio turned away from me to curl into a ball. "Can't I just stay here? I have no desire to be around McCleary people. Especially some bitches that didn't even bat an eyelash when I got chucked from the team. You can go have fun for me while I stay here and jerk off to porn." He curled further into himself and wrapped his arms around his head to prevent me from seeing his face. "Pick up a hot top and tell me the details so I can live vicariously through your ability to be versatile."

"Anyone can be versatile."

"Maybe for the right cock."

I smacked a hand against the swath of flesh that was visible beneath his rucked up T-shirt. "Fine. If you change your mind, give me a call."

Without his interference, I threw on some random items of his clothing and waited for him to comment on my appearance. When he didn't glance in my direction, I grabbed my wallet and spare key and headed out the door.

I took a cab, but still, by the time I arrived, there was already a line, and some of the guys looked like they'd stepped right off the fashion pages of *Out* magazine. The doorman seemed to be selecting people, but to my surprise he pointed at me as soon as I approached.

Judging by the number of white faces when I entered, I wondered if I was fulfilling some kind of minority quota.

I texted Danielle and squinted in the flashing lights, making my way through the sea of bodies to the bar. The place was so loud and cramped that I regretted going out, even if I was morbidly curious about what Danielle had to say.

"Michael!"

She was by the bar, waving at me over the crowd, her dark bangles sliding up her thin arm and glittering in the darkness. Reaching her position was an adventure comprised of dodged elbows and flailing arms, the thick smell of cologne, sweat, and the cloying scent of marijuana clinging to one of the people on the dance floor. I was thankful to reach the bar; I already needed a drink.

My relief was short-lived. Standing by Danielle's side was her best friend Charles, who looked like a cross between a burlesque performer and a model, and David. Fantastic.

"I didn't know this was a work thing."

"It's not," Danielle said, straight-faced among the hordes of glittering gay men. "But Charles wanted me to go out, and I invited David while we were texting."

"You were texting?" My tone made texting sound a lot like consorting with the administrative enemy, and I knew I was being an asshole. I tried to smile. "I didn't know you guys got that close in the four hours you spent together in the past two days."

"What, are you jealous that he's, like, stealing your beard?" Charles leaned across the bar to make a scrunched-up stank face. "You need to learn how to share, Mikey."

"Only Nunzio calls me Mikey."

Charles smirked at that and raised one pink, thinly trimmed eyebrow. "Mm-hmm."

"Yeah, thanks for that insightful retort." I glanced at David, realizing I hadn't greeted him. All I could muster was a faint head bop.

"I was asking her how to do something on the school website. That's why we were texting," he said. "Not for some other weird reason."

"Okay." I turned away like I had no interest in that information and sought out the bartender, but getting a drink didn't seem likely to happen until Charles ducked under the bar. He popped up on the other side with a flourish of his tattooed arms.

"What can I get you, Mr. Rodriguez?"

"Three shots of tequila and a beer."

"Don't you mean four shots?"

"No. They're all for me."

I tried to ignore the guy behind me who kept bumping into my back, and looked at David again. The shirt he was wearing showed every hard line of muscle in his arms and torso. I realized he was glassy-eyed and flushed. They must have arrived much earlier than I had, unless he was just a lightweight.

"Why don't you go dance instead of awkwardly standing here?" I'd expected him to say no, but he just looked around and didn't respond. His movements were exaggerated from the effects of alcohol. "Worried your complicated boyfriend is here?"

"No," he said. "It's just really crowded."

"So? You can make your way to the middle."

"Why don't you come with me?"

Danielle gave a furtive shake of her head. I had to agree with the sentiment. After our tête-à-tête in the classroom, I'd sworn to keep my interaction with David to a minimum.

"Here you go, teacher," Charles said merrily, presenting me with my assortment of booze.

I knocked the shots back one after the other as David looked on.

"Come on." David listed closer and grabbed my wrist. "Let's dance. It can be bonding. Or a better icebreaker game."

"Oh boy," Danielle muttered.

I stared at him over the rim of my mug, took a deep gulp, and set it down on the bar. Good judgment caved under his coaxing smile, and I wondered if this was his way of showing he was normal outside of work.

"One dance," I relented.

"Yes!" His voice was too loud, and the way he bounced on his heels like a child was indicative of how drunk he was. I allowed him to tug me toward the crowd while threading his damp and sticky fingers through mine.

We weaved through darkness with only flashing lights to illuminate our surroundings, but the cluster of bodies was not as annoying now that I was buzzed. When we were finally pinned together and moving to the thrum of European electronica, everything else drifted away. I wished I could clearly see David's face, but all I got was a glimpse of big eyes and wide lips every ten seconds when the epileptic nightmare of a light show switched.

I hadn't intended to touch him except for the press of my front to his with the barest teasing brushes of denim on denim, but he cast the first stone toward debauchery with his increasingly adventurous hands. One palm braced between my shoulder blades and the other found its way to my ass as he guided me closer. I let him get aggressive and handsy for two songs before it escalated to dry humping with a beat.

The feel of his erection bumping insistently against my crotch sent a wave of heat through my body, but when he groaned in my ear, I backed off. It was easy to forget real life and consequences when beguiled by alcohol, a good beat, and the long shadows of a club, but the reality of him being utterly smashed jerked me out of the trance. I remembered his admission about having a boyfriend and his previous horror over drunken antics, and the red flags went up. I would be the one looking like an asshole in the morning if I took him up on any offers now.

It took gold-medal-worthy self-control to pry myself away.

"I'm going to get another drink," I shouted over the music.

"Wait a few minutes."

David clung to me like a lifeline, but I shook my head and cast a quick look around. There were two guys in the vicinity with hawk eyes glued to David's ass, and I nudged him in the direction of the more attractive one.

"I'll be back."

I made a quick escape just as the guy clamped his hands on David's hips and pulled him back. It was a sufficient distraction; David took one look over his shoulder and ground back on the guy with a smile.

I returned to where Danielle was hanging out with Charles at the bar. It was clear that the only reason Danielle was in this establishment was because Charles was working the late shift.

"You two crazy kids have fun?" she asked around a tiny red straw.

"Yep," I said. "But it's time for a few more drinks."

Charles gave me a double thumbs-up and the kind of sharp smile that implied murder if I skimmed his tip. He gave us personal bar service for the next hour.

David appeared once with his new friend in tow, but I made it clear I wouldn't be going for another jaunt on the dance floor. He disappeared while I slurred to Danielle about the possibilities of getting retroactive pay when we finally got a new contract. Once David was gone for several minutes, she bumped my shoulder.

"Don't let him get to you, Rodriguez."

I blinked at her. "¿Qué?"

She gave me a stern look. "Watch your ass. There's enough weird rumors going around without him telling people you hooked up while he was drunk."

"Hey now… he was the one hitting on *me*."

"Maybe, but if he decided to spin it another way, it won't spread around like that."

I shrugged. Somewhere between drinks, I'd forgotten my mission to find out what she'd had to tell me. "What weird rumors?"

"Stupid stuff, but enough to warrant a potential issue in the future. Everyone always says you and Nunzio have been hooking up, and someone has circulated the theory that he was removed from grade team because you guys had drama."

"I already expected that."

"Yeah, but there's more. Now people are claiming Nunzio has it out for David, and that he's jealous of you and David being on the same grade team because he sees the kid as competition in multiple ways. They're saying there's already tension between you and David because of the whole mess."

I was mystified. "They created all of this crap in *two days*?"

"Word travels fast at McCleary. You should know that by now."

"I know, but damn." Craning my neck, I tried to spot David. "So why the hell did you drag me out here to tell me this in person while wonder boy is here?"

Danielle smiled sheepishly. "He showed up after I'd texted you, and to be honest, I didn't think he would come. But not for nothing—I don't think he is behind any of these rumors. I just think you should be careful. If Price has already commented on you and Nunzio's professionalism, allegations of people sleeping with each other and causing drama will just make her want to get rid of you both."

"Got it."

I faced the bar, stress seeping in past the blurry boundaries of my buzz. Charles appeared again and cupped my cheek with a pout.

"Aw, Papi, what's the matter?"

"Never call me that again."

He flicked his fingers at me. "Fine, you cranky-ass motherfucker. I was going to give you a heads-up about blondie over there, but maybe I shouldn't bother."

I blinked slowly. Did everyone have secret info on David, or what?

"What sort of heads-up?"

"Hmph." Charles twisted his wrist, stirring a cocktail in a metal cup. "Let's just say that I know David's boyfriend, and their relationship is ending with some scorched-earth policy shit. So don't get your feelings hurt, sweet pea."

I snorted. "There's very little chance of that, but thanks for the tip."

He smirked. "I should have known better. A hot blond has nothing on a tall, dark, and sexy Italian."

"Shut up."

"Fine." Charles poured the cocktail into a glass for Danielle. "Do you want another drink or what?"

I nodded, and he acquiesced. By the time the alcohol kicked in fully, I was seeing things in slow motion, laughing way too much, and promising Charles enormous tips if he gave me a kiss on the cheek. Danielle put the brakes on my apparent mission to get more deeply into debt and guided me to the door. She hailed a cab and shoved me inside with a wave good-bye.

I mumbled Nunzio's address and threw myself in sideways. My face was smashed into the leather, but I was too drunk to care about whatever had come into contact with the seat that day.

The memory of being in the backseat of another cab with Nunzio and David drifted into my mind—the tangle of fingers beneath my shirt, a hand in my pants, and a bruised mouth beneath my own. It was a good fantasy and had my dick raring to go by the time the ten-minute ride was over. I thrust an unknown amount of bills through the Plexiglas partition and stumbled out of the cab.

I jogged up the stairs, taking two at a time. My body was mistaking the need to get off with adrenaline, so I was only slightly out of breath when I got to the door.

By some miracle I unlocked it on the first attempt, shut it clumsily, and shed my jacket and shoes. The lights were off, but the muted television illuminated Nunzio's lean form stretched across the couch.

I stalked over to him like a heat-seeking missile and threw myself on the sofa alongside him with my face buried against his neck. Wanting some contact with another person turned into me cuddling and nuzzling Nunzio and then transformed into my crotch fitting up to his ass through his baggy sweats. The hint of pressure made my body react without permission of my brain, and the previous hesitations about complications and reliving our one-time fuck session vanished. No intelligent thoughts were left in my head—just base instincts to be spread open and fucked by my best friend. For longer this time.

"What are you doing?" Nunzio mumbled, voice muffled.

I pressed harder against him and made a sound of protest when he shifted and faced me. We sank deeper into the time-worn cushions, his knee between my thighs and our faces not even an inch apart as he stared at me with sleepy, heavy-lidded eyes. It struck me that Nunzio's eyelashes were very long and that he was possibly the most beautiful fucking man I'd ever seen in my life.

I grinned and his lips quirked.

"You're so stupid when you drink."

"You shoulda come. That guy was there."

"What guy?"

"David."

Nunzio's scowl ruined his rumpled sexiness. I regretted saying the name.

"I mean—yeah. Danielle."

"Wait, was it David or Danielle?"

"Uh. Both, I think?"

Nunzio didn't seem too impressed, but the scowl was replaced by a smile.

A burst of fondness swelled in my chest. I remembered why David was the dreaded new guy, and that the rumor mill wouldn't be grinding so aggressively about Nunzio if David had stayed the hell away from McCleary. Why the fuck had I been dancing with him?

I realized that I didn't want Nunzio to know I'd been all over David. I nuzzled Nunzio's face again, hoping it would save me from having to fess up.

"Did you have fun?"

I made a vague sound and kissed his cheek. He felt and smelled so good that I dropped another kiss along his jaw. Nunzio tensed, but his hand slid up and dropped onto my hip.

"How do you look so hot when you wake up?"

"Natural beauty," he deadpanned.

I dragged my teeth against his jaw, and his breathing hitched.

We barely fit on the couch, and we'd have been more comfortable in the bedroom, but I didn't want to move. Being locked together wasn't so bad.

"Clive used to be so jealous of you," I murmured.

Nunzio stroked the skin of my back with his thumb, moving in slow circles. "Really?"

"Yeah, he thought we hooked up when we went out drinking. After he saw us dancing one night."

"I don't blame him. We be all over each other."

"Like now?"

"Yeah, kind of." Nunzio leaned back a little, his face bewildered. "Christ, you're drunk. Go to bed."

"I'm not tired."

"Yeah, but you're making my dick hard, and I don't want to deal with that. Just a few hours ago you looked at me like I had four heads because I teased you."

"No."

Nunzio squeezed my hip. "Yes. Why didn't you push up on David?"

Inebriation leads to the type of honesty that can never end well. "I thought about hooking up with him, but he was too drunk."

A low sigh ruffled my hair. I thought Nunzio would pull away, but he slid his hand fully up my shirt. I arched my back, reveling in the sensation, and nipped at his jaw again.

"You think I'm a good backup?" Nunzio rumbled in my ear.

"No."

"So why's your dick so hard?"

His other hand snaked between us and palmed my crotch, kneading my dick. My eyes slid shut. I couldn't think of a response because every working brain cell zeroed in on the feel of my cock finally getting attention, and the need to keep that stimulation going no matter what.

I latched my mouth to Nunzio's neck, sucking payment into the skin. The soft sound he made indicated that he liked it, so I didn't stop. I was addicted to the taste of him while he rubbed me off through my jeans. His hand spasmed, fingers twitching like he wanted to delve them into the stiff fabric.

I rocked my thigh forward and he eagerly responded, grinding his dick against me with a breathless chuckle. Encouraged, I dragged my teeth over his neck.

Nunzio's breath caught, and then his fingers were yanking at the buckle of my belt and ripping out the tongue with hectic impatience. I attacked his clothing in return—pulling at the waistband of his sweatpants and shoving them down to get at the thick cock beneath. His lack of underwear only made my blood pump faster, rushing to the iron-hard length of my dick.

The situation went from playful to single-minded when the teasing turned into outright desperation. We panted into each other's faces and gripped each other's cocks.

"Shit," Nunzio muttered wetly. "Tighter."

I complied, jerking his cock with a viselike grip while I bucked into the cave of his curled fingers. I didn't try to muffle the sounds that were ripped out of my throat with each pump of his hand. The pressure, each twist of his wrist, the speed—all of it was so perfect that coherent thought was replaced by ecstatic starbursts in my mind.

It was hard to focus on getting him off when I was turning into a useless mound of trembling limbs and needy groans. At one point, I could do nothing but clutch a handful of his hair and gasp while he went all tantric on me.

"Fuck, Nunzio," I gritted out, thrusting up into his hand.

He chuckled. "You like it like that, Mikey?"

"God, yes. Feels so...." The words got lost when he jerked me faster. Heat coursed inside me and dispersed in the way of curled toes and frantic humping. "Oh, shit."

"Yeah...," Nunzio said softly. "You're so fucking hot."

"Shh.... Just make me come. Make me—oh *fuck*."

Nunzio shivered when I blew my load. I sealed our lips together and sucked on his tongue while covering him with my semen. He responded with a hunger that stole my breath and blazed fire through my veins.

I enjoyed the sated feeling for only a moment before I realized our lips were still together, his tongue stroking mine in a sensual way that was fitting for our first real kiss. I'd come all over Nunzio's stomach, and my fingers were still locked around his dick.

A niggle of worry clawed at me, and I pulled away. "Shit."

Nunzio's body was taut with unreleased tension. He pried my fingers off his sticky cock and replaced them with his own. I sucked in a breath and sat up, unable to look away from the sight of my best friend splayed on the couch.

He shoved down his sweats so they were caught around his ankles and fucked his own hand, arching into it and throwing back his head like a porn star. I couldn't stop staring at his parted lips, the way his throat worked with each swallow, and most of all the sight of his cock all slicked up by my semen.

"Michael." His voice was choked and urgent. "Goddamn, I wish you'd touch me."

The words broke through my daze. All it took was one glimmer of pleading blue eyes through the curtain of his thick lashes for me to sink down to my knees and bury my face between his thighs. I ran my tongue over his knuckles, then his fingers, and then he was fucking my mouth with thrust after brutal thrust.

Twice he pulled out when he got too close, and our eyes locked. He smeared the sticky head of his cock against my swollen lips, teasingly tapping it on the flat of my extended tongue, and then he dragged me closer, so I could take the length down my throat again. Nunzio threaded his hands through my hair and held my chin with his other hand, moaning with complete abandon until his voice cracked and he choked out my name.

I swallowed every drop when he came, licking the slit like I wanted more. His stomach quaked and he sighed, thighs parting while I lapped at him like a slutty cat.

"God, you're fucking hot," Nunzio muttered.

I pulled away, and the head of his dick popped out of my mouth. I grinned like a fool, but I was too far-gone to care. He tasted amazing.

"Not bad," I said. "Not at all."

Nunzio sat up, studied me, and then dragged me up by the collar so I was on the couch next to him again. His lips crushed to mine, licking inside, twining with my tongue, and kissing me so deeply that I couldn't keep up. When Nunzio pulled away, he was bright-eyed and I was breathless.

"Go to bed," he whispered. "Before I fucking rape you."

I nodded, thinking that it wasn't rape if I begged for it, but I knew it was better to scramble my ass to the bedroom before this session of fooling around turned into an all-nighter. Judging by the way his hands were roaming all over me, he wouldn't mind at all.

I clumsily got to my feet, and Nunzio reached up to smack my ass. After flipping him off, I tugged up my jeans and stumbled to his bedroom, managing to get there with only one crash against the wall.

I ripped off my T-shirt and threw myself facedown on the bed, leaving the door open. It wasn't quite an invitation, but I wouldn't have minded if Nunzio took it as one.

Chapter Seven

IT FELT bizarre to stand in Nunzio's kitchen cooking breakfast after what had happened the previous night. I had spent the night in his apartment more times than I could count and had cooked a hangover breakfast for us almost every Sunday for the past ten years. Had our fooling around changed that dynamic? There was no way to tell until he woke up, but I worried the entire time I scrambled eggs and poked at the bacon with a fork.

A loud yawn floated in the archway from the living room. I tensed and listened as Nunzio's slow, heavy footsteps headed to the bathroom. My eyes remained on the pan, but I lost focus, hyperaware of every move Nunzio made in the apartment.

An edge of paranoia worked its way through my bloodstream, infecting my flimsy shreds of confidence about handling the situation. I'd leapt out of bed with remnants of regret and a gripping fear that I'd made a massive mistake by throwing myself at him, but resolved to act as normal as possible to see if he followed my lead. The directive had guided me out of bed, through the process of washing up and finding a change of clothes, and to the kitchen. I hadn't doubted the plan... until now.

The bathroom door creaked open, and I took a quick glance at myself in the reflection of one of the glass cabinet doors. The memory of his heated stare and murmured words of appreciation prompted me to run a hand through my spiked-up hair, which was a red flag in and of itself. I'd never cared how I looked in front of Nunzio before.

"Aw, were you gonna make me breakfast in bed?"

"You wish."

Nunzio stood beside me with his phone in hand and looked into the pan of bacon. "Maybe you should just let me do it."

"What?" I looked down. The bacon was starting to burn on one side. "Fuck."

Nunzio nudged me out of the way and confiscated the fork. I hovered by his side for a moment, close enough to notice the damp curls of his hair around his face and smell his minty toothpaste, before I turned to the coffeemaker.

I poured a cup and took a seat at the tiny dinette before giving him a discreet once-over. He was shirtless and wearing a pair of cotton pants that hung just low enough to draw my gaze to his ass.

Nunzio flipped the bacon and glanced at his phone. "Damn, this election is getting ridiculous. I don't know why the union is supporting totally useless candidates for mayor. Dude must have blown someone to get this much support."

The word blown just reminded me of the night before, and I wondered if normal adults could make it through the day without taking everything as an innuendo. Or a reminder of past sexual experiences. Not that six hours was that far in the past.

"Anyone will be better than who we have now." I nodded at the covered pan on the back burner. "There's eggs."

"I'm surprised I had any."

"I am too. They were almost expired. You should go shopping."

"I should start doing a lot of things. I need to start going to the gym again too. I'm going to get all out of shape."

"Yeah, you really look in danger of that."

Nunzio patted his stomach, fingers smacking the bumps and ridges of his abs. I stared at the light trail of hair that went down his stomach and disappeared into his pants. I looked away to avoid ogling his bulge.

Did I use to check him out like this? I didn't think so, but there was no real way to tell if I'd always done it, or if I was just more conscious of it after having had his dick in my mouth.

"Hey, you never know," Nunzio said. "My metabolism could drop, and I could wake up one day with a gut. Anything could happen—we're getting old."

"Speak for yourself."

Nunzio went back to thumbing at his phone, and I settled into the rickety wooden chair. Focusing on how awkward and ungainly I felt sitting at his tiny IKEA kitchen set was preferable to trying to figure out why I was now so obsessed with his body. Casual sex was not something that usually sent me into a high-strung state of overanalysis, but playing ball with my best friend had never been in the cards before.

He glared at whatever was displayed on his phone, and I snorted. Apparently the state of politics in the city had him all up in arms this morning.

"Put your phone away."

"Nah, I'm trying to catch up on this nonsense. I've been out of the loop all summer."

"Yeah, but you also haven't seen me all summer, so I want some attention."

I watched the edge of his mouth curl up in a smile that he wasn't quite ready to reveal, as though it was a secret that my words pleased him. Nunzio made a big show of hitting the button at the side of his phone to shut off the screen before dropping it onto the counter.

"Happy now, needy bitch?"

"Very." I smirked. "You know I like being the very center of your world."

"You are, motherfucker. Like I hang out with anyone else?" Nunzio jerked open a drawer and pulled out a box of cigarettes, then popped one into his mouth. He bent down to light the end off the flame on the stove, and I couldn't tear my eyes away from the way his pants slid down to reveal the seam of his ass.

"You don't like anyone else," I pointed out.

"Facts." Nunzio straightened and let the cigarette dangle from his mouth while flipping off the burner under the pan. "But speaking of needy bitches…. You dropped your phone in the living room, and it was blowing up all night."

"If someone was texting me at that time, I'm pretty sure it's no one I want to talk to."

"You sure?'Cause it was your boy David," Nunzio said, his tone light enough to be completely artificial. "I didn't get a look at the full message, but the notification box started with something a lot like 'I'm a fucking thirst bucket and want your dick in my mouth.'"

I choked on a mouthful of scalding black coffee. "He was drunk and had no idea what the hell he was saying."

Nunzio exhaled a cloud of smoke. "He seemed pretty lucid to me. Go see for yourself."

I stood with a groan and fetched my phone from the living room.

David had indeed texted me multiple times in the wee hours of the morning. He'd begun sending them from the moment I'd left the club and continued on until he'd likely gotten home and passed out.

They started out normal, asking where I was and how I was getting home in typical badly typed drunk-text style, but then veered off into how he wished I'd stayed before claiming he should have come home with me.

Shaking my head, I tossed the phone on the table. A potential ego boost was squashed by the reality that David had zero self-control when drinking. The kid was probably at home burning his iPhone in horror.

"This guy can't have a man the way he acts."

Nunzio moved the strips of bacon onto a plate covered by a paper towel.

"Why not? Not everyone is as noble as you, Mikey. Lots of guys cheat. David and his man might not even be monogamous."

"Yeah, right. Do open relationships really work for anyone?"

"It worked for me back when I was with Gio," Nunzio said, turning to look at me.

"Yeah, until you broke up."

"But that's not why we broke up. It was because I was too young to be that steady with someone. Things would have been different if we were together now. I don't got that frantic need to pound every fine piece of ass I see."

I raised an eyebrow. Ever since we were kids, Nunzio had had issues with preventing his fingers from undoing his fly at the sight of a big ass and a pair of dick-sucking lips.

"Doesn't seem that way to me."

"Just because I do it, doesn't mean I can't live without it."

It was a good point, but the way he was staring directly into my eyes made the comment seem more meaningful than it should have been, and his voice was too even in contrast to the humor I was trying to affect. When the silence stalled and I failed to think of an appropriate response, he shook his head to denounce the topic.

"White bread okay?"

"Sure."

Nunzio grabbed a loaf of bread and tossed it at me before placing the plate and pan of eggs on the table. He sat in the opposite chair, our legs bunched under the table and knees brushing, while I filled four bread slices with crisp bacon and unloaded the eggs equally into our plates. I had a sudden mental image of us cutting school in ninth grade and making the same breakfast for ourselves because we had both been too broke to get anything from the bodega.

I nudged a plate in his direction, and he nodded at me.

"Grazie."

"De nada."

He smiled and stubbed out his cigarette on the windowsill.

I watched him eat without touching my own sandwich and listened to the sounds of Midtown floating in from the sidewalk—honking horns, the random clip-clop of hooves from the horses used for the carriages in Central Park, and a constant hum of voices twined together, indistinguishable but impossible to ignore.

The neighborhood we grew up in had such a different ambiance that it had always felt alien for me to wake up in the middle of Manhattan, even if I had been glad to move out of Queens. Midtown was too crowded, too busy, too expensive, and never slowed down. Lying on my bed with the sound of constant traffic and the steady stream of passing pedestrians hadn't contended with the memory of stretching out in my sweltering room in Queens while listening to the faint sound of salsa outside, and the ringing bell of the piragua guy.

Nostalgia had a way of putting me in a rotten mood, and now wasn't an exception. I slumped in my seat and extended my legs until they slid between Nunzio's. He knocked his knee against mine and jutted his chin at my plate.

"What's wrong?

"Nothing."

Nunzio didn't look convinced, so I picked up my sandwich to appease his concern. I felt his watchfulness even though I didn't meet his eyes. There were multiple pros and cons of bringing up what had happened between us, but avoiding the conversation weighed heavier on the side of *bad fucking idea*.

"So," I said, "about last night."

"What about it?" he asked around a mouthful of bread.

"I was pretty drunk."

"You wasn't that drunk."

"I know, but I wouldn't have been all over you like that if I'd been sober."

"Uh-huh." Nunzio brushed his hands together, raining crumbs on the plate. "So explain to me why you were never all over me when we went out drinking in the past. We used to do it two or three times a week when we were kids."

"Back then I had never—" I faltered, unsure of where I'd been going with that. "Look, I'd never thought about it back then. It was never an option when we were twenty-two, drunk, and horny. But after that night in July, I knew the situation."

"You could be a little more specific, Mikey. You knew what situation?"

I combed both hands through my hair, rolling my eyes at the impatience in his voice. "Jesus, Nunzio, you know what I mean. After July, I had a taste, knew it was amazing, and now apparently when I'm drunk and horny, my brain says it's an option to have some more of the Kool-Aid."

"All right," Nunzio said, spreading his hands. "So what's the problem?"

"There's no problem."

"Then why are you making it sound weird?"

I gave him the what-the-hell-are-you-talking-about squint. "Mira, Nunzio, it's not about weird. I'm not fucking insulting your sexual prowess by saying I was drunk and that's why I stumbled in here and threw myself on top of you."

"Okay, but you're still using the drunk cop-out."

"It's not a cop-out. You're focusing on this minor bullet of information relating to the causes of the event when I'm trying to focus on the effects of the fucking event."

Nunzio pointed at me, finger brushing the tip of my nose. "Don't be whipping out that teacher bullshit on me, talking about causes and effects and bullets. We're not analyzing the fucking Treaty of Versailles. We're talking about my dick and your mouth."

Not bothering to swallow the bubble of laughter that eased my tension, I picked up my bacon sandwich.

"Relax, niño. I'm just trying to make sure it's all good between us, okay? I'm not saying you took advantage of me or trying to pretend it wouldn't have occurred to me at all while sober. I know I can't bullshit you. My concern is whether this is going to be something we should worry about."

Nunzio's broad shoulders rose in a shrug. "Don't know. Should we?"

"I just don't want things to be weird."

"Do you think things are weird?"

Him responding with questions wasn't a good sign. It was a diplomatic tactic he used at work on students, coworkers, and even administrators—gauge the other person's reaction before replying with a lie that would appease them.

"Don't joke around, Medici. I want to know where we stand. Is there anything we need to discuss, or have we just evolved to the stage in adulthood where we can touch each other's dicks without anything more complicated hovering in the background?"

"Hovering in the background? First we were in Global and now we're in English."

The instinct to mush his head backward until he flipped over in his chair grew stronger.

"There's no need for us to have deep, meaningful talks, so calm your tits." Nunzio picked up his fork. "We just got off together. It's just two dudes touching each other. That's it. Don't get nervous."

"I'm not nervous."

"Uh-huh." Nunzio looked down at his plate. "Just go with the flow. We'll be fine."

He sounded so confident that I nodded in agreement, but historically, going with the flow had never worked out too well for me.

I FELT so prepared for the first day of instruction that I was sure something was bound to go wrong. The abrupt start of the school year had given me unfortunate expectations of being set back for weeks, but things were smooth for the first couple of hours.

I knew a handful of the new tenth graders from tutoring after school the previous year, and they seemed like an all-around good group. They were too quiet, but that didn't fool me. The first month of school was a honeymoon period before students' true colors came out, and boundaries were tested after they found their footing with their new teachers.

I delivered my introduction to Global History 10 with my usual straight face and blend of sarcasm and humor, hoping that I was effectively giving off the I'm-nice-but-don't-fuck-with-me vibe.

When the last handful of lingering students exited the room, I grabbed my clipboard and planner and headed to David's room for the team's daily meeting. McCleary required grade teams to have common planning every day during the hour before lunch. Overkill, but I'd adapted to it.

In prior years it had been more like going to hang out with friends. Now that Nunzio was gone and David was running the meetings, I didn't think it would be the same type of show. Especially since I had no idea what David's attitude would be now that we were once again in a professional setting. The guy code-switched between drunk and horny in the wee hours to prim and proper in the daylight like a champ.

My phone vibrated as I made it to the corridor leading to the science wing. I slipped it out one-handed; it was Raymond. He had also called earlier that morning, but I'd let it go to voice mail because class had just begun.

I paused midstep, staring down at Raymond's flashing name, and then up at the clock. I was already a couple of minutes late, but I couldn't ignore his call for a second time.

Making a beeline for the staff lounge, I unlocked the door and slipped inside before the halls cleared. There were a couple of new teachers sitting at the communal computers, so I ducked into the bathroom and locked myself in before answering the call.

"¿Qué pasó?"

"You gotta come home."

I sat on the little table that usually held cleaning supplies, and I pictured my father sick and bent over, choking up blood like he'd done after going on a drinking bender a few weeks earlier. My breath caught.

"¿Está malo?"

"No, but shit is about to get real with me and him. I can tell you right goddamn now."

I exhaled slowly. "Raymond, I don't have time for this bullshit."

"I'm just letting you know. He wants to talk shit, but he can't handle it when I come back at him."

"What the hell happened?"

"He had some people up in here that didn't need to be here, and we got into it."

Great. The last thing I needed, and the thing I had prevented all summer, was Joseph bringing his trifling-ass friends to the house. One of the conditions of our father moving in without me putting up much resistance was that he would not have repeat performances of the not-so-fond days of yesteryear, when he'd turned the house into a spot for his friends while Raymond and I had been at school and our mother had been at work.

My temper flared at the thought of returning home to the place reeking of beer and humid with the sweat of half-a-dozen winos.

"Are they gone?"

"Yeah, they're gone, but he don't know when to shut the fuck up."

I could hear my father rampaging in the background; a steady stream of cursing with the occasional punctuation of "ten cuidao pendejo." The pitch of Joseph's voice activated muscle memory that had me flinching and hunching forward. Suddenly I was ten years old again and expecting a blow.

The reaction was so unexpected that Raymond's rant faded to the background while I tried to ease the feeling of dread forming in my stomach. I pushed through the curtain of anxiety, tuning in again. Raymond was exchanging rapid-fire retorts with Joseph in Spanish.

"Okay, okay. Calm down. You're making things worse."

"I don't give a fuck about things being worse," Raymond's voice boomed in my ear. "I want him gone."

I could picture Raymond so clearly—dark eyes flashing and face transformed into a mask of fury, ready to destroy something or someone. My brother had never been a big troublemaker, but growing up in a house humming with constant tension had put him on edge and always ready for a fight.

"Look, put him on the phone."

"No."

"Well then why are you calling me? Just to rant that he and his bum-ass friends were in the backyard playing dominoes and drinking beer at nine in the morning? If that's the case, I don't give a damn, Raymond."

"I'm just letting you know the situation. I'm not a fucking moron."

"Then how does bugging me at work solve your issue?" I said. "I have a life. I'm at my goddamned job. I can't play babysitter for you and him anymore. If you fight a fifty-five-year-old man and get locked up, don't expect me to bail your stupid ass out. You can stay in Rikers. At least then you'll have an excuse for being unemployed. I'm tired of him, and I'm tired of you. I'm tired of all this fucking bullshit! I should have left months ago."

My voice rose with each word, but by the time my rant was finished, I was more weary than enraged.

The other end of the line filled with raspy, hitched breaths. I winced.

"Ray—"

He hung up before I could say anything more, and I knew I had just set him off worse than he'd been before we'd talked. The phone call had ripped the scab off all the problems that had been festering below the surface.

Despite my aggravation, I wanted to get home and calm the situation, and apologize to Raymond for being a dick. I didn't care about grade team meetings, David, or anything else to do with McCleary. But I couldn't walk out. Not on the first day. Not with administration already watching me.

I left the bathroom with the world swathed in shades of gray. The positivity I'd felt mere moments before had vanished. To make matters worse, the other teachers in the lounge stared at me with wide, inquisitive eyes. Undoubtedly, they had heard every word. I regretted not keeping the conversation in Spanish.

Grinding my teeth together, I hurried to David's room and was instantly on the shit end of his disapproving glare.

"I don't want to call you out," he started, "but I thought we all talked about how imperative it is to start these meetings on time. We've already gotten through the first part of the agenda."

Danielle frowned, but Erica and Kimberly pointedly avoided looking at me.

"Look, something came up," I said without taking the gruffness out of my tone. "I need to step out again and make a call."

"Michael, that's not setting a good tone. I'd appreciate it if you would stay."

"I'm telling you I need to step out and make a few calls. It's not bullshit. I have something going on. A family emergency."

He looked away but not before I caught the glimmer of annoyed skepticism. I'd expected that reaction, but it still set me off.

"You know what, kid? You're not my boss. If I say I have to make a call, I have to make a call. There's nothing on your agenda that can't be relayed to me in an e-mail. You don't need to assert yourself by making a spectacle of me. If you want to think about setting tones, keep that in mind."

Once again, I was ranting without the ability to stop, but this time I could see the person on the receiving end. David's cheeks were flaming as he stared down at his agenda.

I sighed and cursed myself, my father, my brother, and David for being such an easy target. The door shut harder than I'd intended when I returned to the hall.

UPON ENTERING the house, I was greeted by the sound of Héctor Lavoe singing "Aguanilé" with a backbeat of caldero-inspired percussion. The music took me back almost two decades, and this time when I was hit by nostalgia, it wasn't a cause for melancholy. My father listening to salsa while using my mother's rice pot as a conga drum was a fonder memory than most.

I found him in the living room, pounding on the bottom of the pot in perfect unison with the rhythm of the song. I couldn't help but smile. Joseph's shiny black and silver hair was slicked back and damp with sweat, eyes half-shut, and lips moving with the lyrics as if he was in a trance. He didn't notice me until I wandered closer and sat on the arm of the sofa. He jumped, face crinkling in a deep-lined frown. The resounding thumps came to an abrupt stop.

"Did it ever occur to you to get a real drum?"

Joseph set the caldero on the coffee table and reached back to hit the stop button on the stereo. I stared at the device with a hint of disbelief—it had sat unused for so long I'd almost forgotten it worked, and he was using an honest-to-God cassette tape.

"Why are you home so early?" Joseph grumbled, standing.

"Because Raymond called me having a fit. I left since I had a prep seventh period, anyway." I received a blank stare and waved him off, not bothering to explain what a prep period was. The smidgen of fondness diminished when I noticed an empty bottle of rotgut on the shelf next to the stereo. "What's the problem with you and Ray?"

"Your brother is a piece of shit."

The fondness may as well have been nonexistent, because the urge to deck him almost swallowed me whole. "Don't talk about my brother like that."

"You tell your brother to have some respect," he said with a fierce glare. In the past, his flashing eyes had instilled fear and commanded authority, but now they were cloudy and tinged with yellow, telltale signs of disease. "Even you have more respect than he does, and you—"

I raised an eyebrow.

"—are the one who dealt with all of the problems between me and your mother."

"The 'problems'? Is that what we're calling it?"

"Whatever the fuck you want to call it."

"You beating my ass every time you got drunk, arguing with Mami, trashing the house, cops being called—"

Joseph sliced his hand through the air to cut me off. "Enough already. That wasn't my point."

I got his point, but I knew he was going to totally miss mine. Sidestepping him, I grabbed the empty bottle by the neck. I almost expected him to look away with a measure of guilt at how blatantly he was disregarding the wishes of his doctor, siblings, and me by drinking, but he didn't seem to register that anything was wrong. For all that he had changed over the years in some ways, his lack of empathy was the same.

"That's your problem," I said. "You think he doesn't have the right to be angry about anything because he was so young. Okay, fine, fair. He didn't go through the worst of it. But by the time he was old enough to know what the hell was going on, you had stopped living with us and all he knew about his dad was that your rare visits always ended in a fight."

I bristled at the sound of his disgusted sigh.

"You sound like him, making excuses and psychoanalyzing because you watch too much TV. My parents raised me the same way I raised you," he said. "Do you know how many black eyes and busted lips I got from both my mother and father when I got out of line? But I had *respect*, something your mother didn't teach you or that lazy piece of shit you let lay around this house."

"I'm going to say it once more." I squared my shoulders and didn't back down even when he tensed. I didn't step forward, but I also didn't look away from his challenging stare. "Don't talk about my brother like that. It's you and Mami's fault that he is the way he is."

"My fault?" The volume of his voice went from zero to surround sound in two syllables. "I wasn't here all the time, but Vanessa spoiled him rotten. He thinks he doesn't have to work? What will he do when the life insurance runs out?" Joseph turned away with a suck of his teeth and ripped a battered pack of cigarettes from his pocket. "At least you went to school and made something of yourself. When you became a schoolteacher, I was proud. But him? He's going to be a bum like the rest of his friends that stand around in King's Park and smoke marijuana."

"He's young—"

"At his age you were teaching!"

"It's different!"

The smell of the cigarette activated my own craving for nicotine, but I was not about to bum a smoke from him. I strode across the room and looked out the window. Joseph wasn't saying anything that I hadn't told Raymond before, but it sounded different coming out of his mouth—harsher, meaner—and as far as I was concerned, the man who had refused to raise us had no room to judge.

"Growing up the way I did made me want to run as far away as fast as I could, and I knew the only way to make it happen was to work my ass off. But Raymond...."

My eyes slit against the glint of sunlight as I peered through the crisscrossed metal of the screen. I thought I could vaguely make out Raymond's lanky form on the handball court across the street, but I wasn't positive.

"She felt so guilty over my childhood, and was so afraid of Raymond upping and leaving the way I did, that she babied him to prevent it from happening again. She never had the same expectations for him, and he had no fucking motivation to do anything else as long as she was enabling him. And then she was gone."

"So you admit it was your mother."

"No, it was both of you!" I turned and jutted a finger at him. "She let him think it was okay to stay in his room and smoke weed and play video games as long as he was her baby, and you were never here to teach him how to be anything else."

"He had you—"

"An older brother is not the same as a father. I was out of the house before he was even in junior high."

Joseph said nothing to that, but it didn't seem like any of my words were breaking through the invisible barrier he wore to reflect responsibility. His posture was rigid when he picked up his empty glass, gripping it so tight I expected it to shatter and slice through his skin. But it didn't, and when he spoke, the undercurrent in his voice was more weariness than anger.

"I'm proud of you, Michael. I wish your brother was more like you."

"Then act like it. Try to show him how to be a man—help him look for jobs, ask your friends if they know anyone with an opening—do something to help him instead of just cutting him down. Do what you should have fucking done years ago, and maybe he might care about respecting you." I pulled the curtains shut. "Be his father and stop being a burden."

"I'll be dead soon, and then you won't be burdened anymore."

He looked at me, waiting for a reaction, but I kept my face impassive and hard—unwilling to show him how the words twisted my guts and made the bottle feel heavier in my hand. I'd forgotten I was holding it.

I dropped it to the coffee table and shrugged like it didn't matter, like he didn't matter. It was easier to wrap myself in the stubborn resentment than to show him how deeply unprepared I was to lose another parent.

The silence between us grew longer, punctuated only by the distant *thunk* of a ball hitting concrete, before Joseph turned away with damp eyes.

I bit the inside of my cheek to stop myself apologizing and watched him leave the room with his head down.

Chapter Eight

October

"MICHAEL?"

I halted my examination of the crystal statue on Price's desk and looked up. I hadn't heard a word she'd said.

"Are you listening?"

I straightened my back and did my best to look professional and alert. It was hard when I'd rolled into work in a scraggly pair of jeans and a blazer thrown over a black T-shirt to try to make the outfit seem respectable. She didn't have to give me the passive-aggressive lip-purse to let me know I looked like hell; Nunzio did it for her every morning on our way to work.

"Yeah, of course. Sorry."

"Did you hear what I said?"

I clenched my teeth and nodded again, wishing she'd move on and stop dwelling on my obvious inattentiveness. "Yeah, you were talking about the rubric."

Price looked down at the evaluation rubric and the annotations she'd made. I had no idea what she'd been annotating because I'd zoned out as soon as words like "productive struggle" and "rigor" had become repetitive in the conversation.

Post-observation conferences were always the worst. No matter how much we talked about the lesson they'd come in to see, she or the AP would ultimately rate me whatever they wanted.

"Let's put this aside for now," she said in what was supposed to be a gentle tone.

"Why? I want to know how it's going to look before it lands in my mailbox."

"Yes, but first—how do you think the lesson went?"

"I think it was fine. They met their objective, they participated, it catered to multiple types of learners, etcetera."

Her eyebrow arched at the etcetera. "Michael, are you being sarcastic?"

"No. I just didn't think I needed to continue to elaborate when you have your own up-to-the-minute notes."

"I see." Price steepled her fingers together and peered at me, not looking anywhere near the same fifty-yard line as pleased. "You've been having problems lately."

I had been, but my tendency to end each night locked in my room with a bottle of whiskey had nothing to do with Price or her rubric.

"I'm not sure what you mean."

"I've been told that you've been having problems."

It was hard not to get sarcastic this time, so I stayed silent and waited for the lecture that was ultimately heading my way.

"You've been late, you called out once already and it's only October. I've been told that you haven't been doing your part to notify parents about the parent-teacher conferences, and that you've been inconsistent during common planning."

Everything rang true except the last part, and I wondered what David was whining about to give her that idea.

"Oh really? Who told you that?"

"It's irrelevant."

"No, it's not. If my new grade team leader is telling you things, he should tell you the reason why I've been somewhat off."

When she said nothing, I didn't fight the scowl that had already earned me a reputation for being scary among the new tenth graders.

"Did he tell you that my father is ill? I understand that I shouldn't bring my personal problems into work, but there is a lot going on. Sometimes my brother calls me, and I have to rush home. I've explained this to David."

It was a pale shade of the truth. The only phone calls I got from my brother were the kind where he was bitching about our father.

"Perhaps he questions things because of the hostility that exists between the two of you."

My head jerked back. "Hostility?"

"That was the word used."

"That's a pretty radical retelling of the conversations we've had."

Price pressed her palms flat across her desk as if the wood was giving her the strength to deal with me. "You're being defensive."

"Of course I'm defensive. Ms. Price, you're telling me—Never mind."

I had no real way to judge whether she believed my additions to the story, but she picked up the rubric between two fingers and pursed her lips again.

"Forget grade team for a moment. Whether you and David get along, whether you resent him for being grade team leader, or he resents you for not agreeing with his every suggestion is irrelevant to the real problem I have been identifying in your performance since the start of the school year. The heart of the matter is that whatever is going on in your personal life has affected your instruction."

"*How?*"

"You lack energy in the classroom. The rapport between you and the students is not what it has been in the past. They were engaged in this task, but why? Was it because the content was high interest or because of your delivery of the lesson?"

"They met the objectives," I repeated. "I don't know what you mean."

"Yes, they met the objectives," Price replied, a measure of impatience in her voice. "But will they meet the objectives when the subject matter is not as interesting as religion versus science and Giordano Bruno being tortured to death? With your enthusiasm at an all-time low, I wonder how this will affect their performance when you're discussing Enlightenment philosophes and not radical scientists. Which, by the way, you should have been up to by now."

By the time she finished speaking, I was willing myself to implode all over her desk and the goddamned rubric she kept pointing at with a red-lacquered fingernail. I tried to calm down, but I knew my face was veiled in anger. I'd rather be burned at the stake with Bruno than listen to her bullshit.

Criticizing me for things that had yet to happen had always been Price's strong point, but it had never been about my teaching. I may have been a disaster in most other areas of my life, but my teaching had always been on point.

And if the ninth grade history teacher had gotten up to the 15th century, I wouldn't have had to backtrack so far in September to review. The words gathered in my mouth, but I held in the string of retorts. The fire of my defiance fizzled before I could put up a fight.

"Okay. I'll do better."

She looked surprised. The papers made a slapping sound when she dropped them onto the desk. "I hope your father is well."

"Thanks."

THE NIGHT of parent-teacher conferences, I ditched my jeans and jacket combo for a button-down shirt and slacks. I'd called all the parents on my list in the days after my meeting with Price, and because I spoke Spanish unlike the rest of my grade team, I was able to schedule appointments with most of them.

David poked his head into my classroom twice to "check up on things," and each time I had to resist the urge to slam the door in his face. That desire didn't fade even after three hours of nonstop parent meetings and another half hour of cleaning up my room for the morning.

I was in the midst of dragging desks back into their quads when I heard keys clinking behind me. I looked over my shoulder to see David standing in the doorway looking tired and disgruntled.

"How'd it go? You looked busy all night."

"I was." I finished lining up the desks, scrutinized the layout of the room, and then grabbed the stacks of report cards and transcripts. "I heard your outreach didn't pan out so well."

David didn't miss the cheap shot. "You can't resist making fun of me, can you?"

"Nope." I shoved the paperwork into a folder and crossed several names off my list. "You can't resist the desire to talk shit so I'm following your lead, Papi."

His forehead wrinkled. "What do you mean?"

"Forget it."

"Why can't we have a decent conversation?"

"Because you're just as bad as I knew you would be, and I hate it when people live up to my low-ass expectations." I walked to my desk and dropped the folder on top. "You went behind my back and complained about me to Price."

"No, I didn't."

"Don't play me for a sucker, kid. She told me all about it during my last post-observation. She said there was *hostility* between us."

David recoiled, his features locked in an indignant expression. Some of my conviction crumbled.

"I never said any such thing to her. Why the hell would you believe I'd do that?"

"Because we don't get along, and I second-guess you in front of the others."

"Yeah, but why would you think I'd go running to Price after what you said to me about setting a tone? I know you think I don't listen, but I do. You've been teaching much longer than me, and I have a lot to learn."

I contemplated his earnest expression. "Then who did you talk to?"

"I didn't—" David broke off when I glared. He smoothed his sleeves from where they had bunched at his elbows and tried to straighten out the wrinkles. "I just spoke to another teacher. I was frustrated with you, but I never said that we had hostility between us. I didn't even go into detail. I'm just as much a problem in this as you are."

"I'm glad you know that."

David gave me a scornful look. I couldn't help but smile.

The guy was so high-strung it was hard not to poke at his flaws. In the month and a half we'd worked together, I'd realized how contradictory he was in terms of expectations and actions. He wanted to seem like an indestructible automaton with the best strategies and classroom practices, but didn't have the patience to wait for the experience that would get him closer to that goal.

I had no doubt he would burn out after his third or fourth year. No one could run on fumes for so long when they were so demanding of themselves and everyone around them.

"Why don't we talk like adults and forget this kiddy shit?"

I sat on the edge of my desk and patted the spot next to me. David moved closer, watching his step as though my room was hazardous and full of landmines. He leaned against the whiteboard nearest to my desk.

"What do you want to talk about?"

"I want to know which teacher you spoke to."

David shrugged. "Too bad. I'll discuss the situation with them myself. I'm sorry I trusted the wrong person, but I'm not going to throw them under the bus before I have the facts."

It wasn't the answer I wanted, but at least the little fucker was loyal. I studied him and switched gears. "Where are you from?"

"Connecticut."

I nodded, unsurprised. "Where'd you go to school?"

"Brown. Why?" It seemed like he was waiting for a punch line that would land him on the butt end of a white-bread joke. "What about you?"

"All city colleges."

"Oh."

"Is that a problem?"

"No! Why the hell are you so defensive all the time? It's like you walk around with this chip on your shoulder and think everyone is always trying to say they're better than you."

"People usually are." When he opened his mouth to protest again, I held up a finger to thwart the words. "You have no idea what it's like being me. You've got no fucking idea how it feels to be scolded by a twenty-four-year-old kid about professionalism while in a room full of white people. It's bad enough that this system makes it seem like teaching experience is inverted—the more time you put in, the worse you get according to the city. Better trust things in the hands of baby grads who have their head full of ideals and are easily brainwashed by the admin."

"No one thinks you're a fuckup because you're not white."

"Don't turn this into race baiting—that's only a fragment of what I said. I'm not saying you have problems with me because I'm Puerto Rican. I'm telling you how your attitude, and how Price's attitude, makes me feel. And why that leads to it looking like I have a chip on my shoulder."

David nodded, but I could tell he didn't see what I meant. I bet he'd grown up in some safe household in a whitewashed suburb where everyone played at politically correct activism. He had likely never considered the possibility that a guy like me could still feel uncomfortable in a school full of people like him. No matter how liberal he thought he was.

"I don't think I'm perfect," he said after a breath of silence.

"I sure as hell hope not."

"I don't. I'm messed up and stressed all the time. I'm sure… I'm sure my stuff sounds stupid compared to your dad being sick and everything, but it's not like I'm thrilled with my situation either."

David inched closer to the desk and looked at me from beneath a fall of platinum hair. The kid's face belonged in a Botticelli painting.

"Is this about your complicated situation?"

"Not entirely, but kind of. I mean, it relates." David adjusted the collar of my shirt, smoothing it down; a minor imperfection that had nagged him and his unceasing need for order. "My parents were by all accounts perfect, and I'm their only son, so I have to live up to that. I seek out these situations that should be ideal and work really hard to achieve things, but I never feel successful."

"Financially successful?" I pushed his hand away from my shirt.

"No. I wouldn't have become a teacher if I cared about the money."

Spoken like a true trust-fund baby.

David widened his eyes again, turning the conversation into a confessional. "I mean intrinsically. No matter what I do, there is no intrinsic sense of accomplishment. I always feel like I'm trying to catch up to something that's out of reach. I plateau when I hit a milestone and then can't move up no matter what I do. And my relationship with my boyfriend is just like that."

"So you do have a boyfriend."

"We've been separated a couple of times but…." David looked at the ceiling for answers. "I always know I'll end up going back to him, and I'm always disgusted when I do. And then I get angry that I'm such a dick about it because there's nothing *wrong* with him. It's just… not what I wanted. Not how I thought I'd feel with another person. But he's perfect, so there's no real reason to break up."

"Your generation is so messed up."

"It's true." He didn't appear surprised by my assessment. "The Millennials are screwed up in a lot of ways, but which one do you think applies to me?"

"People your age either use the recession as an excuse to not even attempt adulthood, or try to fight the reality of the economy by expecting 200 percent from yourselves—like that will change the situation. A lot of teachers here are like that. They do everything they can to capitalize on this system's idea that youth is superior to time put in by vet teachers by racing to leadership positions. But then their stamina fizzles out because they take on so much."

David's gaze turned imploring, and he nodded slowly. It was almost like he wanted me to explain what was wrong with him so he could go out and try to fix it. Watching him look so lost was depressing. The kid was doing a lot better for himself than most.

"My boyfriend is like that too," David said. "He's achieved more than most of my friends from college, but he still thinks it isn't enough.

He's a wreck because of it, but he also has a lot of guilt over his privilege and wealth. His father owns some hedge fund. He's like a billionaire."

"Is that why you don't feel the same way about him?"

"No... not just that."

"So, then, what? You're waiting for a soul mate, and he's just good on paper?"

David shrugged and tried to affect nonchalance, but I saw his mouth twitching up in a guilty smile.

"Am I right?"

"Kind of." David studied the Enlightenment books the kids had created and then a map of Versailles I'd stuck to the whiteboard. "The problem is... sexual chemistry. Or lack thereof."

"Oh."

His gaze settled on me again. "Yeah."

"And that's why you push up on me when you're drunk and feeling all naughty and brazen."

The answer came slower, his voice quieter, "Yeah."

I wanted to laugh at the cliché of it all. The Ivy League graduate, buttoned-up and shiny blond, earnestly trying to make a difference in the inner city, but bored with his yuppie boyfriend—a lawyer, premed, maybe some executive at a start-up—because the sex was vanilla, and I was the macho Latino dude with the answer to it all.

It was so corny that I wanted to tell him I wasn't the firecracker Puerto Rican to spice up his sex life, but my mind was already cranking out the possibilities of how I could do just that. No wonder the kid had come so hard from being used by me and Nunzio's hot, Sicilian ass. I could clearly see him deep throating Nunzio while I ran my tongue all over him, and my gears shifted from castigating lecturer to willing participant in his undoing.

I tried to look away, but David's lips were parted, and damned if he didn't look like he wanted a repeat performance right then and there. Just admitting to his dirty little secret seemed to have turned him on. He moved in a step until he was standing between my thighs and dropped his hands on either side of me.

My thoughts hurtled ahead, and I wondered how bad he wanted my dick—if he'd let me do him right there even if it meant him cheating on his poor bastard of a boyfriend.

The idea was at once delightfully filthy and a massive turnoff, but the notion of someone wanting me so much was enough to make me shoot my load. Too bad it was never going to happen.

David listed forward, and I leaned back inch by pathetic inch until a figure shadowed the doorway over his shoulder.

Nunzio's hands were in the pockets of his bomber jacket and a book bag hung from one shoulder as he stood in the doorway. I waited for him to smirk or joke, to make some inappropriate comment referencing our threesome, but he was just silent and staring.

I planted a hand against David's chest and shoved him away. Confusion flashed in his face, but then he noticed Nunzio looming behind him.

"I didn't know the market was still open on your ass," Nunzio commented with a hint of his usual drawling smarm. "I'd have been all over that, Mr. Butler."

David reddened and muttered something, but I'd already quit paying him any mind. I wondered if Nunzio was serious. After that night in July, he'd never given any indication that he still found David attractive, and the possibility wasn't as pleasant as it had been thirty seconds ago when my brain had provided a play-by-play of us wrecking David on a sweat-soaked bed.

I didn't realize I was frowning until Nunzio's smirk finally made an appearance, hard-edged and teeth flashing white at me.

I stepped around David and he looked at me sidelong, but I followed the route of pretending nothing out of the ordinary was happening. I jerked my chin at Nunzio. "You want to head out?"

"Nah, why don't you finish up with David."

"We're finished."

David nodded, but it may as well have been in slow motion. The baffled look he was aiming at me only heightened my sudden desire to kick him out of the room.

"Nope, I'm gonna head out on my own. I need to get the fuck out of this building before I slaughter someone." Nunzio gave me the same tight-lipped smile, unreadable and completely fake, and backed away. "But you should tell David about the happy hour tomorrow."

Now I was dumbfounded. He'd informed me that David was persona non grata at his annual post-PTC shindig, as were Kimberly and Erica.

"Okay, then," I said slowly.

"Catch you kids later."

Nunzio turned away, and I listened to the sound of his receding footsteps until they faded completely when a door opened and closed.

"That's cool that he invited me," David said, face lit up and oblivious like a kid on a summer morning. "Who else is going?"

"I don't know. I didn't invite them. Probably Karen and Danielle."

David asked me another question, something about the venue and what time people were meeting, but I didn't respond right away.

The tension and flirtation between us had drifted to the back of my mind like a lecture on educational theory—interesting in the moment but easy to forget once it was over. I was much too worried about what was going on in Nunzio's head and wondering why I was suddenly in the dark about what he was thinking.

Chapter Nine

TEACHER HAPPY hour started at four thirty. By the time the typical party crowd showed up, the remaining stragglers from McCleary were well and truly shitfaced. Nunzio and I were among them, which was a surprise to nobody at all.

The good thing about the outing being at a so-called beer garden in Williamsburg was that it was spacious enough for conversations to be carried out in the brisk October wind, and I was a good distance from the rest of our colleagues. Things were fine until I saw David and Nunzio getting cozy at the bar.

I choked on my beer, causing bubbles to rise in the Viking-style stein that I was holding with both hands. My throat burned in protest, and I gasped a couple of times before setting the stein on the table I'd moved to on the side of the patio. Nunzio had only invited a select group of teachers from McCleary, but they talked about work with a single-minded focus that I couldn't handle—especially not when Nunzio was playing games.

All of a sudden, Nunzio was leering at David and giving him come-suck-me smiles. Even David had seemed caught off guard by the sudden shift in Nunzio's behavior and had avoided him for most of the night.

Until now.

An enormous guy with a blond beard and a faux-hawk got in my line of sight, and I had to stop myself from shoving him out of the way. He stood there with his miniature can of PBR and ranted on like a goddamned idiot about being a bona fide zombie survivalist. The conversation was so absurd that I quit eyeballing Nunzio and David to sneer at Mr. Faux-Hawk and his skewer of minisausages. He beamed up at me, oblivious to my hatred, and asked if I watched *The Walking Dead*.

I shot him my most baleful stare and walked around him to return to my spying. David was close to Nunzio's side, grinning as they looked at his phone while one of his hands rested on the small of

David's back. The motherfucker was rubbing it, but the movement was so subtle, I wouldn't have noticed it if I hadn't zeroed in on it with guided-missile precision.

What the hell was wrong with me? What did I care if Nunzio suddenly wanted to bang David? We both hooked up with random people all the time. Why did it matter if his fingers were slipping under the hem of David's T-shirt? When had I reacted this adversely to the sight of Nunzio about to score?

For the past two decades, I'd watched him suck in scores of guys and had never felt this level of irritation, but I wanted to punch someone in the face at the sight of Mr. Ivy League leaning into Nunzio's touch.

I could suggest a threesome, but David was off the table for me. There would be no nooky and no helping this poor, confused baby gay cheat on his oblivious premed/lawyer boyfriend.

With that in mind, I decided to inform my best friend of that decision. Just to give him the option of following suit.

A phone rang—the ringtone a blend of pop and dubstep—and David hightailed it like his ass was on fire. He answered and made his way to the entrance of the bar.

I took his place at Nunzio's side. "Having fun?"

"Why are you standing in the corner and watching us like a creep?"

I grabbed Nunzio's glass. It looked like cranberry but smelled like vodka, and I confirmed that by draining it. "I didn't want to interrupt."

"So you just stood there?"

"Yeah, why not? I was curious."

"About what?" The sides of Nunzio's mouth curled up.

"About your plans. So are you going to smash him all of a sudden?"

"Maybe. He's a cute kid."

"I'm just letting you know"—I scanned the row of bottles behind the bar instead of looking at my best friend—"that he's got a man."

"Yeah, but I don't."

"So where's your moral compass?"

"I left it in the West Indies with Christopher Columbus."

I wasn't going to laugh at Nunzio's stupid jokes. I refused to humor him no matter how adorable he was when his eyes crinkled at the sides.

"You know, what if it was me? What if I was David's man and you were helping him to do me dirty?"

It was a weak line of reasoning. I knew it, he knew it, and the bartender with the eight-inch chops hanging off the side of his face most likely knew it. My desperation to keep Nunzio out of David's pants was so crystal clear that a voice in the back of my head screamed at me to shut up and quit being so pathetic. I was embarrassing myself and the inner part of my psyche that still had a mote of pride. I crushed it mentally and tilted the glass to eat the ice.

"That's really all you got, Mikey?"

I crunched the ice with my back teeth. "Whatever, Nunzio. I'm just saying—if I was you, I wouldn't mess with him. He has a man. He's like a little helpless baby gay who needs guidance and not cocks up his ass every time he gets drunk. Be a better gay guide, sucio."

Nunzio's elbows thumped on the top of the bar, and he listed forward, smelling like vodka and cigarettes. I wanted to lean in and inhale him, bury my face in his neck and just breathe. It was a weird urge, but this whole situation was weird. Including the fact that I now found his angular jaw so tempting and the way I kept admiring how his shoulders looked covered in a tight Henley.

"This is what I hate about queer people," Nunzio said. "They always think you have to be some kind of activist. Why can't we just not care about shit like everyone else?"

"Because that's what's wrong with this country."

"What are you? My mother?"

"No, because your mother is part of the problem with this country."

"And those are true facts." Nunzio laughed, slapping his hand on the bar and so cheerfully drunk that I nearly regretted coming down on him for his life choices—but not if it kept his dick out of David.

"Look—don't do it. Just leave him alone. Let him figure out his life. Don't be a scumbag."

Nunzio sighed through the remaining bursts of chuckles, wiping his face with the back of his hand. The music changed and grew louder, a remix of a song I hated even more with the inclusion of dubstep drops. The bass vibrated so loud that I winced and ducked my head as if we were under siege. I didn't protest when Nunzio grabbed the front of my shirt to drag me closer so he could be heard.

"But maybe I just don't want to go home alone?"

"Why not?"

"Maybe I'm lonely."

"You can go home with me."

Nunzio dragged his fingers across the bar, tapping a beat until they bumped into my hand. His skin was cold, and I covered the back of his hand with my palm, rubbing in a halfhearted attempt to warm him up.

"Yeah, but what if I need to let off some steam?" He looked down at our hands. "You know?"

Behind us, a cheer went up and filtered in from the patio. I didn't have to avert my gaze to recognize the voices—Danielle, Charles, Karen, a couple of other teachers from our floor and at some point David had returned. He must have taken a roundabout route along the perimeter of the bar to avoid me and Nunzio, which was smart, since I was almost positive he'd been on the phone with his allegedly ex-boyfriend.

It solidified my own decision to keep off him. At some point the kid would figure out what he wanted, but I had a feeling he wasn't the type to be satisfied with being passed around like a toy, which would be the case whether he slept with me or Nunzio. He wanted perfection, and not being someone's top choice didn't fit that goal.

David's laugh rang out again, and I almost turned to seek him out in the crowd, but I kept looking at my best friend and the tiny grin playing around his generous mouth.

No, David would never be my or Nunzio's top choice. Not even for a casual fuck. Not anymore, anyway.

"We can figure something out," I answered finally.

The grin got wider and Nunzio slid off the barstool. "Bet. Then let's go."

WE TOOK two trains to get back to the West Side of Manhattan, and the entire time Nunzio's gaze was on me. The Medici bedroom eyes were near infamous for those who knew him, but I'd never had them aimed at me other than on that one drunken night.

Since high school he'd always been the playboy, even though I had become sexually active first. I'd gone for whatever I could get as a teenager, but Nunzio had always set his sights on the hottest and the most unattainable. One look into those Sinatra-like baby blues and even the straightest of the hottest jocks or thugs at our school in South Jamaica melted in front of him and wound up with their knees in the air. Everyone I introduced Nunzio to always went on about how fuckable he was but I'd known him for so long I'd never truly understood what they meant until I'd felt his hands and mouth on me.

Was this what other people felt once they'd had Nunzio's hard, muscular body against them? Did their stomachs go all hollow and fluttery when he pinned them with that filthy eye-fuck? I was hard just from the expression on his face, and I felt like the other straphangers had to know that he was thinking something dirty—about me. About whatever he wanted to happen in the next hour.

Jitters crawled through my body. I licked my lips, overly aware of how warm I was and of the sweat gathering beneath my jacket. When we arrived at our stop, I was grateful.

The station at 50th was deserted when we got off the train. As soon as it took off through the tunnel, rushing by and causing my hair to fly about wildly, Nunzio dropped his backpack and shoved me against one of the columns lining the platform. My heart caught in my throat.

His tongue slid between my parted lips and caressed my own. I dug my hands in the folds of his leather jacket and tried to regain a measure of control.

Everything about him drove me crazy—how good he smelled, how strong he was, the menthol and vodka taste of him, and the way he immobilized me so casually with one arm pinned alongside the column above my head and the other cupping the side of my face.

He knew what he was doing, and he knew what he wanted, and I was just along for the ride.

I peered at him, but all I saw were lashes and delicate eyelids as Nunzio coaxed a response out of me with talented strokes of his hot velvet tongue. He made a sound low in his throat, a soft hum of pleasure, and it cut through my scattered thoughts.

I returned his kiss, intending to make him as breathless and frantic as I was, and released one hand from his jacket to tangle it in his hair. I gripped hard and attacked his mouth. I didn't resist when he pushed me harder.

Nunzio rocked against me, but the layers of denim made the friction less intense. He hissed in frustration and dropped a hand between us, aggressively pawing at my belt and fly before yanking his own.

"Wait," I muttered when my jeans loosened and sagged.

He shushed me with his lips, and I heard his zipper slide down. "I just wanna touch it."

My heartbeat spiked again. I wasn't nearly drunk enough to get through this. I was too conscious that this was Nunzio playing me like a goddamned symphony and making my dick ache. This was Nunzio turning me into a wreck in an empty subway station in the middle of the night.

I started to say something, but the words dissolved into a hoarse gasp when he stroked both our dicks with slow, measured tugs of his hand. I arched my hips into his touch, using the column for leverage.

My concern about our state of undress, and the faint sound of voices on the other side of the platform, disappeared. Every thought centered on his fingers sliding along the veiny slickness of my dick, and the way he explored the inside of my mouth.

He sucked on my tongue, nursing at it and then released it to nip at my lower lip. My fingers tightened in his hair, a death grip that kept his face close to mine so I could kiss him with bruising force. I didn't let him pull away, didn't want to see his knowing smile and hooded eyes. I wanted to taste him without thinking, feel him without seeing, and enjoy the sensation of my body turning inside out with a fierce desire to never let this end.

His hand moved just enough to stimulate, but the intensity of our kiss swelled until my mind was void of everything but him. The sound of his breathless sighs, the feel of his hand releasing my dick to slide upward so he could hold me tighter, our bodies grinding languidly together, and the way we both poured everything into the other until we were raw and undone.

A tremor stole over me, and, finally, I had to pull away. He stared at me wild-eyed and shattered with his lips damp and parted.

"Train coming," I said, voice scraping out low.

"Oh." Nunzio fumbled with his pants. "Yeah, okay." He zipped up around his erection and winced a little.

I did the same, fixing my jeans, and trying to ignore the sharp pang of unsatisfied lust. "You good?"

Nunzio nodded. "Yeah. Yeah, of course."

"Okay, then. Let's go."

I shifted away from the wide column that had shielded us, but he jerked me back. "Wait a sec," he muttered and leaned in for one last kiss. He licked in slowly, deliberately, and then traced my swollen lips with his tongue before pulling away.

I stared dumbly and was forced into mobility by the sudden rush of the train hurtling through the tunnel. No one departed from the car nearest to us, but we started walking anyway, acting as though we hadn't just spent ten minutes kissing on the filthy platform.

I stole glances at him as we strolled toward the staircase, but he looked no different than usual, as if us fooling around was now just a normal part of our friendship.

Maybe it was and I was overreacting, but I couldn't stop myself from analyzing his every move, like a teenage boy with a crush. Things were better off with my dick in his hand, when I was too distracted to think about the implications of what was happening between us.

"Damn, it's cold out here."

I nodded but didn't feel it. It was after two in the morning, but crowds of people stood in front of restaurants and bars along Eighth Avenue. I nearly asked Nunzio if he wanted to get a drink or go dancing, but got tongue-tied when I noticed his eyes locked on me. It was the first indicator that this was going to veer off into the land of *complicated* really fast.

We stopped to wait for the light and I shot him a nervous smile.

"So what do you want to do?" he asked.

A flood of taxis rushed by, lights flashing in the darkness and nearly blinding me. I looked away, back down the street and toward a large gay sports-themed bar that had just opened.

"I could go for another drink."

"We could just pick up some bottles at the liquor store and go to my place."

"We could pick up another little friend."

"What do I need someone else for? I got you."

I turned my head so fast I nearly gave myself whiplash. He looked serious and a little annoyed.

"You had fun last time."

"Mikey, I thought you were cool with this. If I wanted some little twink, I'd have stayed with David. You know?"

"Yeah, but are we seriously just going to your place to screw around?"

"Yes."

"Jesus Christ, you're such a horndog."

Nunzio shrugged, unashamed, and snagged my hand. "Come on, gorgeous. It's so much better when it's just us. We can just get off and then we can chill. Sex without the song and dance and having to spend a fortune on drinks."

I didn't know what to say, so I said nothing, opting to cross the street when the cars stopped. It was more than a little absurd that I couldn't bring myself to discuss the situation when I'd just had my tongue in his mouth, but it was different when we were out in the real world.

He didn't let go of my hand, and I didn't pull away, so we wound up walking to his door looking like we were about to go skipping through a field with flowers in our hair. I was momentarily embarrassed when his neighbor ran into us and gave Nunzio a knowing grin.

Once we entered his apartment, déjà vu hit me like a mallet, and I saw myself stumbling into the dark living room on wobbly legs before throwing myself on top of Nunzio as he slept on the sofa. Flashes of wet mouths and soft gasps accosted me, and the memory of my name dripping from Nunzio's mouth in a sultry groan rang in my ears.

Swallowing, I snuck a glimpse of him in the dark, but he was just a rangy form moving through the apartment before jerking the cord on a lamp. Golden light flooded the room.

Nunzio kicked off his boots. "So what are you in the mood for?"

"Regarding what?"

"Regarding alcohol." Nunzio shrugged off his leather jacket, then took mine, and threw them over the back of an armchair. "How drunk do you need to be right now?"

"What do you mean?"

"It means whatever you want it to mean, Mikey." Nunzio dropped onto the couch, extending his legs in front of him and folding his arms behind his head. "How drunk do you need to be for your best friend to rail you?"

There was an implication in there that was wearying. I just shrugged and watched him snag a bottle and two shot glasses from the bar. It was not more than a narrow, beat-up cabinet wedged between the wall and the door leading to his bedroom, but Nunzio had arranged the bottles inside with meticulous precision.

"You cool with vodka?"

"I guess. Especially since you're trying to imply I need to be drunk to get it on with your ugly ass."

"Oh, screw you."

"I'm so serious."

Nunzio flipped me off and poured two shots. We downed them, and I nearly gagged. It was sweet.

"Ugh."

"Want me to change it up?"

I smacked my lips, tilting the bottle so I could see the flavor. Coconut.

"It'd be better with some pineapple juice, but it's fine if we're going for gayest drinks ever."

"Shut the hell up." Nunzio watched me measure out the next set of shots. "So you really never thought about having sex with me?"

"Not really."

"Seriously?" He threw back the next shot. "What about when we sleep next to each other or whatever? All those times we wound up in the same bed on a trip or even after going out drinking?"

"Nope."

Nunzio's brow knitted together. "When we used to pick up guys and spend the whole night wrecking them in the same room?"

"Nope."

He seemed so disbelieving that I chortled, sliding my shot glass back onto the coffee table. "I'm not joking. I never considered it before we had that threesome with David."

"That's messed up."

"How the hell is that messed up?"

"Because, that makes it seem like you don't find me attractive or something." Nunzio jutted his chin at me. "That ain't what you're saying, is it?"

It was tempting to say yes and make up some flaws about him, but I just waved him off. "We've been friends since I had braces and you had acne. I didn't see you that way for a long time. You remember how weirded out we both were after kissing in middle school."

"Uh, yeah, that was before I knew how to use my dick."

Even while flipping a shot glass between his long fingers, Nunzio's features were creased in an accusatory glare.

"Are you really that offended?"

"Hell yeah. You're trying to play me."

I snickered again. "You need to relax."

"Who's not relaxed?" Nunzio put the shot glass on the table with a *thunk*. "I'm fine. Just wondering where your head is."

Unconvinced, I spread my hands. "Anything else to this inquisition?"

"Yeah. You said you never thought about it before this summer, so what about after?"

I'd backed myself into a corner with that admission, and the sharklike smile sliding over Nunzio's face made it obvious he'd clued in to that same detail.

"I thought about it sometimes."

"What'd you think about?"

A tableau of pornographic stills flitted through my mind like a slideshow on fast forward, but I hesitated to say which one I'd gotten off to for the past three months. Especially since I'd analyzed each one while naked under my ceiling fan and fucking myself with a dildo.

"C'mon," he cajoled. "I'm curious. If you never considered touching me before that night, there must have been something that stood out. Like for me...." Nunzio raised one broad shoulder, face intent and one hand curling around the edge of the couch cushion. "I kept thinking about you sucking on my fingers and grinding back on me like you wanted my dick."

"I did." The words were out before I could stop them, but his eyes were hypnotizing me. "I wanted you in my ass. I thought about you shooting inside me all summer."

"Yeah?" His voice was so low and husky I barely heard it over a fire truck careening down the street outside.

"Yes. I hardly even let Clive fuck me raw."

One of his hands dropped to his crotch, squeezing and adjusting his dick. It was an unconscious gesture, but I could see the outline of his cock snaking down the thigh of his jeans. My mouth went dry.

"You like it raw, Mikey?"

"With you I do."

"Mmm."

Nunzio slumped down on the sofa, spreading his thighs wide and giving me a better view. The slow slide of his smile and the twitch of his eyebrows were so arrogant that I wanted to laugh him off, but my dick throbbed at the sight, demanding stimulation and diverting all coherent thought to its needs.

I grabbed the vodka and poured another couple of shots. I shoved one in his face and the clear liquid sloshed over the rim and onto my hand. When Nunzio declined to take it, I pushed it to his mouth and forced his head back until his lips parted.

He drained the glass and dropped it on the table before turning his face to lick the spilt vodka off the back of my hand. Nunzio closed his fingers around my arm, kissing up higher until his mouth warmed the inside of my wrist.

"Nunzio, don't be a weirdo."

It was meant to be light, a way to laugh him off, but my voice dropped an octave. His only response was to part his lips wider so the warm wetness of his mouth enveloped my skin before he pulled away with a sucking sound.

"Come on, Mikey," he said. "It's just us. No one watching. No one's going to find out." He shifted so he could straddle me and hold my shoulders against the back of the couch. "Just have fun with me. No one's gonna know."

"It's not that." I swallowed again, and my eyes slid shut when he dove in, mouth attacking my throat and sucking on the bobbing lump of my Adam's apple. "Jesus Christ, Nunzio. What's with you?"

His tongue dragged along the rough stubble on my throat. "Just really horny, and you're right here. And I haven't stopped thinking about stretching that ass out since July."

His hand slid between us, massaging the hard length in my jeans. I groaned.

"I like when you make noise," Nunzio whispered. He pressed down harder, drawing another gasp out of me. "Sexy motherfucker."

"You're so full of shit," I whispered, arching up.

"I'm speaking facts, son. You have no idea what you do to me."

I tilted my head back to look up at him, but his face was cast mostly in shadow.

"Nunzio, this is just fucking, right?"

Nunzio's hips jutted forward, and the movement sent zings of fire spreading through my nervous system, making my toes curl.

He dipped down again and this time his mouth latched onto the side of my neck. The sound that poured from my mouth was uncontainable, but I tried anyway, biting my lower lip.

"Yeah," he murmured.

I clamped my hands onto his hips, guiding him faster. "You swear?" I gritted, releasing my savaged lip.

"I swear."

The words were muffled in a flurry of movement. Nunzio slid off my lap and evaded my desperate, grasping hands. With rough, impatient motions, he wrenched me around, undid my belt and fly, and pushed me down with my arms digging into the back of the sofa. The blunt edges of his fingernails dug into my skin when he tugged down my jeans. He let out an annoyed growl when they caught around my boots and tossed them aside before arranging me on the couch so my knees were bent and my ass was sticking out.

The sound of him panting and swearing, so impatient to touch me, to fuck me, caused everything I had been trying to hold back to release in a trickle of precome from the tip of my cock. I pressed my mouth to the microfiber fabric and rocked against the throw pillow that was trapped between my abdomen and the back of the couch.

The fire in my gut threatened to spread, and overtook me until my hand twitched with the need to grab my dick. I gripped the cushion with clawed fingers to prevent jerking off even though the throb was unbearable.

Behind me, I heard the metallic glide of a zipper, the thud of clothes hitting the floor, rustling, and the jingle of keys.

"What—"

Something cold and gooey slid down the cleft of my ass. I recoiled in surprise and hoped that he had lube or lotion in his backpack because using hand sanitizer to slick up wasn't my idea of a good time.

I planted one foot on the floor for leverage when he splayed me open and rubbed my pucker with the pad of his thumb. My ass clamped up, resisting the sudden intruder. He replaced it with the blunt tip of his cock, and the part of me that was starved for contact—for a hard, thorough pounding—crested. I pushed back on him and bit the sofa's padding as the sweet burn of him sliding home overshadowed the ache of my cock.

"Yeah," he uttered, freezing in place once he was fully sheathed in my ass.

Nunzio sucked in deep, shaky breaths while allowing me to adjust to his girth. But I didn't want to wait.

The feel of him raw and buried balls deep was like a drug. I couldn't think straight, and I couldn't react to anything but the unquenching desire to be ridden without any consideration or care.

I took the initiative and flexed my ass around his dick. Nunzio dug his fingers in tighter before slamming me back with a rough pull that descended into a brutal railing. He punched into my ass so hard it seemed he would screw me through the couch.

The constant mash of pressure against my hole made me see stars, and was intensified by my dick grinding along the pillow. It shouldn't have been enough to make me peak, but I could feel it coming in the way the flames licked up from my balls, spread to my belly, and turned me into a babbling mess.

A mantra of *right there* and *yes* filled the room while I clutched the sofa with one hand and reached back to grip his thigh with the other. I tried to guide him faster, but my hand slipped on his sweaty flesh, so I settled for ramming myself back on his cock.

The repeated words lapsed into a series of senseless groans, and the fabric beneath my gaping mouth grew damp from drool. I didn't care. I had no shame. I didn't even know who I was anymore, because Nunzio's gorgeous cock was nailing my prostate over and over until the combination of such sweet precision and the friction of my erection against the pillow caused me to seize up with a strangled shout.

I felt the orgasm approaching, but I wasn't prepared for the hands-free eruption that led to me shooting all over his sofa with a wild cry. I blanked out in a daze of boneless limbs and tingling nerves, and returned to reality once Nunzio pulled out.

I expected to feel the warm spatter of his jizz on my ass, but Nunzio manhandled me onto my back and splayed my thighs open wide enough for them to burn. He slid back into me and I spread my knees as wide as possible, steadying one foot against the coffee table, and replicated the filthy smile he'd given me earlier that night.

I watched his face flush darker and could tell he was about to bust. I knew it by the way his cock pulsed, the way his fingers tightened hard enough to break capillaries beneath my skin, and from the steady stream of nonsense he guttered out.

"Your ass feels so fucking good."

I tightened up around his cock, and he tilted his head forward. Sweat dripped down to my chest.

"Yeah—oh *fuck*, squeeze that dick, Mikey."

Nunzio's hips battered my ass. He didn't try to swallow the rising volume of his voice as I did my best to rip the orgasm out of him. When he came, he filled me deep while moaning my name so beautifully that I had the senseless urge to drag him down and suck his tongue into my mouth.

The delicate arch of his brows winding together and the red, abused curve of his mouth combined to make him look raw and open. His thrusts slowed and he pulled out with a quiet, "God."

He licked his lips and blinked before clumsily trying to fit us both on the couch without having to unstick himself from my chest. It felt so right that my first instinct was to shove him away, which couldn't be healthy at all.

"Damn, Mikey. You got me feeling some type of way."

I bucked my hips, spent dick trapped against his thigh, and ass still holding in the streams of semen he'd shot into me. "What way?"

"Like I could get by pretty well fucking only you and be really okay with that."

I snaked my hand around his waist and rested it on his ass, squeezing the plump cheek. "Thought this was just about sex."

"It is. But fucking you is like shooting up, and I don't think one more time is going to be enough."

Nunzio skimmed a sluggish kiss to the side of my jaw, flicking out his tongue. I shivered, and he followed it up with a kiss.

"Does that freak you out?"

I shook my head, but truthfully, I didn't know.

Chapter Ten

November

"THERE'S NOTHING I can do to make it up?"

I studied my laptop and the electronic grade book with rows of assignments, scores, and student averages. The column of zeroes beneath Shawn's name was almost impressive. He'd missed everything from the past two months due to a combination of truancy and falling asleep in class. Now here he was, staring down at me and seeming five seconds away from a meltdown. He was probably expecting me to say he had to make up the credit in night school next semester.

"There's not a lot of ways I can fix this for you, buddy."

I turned the laptop so he could see the numbers that were damning him with unyielding objectivity. I'd tried to give him a couple of random points for participating—even though his participation had been limited to breathing—but it had merely managed to lift his average to a measly 3 percent. None of his homework was done, and he didn't even know who Napoleon was, which indicated that he deserved to fail. Still, something about Shawn kicked in my overprotective nerve, and I wanted to help him out.

Shawn skimmed the screen once, then again, and I could practically hear the wheels in his head churning while he tried to figure out a way to scrape by with a passing grade. Every few seconds he started to speak, paused, and then shook his head. He had to know that every scheme he came up with would not work. Not with me, anyway. I was infamous for my strict policy on makeup work.

"Fuck."

I nodded in agreement. "Why did you wait until now to show concern? It's the damn middle of November."

"Because." Shawn shifted from foot to foot, fidgeting and biting his lip like I was interrogating him about something more serious than cutting out on every group project. He looked at the open door of the classroom, then back at me, and walked over to push it shut. "Look, it's some real personal shit, okay? My dad is in jail, I got to be picking my little sister up from school all the time, and I work at night."

"Work where?"

"Rodriguez, come on...."

I turned the laptop screen back to me and tapped my fingers on the track pad. Shawn's reputation had found its way to my ear long before he'd stepped foot in my classroom. Typically, I disregarded rumors about a student until I taught the kid for myself, but him being truant for three weeks at the start of the school year had not made a good impression at all. He'd managed to live up to every expectation— bad attitude, short temper, and constantly LTA (long term absent)—but there was still something about him that activated my guidance counselor instincts. He wasn't a well-behaved student, but I'd seen worse, and I could tell he had a story buried beneath all of the sarcasm and defensiveness.

"You gotta help me out, Rodriguez," Shawn insisted. He combed his fingers through his dark blond hair, knotting them up and then releasing with a loud exhale. "Look, I can't do p.m. school or summer school. I got no one to watch my sister."

"Who do you live with?"

"People. That ain't the point. I can't get stuck being in this building every night and over the summer!"

"Shawn, you're not even here during the day, which is why you're in this position."

He opened his mouth to protest, but then the side of his mouth twitched up into a silly grin. "Okay, good point, but still, you gotta help me, Mister."

"I don't have to do anything."

"*Please.* I'll buy you breakfast for the rest of the year."

"You don't get here early enough."

Shawn thumped his hand down on the desk. "Come on, Rodriguez. I thought we were cool."

Hiding a grin, I crossed my arms over my chest and studied the rows of assignments again. "Let's make a deal."

"What deal?" He was instantly wary. "I can't be doing no after-school stuff."

"I don't care where you do it, but you need to start putting in that work or you're screwed. The only way this is going to happen is if you make up both assessments and every homework from this marking period, and do the chapters on the Scientific Revolution and the Enlightenment in the prep book."

I ignored the dawning look of horror on his face and jerked my thumb at an orange textbook on my desk. "Don't give me that face, because this is a good deal. And I can tell you now that this is a one-shot deal. I don't believe in magical makeup packets and get-out-of-p.m.-school-free cards for kids who can't be bothered to show up. You feel me?"

"Yeah, I feel you, Mister." Shawn leaned against the desk behind him. "But what if I don't finish in time?"

"You have no choice."

"Yeah, but what if I can't?"

I snorted. "Stop making excuses before you even try."

"I don't got time for—"

The door opened, and Shawn stopped midsentence. David poked his head through. Brow furrowed, he looked from me to Shawn.

"Hey guys. Try to remember to keep the door open during all after-school meetings, okay?"

The look I nailed him with should have shriveled his insides until he keeled over on the linoleum, but he was riveted on Shawn. The kid looked like he wanted to punch David in the face.

"Wow, son. We're talking about some shit, and I wanted the door closed."

"I understand that, but it needs to stay open."

"What the fuck for? What are you trying to say?" Shawn's voice rose.

I stood up and clapped a hand on Shawn's shoulder while giving Mr. Oblivious an exasperated look. David was definitely not picking up on the vibes Shawn was throwing, and continued to stare into the classroom like he was waiting for a PowerPoint presentation on how to deal with irrationally angry children.

"Did you need something, Mr. Butler?" I asked when he failed to speak.

David didn't get the hint and kept staring at Shawn, who had drawn himself up to his full six feet. The kid was big for a fifteen-year-old, and looked like an undergrad instead of a sophomore in high school.

Finally David turned to me. "They're looking for your attendance."

I knew it was an excuse, but I pointed to the blue folder with my bubble sheets. "There you go."

"Thanks."

David shot me a harried glare and grabbed the folder before marching out of the room with a click of his boots. Once the sound faded far enough down the hallway, Shawn stormed across the room to shut the door with a defiant kick.

"I can't stand his faggot ass."

"Watch it, Shawn." I dropped into my chair. "Number one, you don't say that word, and number two, you shouldn't talk about your teacher like that or give him that attitude."

"But he be getting me tight in class, Mr. R. Always talking shit and calling me out to make me look stupid. He pretty much told me his day was better when I didn't show up. Little homo ass bitch."

Nice one, David.

"I'm not going to tell you that Mr. Butler has to be your favorite teacher, but you have to respect him. And the gay slurs are unacceptable. Next time I hear it coming out of your mouth, you can pretty much count on me writing you up and making sure it leads to a suspension."

"What's the big deal? I'm not talking about *you*."

"Okay, so can I go around making racial slurs just because I'm not talking about the person standing in front of me? Can Ms. Price go around talking about spics just because she isn't directing it at me? Can I kindly request her to stop hiring so many crackers because I'm starting to feel like the last man standing?"

"No, that's some crazy shit."

"Yeah, so what you're saying is some crazy shit. Talking about gay people is the same thing, kid."

Despite all the tough-guy talk, he still seemed surprised to hear me curse. After a moment of giving me the side-eye, Shawn sucked his teeth and shoved his hands into the pockets of his black jacket. "Whatever. I don't got no trouble with gay people. They're everywhere in this fucking school. They don't call it McQueery for nothing."

And that was the damn truth. The nickname was widely used because the school had such a high population of gay students and gay teachers, but his excuse just made his lack of wherewithal even more unacceptable. It was starting to frustrate me, so I ended the conversation with a wave of my hand.

"Shawn, I need to get going. Clean up your attitude and download your assignments from the website. The marking period ends in two weeks."

"Aiight, Mr. R. Thanks."

I nodded and watched him go. The annoyance didn't dampen the concern, and I was unable to stop wondering what he did for money that caused him to fall into a coma-like sleep every day in class. I had another student who worked nights in a Laundromat, but something told me Shawn wasn't folding clothes to make cash. Between me, David, and the guidance counselor, we'd tried to get in touch with a parent almost ten times, but never received a response. It was coming to the point where I knew a caseworker would be put in charge of the situation, and even though I hated to watch that go down, I suspected it might be for the best. The burgeoning mental image of Shawn raising his little sister by himself would not fade.

Slamming my laptop shut, I groaned and put my head on the desk. There were piles of papers, folders, and student work beneath my face, but I didn't care. The day had been long, and due to my students having serious misconceptions about geography, my lessons were behind once again.

I shut my eyes and thought about the long commute home, the crush of people on the train, and the mind-numbing volume of music my father or Raymond would inevitably be playing. In the past couple of months, my house had transformed into a messy bachelor's pad, and even though I was nowhere close to being a neat freak, the place disgusted me more often than not when I took a moment to look around on Friday night. Apparently being the responsible one also meant being the clean one, and all of a sudden the motherfuckers had me mistaken for the maid. Going to my favorite dive bar to get toasted for the trek home was better than rushing back to that disaster.

My life choices were narrowed down to either arguing drunk or arguing sober, and the latter always left me ten times more stressed than I'd been at the start of the fight. The internal debate ping-ponged in my head, back and forth, left and right, until the only thing I was certain of was that the predicament I'd found myself in was going to give me an ulcer and a ton of gray hairs.

I sat mulling over my options until I heard another pair of footsteps moving down the hallway. After twenty years, the tread of Nunzio's motorcycle boots and the jingle of his wallet chain were unmistakable, so I didn't look up when he strode into the room, shut the door, and stopped by my desk. His fingers wound into my hair and combed back, petting me like he was trying to soothe a feral cat.

Leaning into the touch, I released a soft sigh and kept my face pillowed in my arms. The feel of his long fingers dragging through my hair, scraping my scalp, and the rough pad of his thumb brushing along the curve of my ear almost drove me to wrap myself around him and enjoy being spoiled.

There had been a time when I could do that—stretch out beside him, on top of him, or cuddle up with him—and not feel anything more than the contentment of unconditional friendship, but after fooling around with him, things had changed. Now, as he chuckled quietly and let me bask in the attention, my mind was playing tricks on me and whispering that going back to his place to extend this mostly innocent show of affection would be a good idea. But the logical part of my brain that acted on more than base desires and instincts knew better.

Evidence of that had come the week before, when I'd spent the night at his apartment after a spectacularly shitty day at work.

Vegging out while sprawled all over each other had been anything but platonic when I'd been incapable of not ogling his bare chest, the V of his torso, and the crotch of his sweatpants. In turn, I'd felt him tracing my mouth with his eyes, and his casual touches had grown frequent; his hands had wandered all over me until he'd wound up squeezing my thigh with his knuckles grazing the bulge under my fly.

After two hours of simmering tension, Nunzio had turned on the hardest-core gay porn he could find. We'd watched each other jerk off while two guys played edging games on his television. We hadn't touched until the white-hot surge of an oncoming ejaculation had led to me kissing him.

There had been no fucking, but making out for a half hour after shooting our loads only led to a conflicting series of feelings and fantasized scenarios that had nothing to do with the *just platonic sex haha* story I kept tossing around in my head. But we'd slept in separate rooms, and everything had been normal after that, so who the hell knew?

"Hey." Nunzio's hand slid down to glide along the side of my face. "You okay?"

"Just have a headache." I turned my head to peer up at him. His dark hair was messier than usual and his blue eyes shot through with red. "Are *you* okay?"

He shrugged. "This day just needs to end."

I nodded in agreement. "Are you heading out?"

"Yeah. Why don't you come with me? Get some dinner." His hand moved to my shoulder and rubbed out the tension. I made an appreciative sound. "We could order something or whatever."

"I should go home and make sure no one has died today."

Nunzio pulled away. "Are you serious?"

"Unfortunately." I shrugged. "Sorry."

"Don't apologize. I feel sorry for you, not me." Nunzio crossed his arms over his chest, the leather of his jacket creaking. "What are you doing next week?"

"What's next week?"

"Thanksgiving, man. Are you doing shit with the fam?"

I'd forgotten all about the upcoming holidays. Either that, or I'd buried them in my alcohol-saturated brain, since it was the first holiday season since my mother's death. Just the thought tightened my chest, and I wanted to go back to burying my face in my arms.

"Either my aunt will invite us over, or they'll ask to do dinner at the house."

Nunzio grabbed a student chair and straddled it. "They're still gonna do all that even now?"

"I don't know. I haven't thought about it, but no one has said otherwise, so I'm going to assume they have the same plan. It's not like there is anywhere better to have a get-together. Both my aunt and uncle have small apartments."

He continued to stare at me, so I pushed on, desperate to change the topic. If someone had told me adulthood was equal parts being broke, depressed, and taking care of my family financially, I would have opted out and tried to find a one-way ticket to Neverland.

"What about you? Your parents doing anything?"

"No," Nunzio scoffed. "Apparently they don't celebrate holidays anymore. Besides, I haven't seen them in almost a year."

I remembered that—the past Christmas, Nunzio had wound up having his own family drama when he'd walked out on them in the middle of Christmas Eve dinner and fucked and drank his way through New Year's. He'd never given me the details about what had happened, but I suspected it had a lot to do with his parents coming down on everything he did. It had been that way for as long as I remembered, and watching him grow up being rejected for not being the perfect Italian son had played a large part in my own decision to stay closeted.

As much as Nunzio said he didn't care about having the approval of his parents, I knew it hurt him to be considered a disappointment, and that had been the Medicis' consensus, even before they'd walked in on him railing some frail blond boy in high school. His gayness wasn't the root of the problem, but it had been the final nail in the coffin of their relationship.

"You can come over and spend it with us. My aunt will cook a pernil and pasteles. You can chill and watch football with Raymond and keep him entertained while I try to talk my dad out of drinking himself to death. Sounds like a blast, right?"

It sounded like a goddamned tragedy, but Nunzio grinned like I'd just offered him a gold bar.

"You sure? Because I'm gonna come. Don't offer if you're not sure."

"Of course I'm sure. I can have something normal to look at when everyone else starts driving me insane."

"If I'm the only piece of normalcy you got, then you're up shit creek without a paddle."

"I think I'm there anyway." I forced myself to stand, arching back in a stretch. I wished I could teleport back to Queens. I could take a cab, but I didn't feel like shelling out forty bucks because I was too lazy to sit my ass on the train for an hour. "So you going out or going home?"

"I wanted to go with you," he pointed out. "You don't even want to grab something before getting on the train?"

"Nah, I don't want to spend the money."

"It's okay, I got you."

"Nunzio, stop asking me."

He scowled. "Fine. I'll just go to the gym since you want to be a fucking lame ass."

"I'm fine with being a lame ass."

Nunzio picked up a piece of student work. His mouth crooked up in a half smile, and I wondered if he'd grabbed the essay in which one of my kids had referred to Marie Antoinette as a thot—"that ho over there."

"David was lurking around and waiting for you," he said. "He made tracks when he saw me, though. I think I still make him nervous."

"Maybe because you're really aggressive."

Nunzio dropped the paper on the desk while I packed up. "Oh please. I haven't even looked twice at his prepubescent ass since that night at the happy hour. He's lucky he got to touch my dick the one time that he did."

"You seemed into it at the time."

"Yeah, because I was drunk at the time."

I avoided his gaze and stuffed folders of ungraded work into my backpack. Whenever David came up, the intensity of the conversation took on a vibe I wasn't altogether comfortable with. It was in the way Nunzio's voice sharpened, the way his eyes narrowed and mouth pursed into a slash.

"Why? Are you still into him?"

"No. He's a good-looking dude, though."

"If you say so."

I met his gaze. "I already told you I have no interest because he has a boyfriend."

"I heard they broke up."

"Did they?"

"Yup. You could jump on that now if you wanted, and your morals wouldn't be corrupted. I bet that's what he was coming to tell you—that his ass is now free to be claimed by random dudes at the club, but he'd rather be full of your dick since you turned him out so good last time."

"Wow, you really went in with that scenario."

"Shut up."

I jerked the zipper around my bag, but it was a tight fit with the amount of folders and papers. I hadn't graded in two weeks, and I was two major assignments behind. It seemed like I'd been playing catch up since the first week of school.

"He didn't want to bring himself in here to say whatever he had to say, so I'm going," I said.

"You sure you don't want to wait around and make sure he isn't going to offer up his hole?"

"You're obsessed."

"No, I'm not."

He was, but I let the issue drop and grabbed my jacket from the back of the chair. "Walk me to the train. Maybe David will show up so you can make fun of him some more."

"If only."

We left the building and parted ways. I spent my subway ride slumped in the seat, nearly dozing off twice before I was disrupted by an overexcited religious zealot preaching about hell and damnation. She was followed by a guy who was panhandling while wearing a brand-new pair of Jordans. By the time I was in Queens and getting off the train at Sutphin Boulevard, I was done with people for the day.

I made the walk from the train to my house without looking up, pretending not to hear the voices of numerous people calling out to me as I crossed the avenues and wound my way through the park. Living in the same neighborhood I'd grown up in was a pain in the ass primarily because I knew everyone, from the crackheads who hung out by the LIRR to the guy in the bodega who used to sell me loose cigarettes back when I'd been too broke to buy a pack.

Running into old high school friends wasn't exactly a blast either, unless it was one of the curious guys I'd brought over to the gay side for twenty minutes in heaven on one of the rooftops. They always wanted to relive those old times, but I wasn't even in the mood for that these days.

The grit and grime of South Jamaica didn't make me reminisce about running through the streets with Nunzio back when the subway had taken tokens, Mister Softee had been seventy-five cents, and we'd been just fine sweating it out on the pavement as long as we could do it with a bag of chips and a quarter water. All I could see were the same sorry-ass bums hanging out on the corner, the avenue filled with litter, and the loitering undercover cops who still thought folks in the neighborhood were too oblivious to spot a DT.

Morale sank to an all-time low and deteriorated further once I turned onto my block. The house my mother had worked her ass off to pay for was starting to match my dismal perception of the entire neighborhood. I couldn't tell if our lack of attentiveness was finally setting in, or if the depressing reality of the holidays was casting everything in shades of gray.

It was hard not to think I had let her down. Try as I might to convince them, Raymond wouldn't get a job, my father wouldn't stop drinking, and my childhood home was all but falling apart. The fact was cemented by the handful of bills in the mailbox—one was a cut-off notice for the electricity, another was a letter from the bank reminding me I was late paying the mortgage.

I crumpled the envelopes in my hand, shame warring with frustration after I stepped into the house. The heat was cranked up so high it was oppressive, and I caught a whiff of stale beer.

Dropping my backpack by the door, I kicked it shut and strode through the house. Each room was messier than the last, and every light was burning. The kitchen counter was littered with dirty dishes and glasses, the garbage was overflowing, and there was an array of laundry tossed here and there in different rooms.

I stomped up the stairs, ready to unleash my rage on Raymond or my father, but stopped dead at the unmistakable sound of bedsprings creaking. For one horrifying moment, I thought it was coming from my mother's bedroom—the bedroom my father now occupied—but then female moans emanated from Raymond's side of the hallway.

My relief was mirrored by revulsion, and I clenched my jaw. Great. Now I would have to listen to him fuck all night.

More aggravated than ever and spoiling for a fight, I peeked into the master bedroom. Joseph was sprawled on the bed, snoring and nearly sliding off the edge of the bed. He was drunk again.

I deflated.

Moving farther into the room, I examined the man who had been in and out of my life without ever pausing to stay for more than a moment at a time. Beneath the haggard face and unkempt appearance, he looked like me and Raymond. He was tall and lean, had once been attractive and strong, and I knew him to be far more intelligent than anyone would ever assume. But he'd wasted all of the things that should have made him successful.

Even now with his barely functioning liver, even after my mother had died so abruptly and so young, he was still knocked out and reeking of booze. Sometimes I wondered what had happened to make him give up. I'd asked him those questions for years and had never received an answer more substantial than, "I'm just no good. It's not in me."

For reasons beyond the realm of my comprehension, I tugged off his tan boots one by one. They thudded to the floor, but he didn't even twitch at the sound. Shaking my head, I removed his jacket and wrenched off a scarf twisted around his neck. It seemed like he'd stumbled in after a bender and keeled over right after stepping into the room.

"C'mon, Pops," I muttered and guided his limbs to coax him beneath the blankets. "Get in before you get cold."

Joseph mumbled something unintelligible, but didn't protest when I covered him up. His mouth shifted into a brief, tired smile before he began to snore once again.

I almost backed away, but something caught my eye. On the floor by his now discarded boots was an old picture of my parents. They couldn't have been older than seventeen or eighteen, were grinning at the camera with big white smiles, and were wearing New Year's party hats.

The anger that had sluiced through me in hot, violent waves transformed into a depression that sank into my bones like lead. I placed the picture on the bedside table next to him, careful not to set it in the sticky spot that had gathered from a long-dirty glass, and hurried from the room.

The sound of my father's deep breathing, my brother and his girl, and the more distant laughing and music emanating from the neighbors culminated in my mind until all I wanted was to go upstairs and figure out which bottle to open first.

Chapter Eleven

Thanksgiving

"ARE YOU sure this is a good idea?"

"Why wouldn't it be? It's not like they don't know you or something."

Nunzio shoved his hands into the pockets of his leather jacket as we walked. The day was bitterly cold, the sky an oppressive gray, but even a promise of snow on Thanksgiving wasn't enough to make me feel more festive. Being around Nunzio helped, but his pinched, worried face and lip-biting paranoia was catching.

"Yeah," he agreed. "But your mom was always there in the past. You know your dad hates me. Always has."

It was true. Something about me and Nunzio as a unit had put my father off since the very beginning. It was like he could smell our impending gayness, even though I'd never come out.

"And," Nunzio added when I failed to respond, "your uncle vocally hates gay people. At least Joseph shuts up about it around me."

That was also true.

"Just chill out. If anyone gets out of line, I'll straighten them out."

"Mikey, no. The last thing I want is for you to be fighting with your fam because of me. I should have stood my ass home."

The wind gusted, blowing my scarf to the side. I grabbed the end before it unraveled, and swore when I lost my grip on the twelve-pack I'd just bought from the bodega.

"Just calm down. You're acting like it's a big deal when nothing has happened yet. I told my pops you're coming by, and he didn't flip out about it."

Nunzio fixed my scarf, handsome face creased with worry. His hair was smashed down by a knit hat, and unruly strands escaped the sides.

"I just feel weird without your mom. She's the only one who was okay with me being around so much."

His hands fell away, and a fierce protective streak shot through me.

"It is okay. It's my house and I invited you."

Nunzio didn't reply. I stalked off again, and he trudged after me. He'd been going back and forth with this ever since I'd met him at the train station a half hour ago, and hadn't stopped even as I went from store to store looking for some aluminum pans I'd apparently neglected to get enough of, according to my aunt.

We entered the house, but Nunzio hung back and watched me wipe my boots on the mat. I rolled my eyes, and he followed my lead, removing his jacket and scarf while peering through the archway like he was expecting a guerrilla attack.

"Those are not big enough," Aida crowed, barging into the entryway. "Carajo, Michael."

"Look, that's all they had. I don't know what you want me to do. I'll use the twelve goddamned pounds of—"

"Who do you think you're talking to with that language?"

"Sorry." I looked at Nunzio. He was finally smiling. "I'll use the twelve pounds of foil that Jackie made me buy to make a pan for you, okay?"

"Smart-ass." Aida glared at me before turning to Nunzio. He removed his hat and averted his gaze, but she bustled over with a huge grin.

"Nunzio! I haven't seen you since you were a skinny little thing!"

"Yeah," Nunzio's smile returned. "Yeah, I came over for Christmas and you were here one year. You felt bad I didn't have any presents and tried to give me money to go to Rite Aid and buy myself something."

"Poor baby. You want something to eat?"

I could sense Nunzio was about to say no, so I gave a furtive shake of my head.

"Uh, yeah, I could eat," he replied.

"Good, good. Jackie, Michael's cousin, was just talking about you. Do you remember her?"

Before Nunzio could give an affirmative, Aida looped her arm through his and guided him to the kitchen. I knew she would poke at his lanky frame and dub him flaquito before giving him a predinner meal. It would inevitably lead to an interrogation about why his parents had left him alone on Thanksgiving.

Satisfied that Nunzio was being indoctrinated in a positive way, I entered the living room to deal with the inevitable shitshow of my male family members trying to coexist in the same room.

My father and his brother John had hardly tolerated each other for as long as I could remember, but after John's wife walked out on him, they'd made an attempt to bond.

The Rodriguez family didn't have luck when it came to significant others. Both John and my father had driven their wives away, and Aida's husband had died of cancer only a handful of years after they'd gotten married. She'd never had any kids of her own, which was why she was so active in her brothers' lives. More often than not, she acted in the role of peacekeeper when John and Joseph drank a little too much and shit got too real.

But they hadn't reached that stage. Yet.

The two brothers sat side by side on the sofa with identical glares fixed on a football game. Raymond was half-turned in the armchair by the window with his phone clasped in one hand.

"You're missing the game," John barked. He cast me a sidelong glance, disapproving even though he had no qualms about reaching for the beer I was still sheltering under my arm.

"I don't give a flying fuck about the game."

The degree of scorn in John's expression heightened to blistering.

Raymond shook his head, clearly thinking I was an idiot. "Is Zio here?" he asked.

"He's in the kitchen with Titi."

"Ask him if he's up for some Black Ops later. I borrowed a controller from Chris."

He sounded exactly like one of my students, and that facet of his personality was getting more grating as time wore on.

"Yeah, I'll get right on top of that, Ray."

"You better. I don't get to chill with him these days."

Raymond sounded genuine, and I almost felt bad for being annoyed by his request. If there was any ally better than me to defend Nunzio, it would be Raymond. Even if he talked shit every once in a while, Raymond had always been keener on Nunzio than he was on me. He'd trade us if he could.

"I'll see what he wants to do," I said. "He just got here, and Aida has already dragged him into the kitchen to fatten him up."

"Oh. He'll be there for a while, then."

The game went to commercial, and Joseph turned his glassy eyes to me. "Why don't you bring a girlfriend home for Thanksgiving for a change?"

John snorted into his beer, still staring at the television. It was amazing how such a low, petty sound, could make my hackles rise. A witty retort waited to be unleashed from my mouth, but I settled for a wintry silence.

"Naw, he has too many different chicks to just pick one," Raymond butted in. "If he brought one over, she'd get the wrong idea."

The statement washed over me and left me blank, but then the meaning sank in, and my attention snapped to my brother. He was thumbing at the screen of his phone, not looking at me or our father, and appeared to have released the lie without giving it much consideration.

I didn't know what to make of it, and judging from the cloud of confusion ghosting over Joseph's countenance, he didn't either. But he was already dangerously close to sliding down the slippery slope of drunk-before-dinner, and probably couldn't make the connection between Raymond's claim and the obvious lack of evidence, since I'd never brought a girl home for any length of time at any point in my life. It did shut my uncle up, though.

The football game resumed, and some of the tension bled out of me. Joseph and John shouted in a mixture of Spanish and English, yelling at the game and then debating with each other about every random thing that transpired. Meanwhile, I sat next to Raymond, trying to catch his eye while doing my best to pretend I gave any sort of damn about football. I largely failed.

I threw in the towel on trying to get my brother to make eye contact and went back to fantasizing about my bed and a book. The day was panning out as I had expected—uncomfortable, long, and full of awkward moments and tense exchanges that drew an iron curtain between me, John, and my father. It was only a matter of time before the side-looks and smart comments escalated into something that couldn't be ignored, and by then we would all blow up like Hiroshima.

The best option for avoiding fireworks was to avoid alcohol, but Joseph broke the label on a bottle of Brugal, and the first stone was cast.

By the time the sun retreated from the blanket of clouds that had masked the sky all day, the volume of our voices had risen, and I had a nice buzz going. At some point Nunzio and my cousin Jackie joined us in the living room, but Raymond whisked Nunzio away to play Xbox before he got the chance to pick up on the thickening tension. I was left alone with the two elder Rodriguez men, and only John's daughter to run interference. When my phone vibrated in my pocket, I was grateful to have a distraction.

How's your holiday?

David.

Sucks. You?

It could be better.... I'm in CT with my parents. Is Nunzio with you?

Yes, how did you know that?

He told me.

Any number of scenarios would have led to the conversation of Thanksgiving plans coming up, but something told me Nunzio letting David in on that detail had been deliberate. I rubbed my chin and wondered, not for the first time, what Nunzio's deal was when it came to David.

The more thought I put into it, the more it seemed like he'd been cockblocking from the start. Even the threesome had been out of character. That night in the club, Nunzio had swooped in and inserted himself as soon as David and I had started to talk.

These days he claimed to not even find David attractive, but more than that, he went out of his way to be outright hostile to the kid.

My phone vibrated again.

Do you want to meet up tomorrow?

I stared at the words, fingers hovering over the screen, but I ultimately put my phone away without typing back. I didn't know if he wanted to have lunch or suck my dick, and I wasn't in the mood to come up with a response for either proposition.

"Who's sending you messages?" Joseph jerked his chin at the phone.

"Somebody."

"A woman?" Joseph took my lack of a response for an affirmative and went on. "I don't understand why you spend the holidays with that maricón and not a woman."

The casual disrespect of my father's words boiled my blood.

"You shouldn't say that, Tío," Jackie scolded. "Nunzio is like family."

"I don't mean anything by it." Joseph waved his hand and added a dismissive flick of his fingers, but his shoulders were stiff beneath a sweatshirt that smelled of sweat and a double dose of annoyance. Once upon a time, the sideways cut of his dark eyes and an ominous edge in his cigarette-hardened voice would have backed me into a corner until I said whatever it was he wanted me to say. But now, I matched his mean mug with one of my own. He didn't miss the coldness in my expression.

"You always have to find a reason to be angry with me, don't you, Michael?"

"Keep your mouth shut about Nunzio if you don't want me to get upset. He's more family to me than you are."

"I bet," John grunted.

Jackie put her hands on John's shoulders and dug her fingers in.

"I'm going to say this once." I stood and looked between my uncle and my father. They were five years apart but bitter and hateful in varying shades, with quicksilver tempers to match. "If you want to be in this house, you will respect my friends. Especially one that I've known for twenty years and has had my back every fucked-up step of the way. He was the one who helped me with funeral arrangements when you were out drunk and worrying about the will," I spat, pointing at Joseph. "And while Raymond was too traumatized to leave his room."

"I didn't say anything about him. I just wonder why the hell you always have him around and not a woman." Joseph grabbed his glass and drained it, eyes flitting to Jackie like he wanted her to get a refill but knew better than to ask. The glass dropped back to the table smeared with greasy fingerprints. "You're telling me your mother never asked why you're always alone?"

"Maybe she did, but she didn't judge me for it."

"What about you am I judging? I didn't say anything about you or your life. I only asked a question, and you jump down my throat, rushing to defend his honor."

"Because as far as I'm concerned you're nobody, and I don't owe you a fucking explanation," I said.

A slurry of Spanish swears crept out of Joseph's mouth. His leg hopped, fingers gripping the arm of the sofa, and he looked two seconds shy of flying into a rage. The curtain of tension was lifting, but in a way that would ensure a battle instead of an armistice.

I wanted to break it down and explain that every time he called Nunzio a faggot, every time he used words like maricón or pato, he might as well have been spitting his hate at me. The worst part was my father failed to understand that hate said in a joking tone still shriveled and hardened my heart. Even if I never told him I was gay, and even if he never directly aimed his insults at me, he would lose all respect for me if he knew. It was evident by the wary way he kept Nunzio at arm's length and had always muttered to my mother that she should keep us apart.

My father exhaled slowly and glanced up at Jackie. She hovered behind the sofa, supremely out of place with her pink sweater, rosy cheeks, and waist-length curls—a school girl stumbling into the middle of a brewing bar fight.

"What time is dinner ready?" Joseph gritted out.

"Soon," she replied, relief in her voice.

"Fine. I'm getting another drink."

Joseph wobbled when he got up, teetering to the side before he regained his balance. I could tell he was upset just by looking at his profile, and the way he strode out of the room with slow deliberate steps drove the point home.

"You're not fooling anyone, Michael," John said once my father was out of earshot.

"Jesus, Daddy, can't you leave him alone?" Jackie hissed. "Why did you want to come to his house if you're going to keep bullying him the whole time?"

"Don't worry about it, primita. It's only bullying if I gave a fuck about what he or my father thought."

John didn't seem the least bit concerned about the amount of fucks I had left. He waved me out of the way of the television.

Jackie muttered an apology to me, and I dropped a kiss on her head. She was no more responsible for her father than I was for my own.

I jogged up the staircase to seek out my wayward brother and friend. I found them in Raymond's bedroom, sprawled on the bed and focused intently on whatever game they were playing. They were surrounded by a cloud of sickly sweet smoke and illuminated only by the glow of the television.

"Jesus, Nunzio. Really?"

"What?" The word came out in a wheeze, surrounded by billowing smoke.

I fought the urge to stand in front of the television to fuck up their game.

"You really had to smoke up with him? Now? I already got my pops talking shit to me about you being here."

"Why?" Raymond bolted upright like my words had jammed a lightning bolt up his ass. "Zio always comes around on the holidays."

"Yeah, when Mami was here. Now that dickhead thinks he's king of the castle and keeps throwing underhanded comments."

"Like what? Want me to go—"

I held up a hand to thwart my brother's charge down the stairs. "Relax. Let Jackie and Aida tell them a thing or two. I'm tired of fighting."

"Jackie?" Raymond considered me, his mouth pulled to the side. "What's she going to do? She's dumb as a box of rocks. We could straight up have a brawl, and she'd sit there like an oil painting until someone got shot."

It was a struggle to mold my face into disapproving lines. "That's not nice, Ray."

"I know it's not. That's why I said it."

Nunzio dug his elbow into Raymond's side. "Hey, she's sweet. Don't be a jerk."

"Whatever." Ray passed the pipe to Nunzio. "What the hell is he busting your balls about, anyways?"

"Same old crap. Pops has forever been trying to imply that Nunzio is slowly turning me gay."

"So just tell him you was gay even before you met Nunzio."

Raymond said it just as Nunzio started to toke. He sucked too hard on the pipe and went spiraling into a coughing fit.

I gaped at my brother. Now it was my turn to do a rendition of an oil painting. I willed my brain to jump start, but all I managed was a vague "huh?" while Nunzio wheezed and slapped his hand against the mattress.

Raymond rolled his eyes. "You must think I'm an idiot. We used to share a fucking room. Also I used to follow you everywhere when I was a kid. You don't think I never noticed you going up to the rooftop or behind the bathrooms at the pond?"

The bigger question was why I'd been so positive that my expeditions up to Captain Tilly Park had been so clandestine, or why

I'd never considered the possibility of my bratty little brother tailing me after being brushed off one too many times.

The idea of mini-Raymond getting an eyeful of some dude balls deep in my mouth or ass was enough to make me want to fling myself off the nearest bridge.

As I worked myself up to a stroke, Nunzio was still hacking, his eyes tearing up as he doubled over and held out the pipe for Raymond. My brother took it with a self-satisfied grin. It was halfway endearing now that I knew he'd been onto my secret for years. *Years.*

"Why didn't you ever say anything?" I asked, finding my voice.

"'Cause you clearly didn't want me to know. I guess you thought I was going to call you a fag and hate your guts?"

The answer to his question was not a quick find, so I sat on the edge of the bed. With my feet planted on the floor and the weight of the mattress under me, it was easier to gather myself enough to form a coherent response.

"I wasn't going to come out to our parents, so I decided not to tell any of you. There were times when I wondered if you were onto me, but that was when we got older."

"Shit." Nunzio grabbed a beer from the nightstand and gulped it down. "Jesus, Ray. That messed me up."

"Good for you." Raymond put his pipe in the drawer of the nightstand. "You all are some pussies, all scared of being honest and getting judged. I don't even know why you thought I'd give a damn about you being gay when I was still cool with Zio after he dropped the homo bomb. What, you thought I'd tell Pops?"

"I don't know what I thought, but I didn't want you to find out." I lay backward on the bed. "Don't take it personally, okay? It's no one's business who I like to sleep with, and I didn't want to discuss it."

"I can relate to that," Nunzio chimed in, voice still strained from the toke gone wrong. "I did that ceremonial rite of passage coming out to the parents bit, and it was the worst idea I ever had beyond shaving my nuts with soap and water."

Raymond shook his head. "No one needed to know that shit, man."

"Look, I'm just saying, it don't always go right." Nunzio put a hand on my forehead for no reason that I could discern besides wanting to touch me. His fingers slid into my hair and scratched along my scalp. "He didn't even tell me for a while, and I'm his best friend, and he already knew I was pretty fruity based solely on my appreciation for Nick Carter."

"You even had those fucking trading cards," I said, smiling at the memory. "You were a lame kid."

"Shut the hell up." Nunzio gave my hair a tug. "Anyway, don't get mad, Ray. He's just a secretive asshole. Like how he's always trying to front and act like he's not trying to get with this guy we work with."

I shoved his hand away. "Okay, time to change the subject."

"What dude?" Raymond asked, looking between us with obvious curiosity. "Yo, I always wondered—do you take it up the ass?"

"Wow."

Nunzio cracked up. His shoulders shook with the force of his laughter.

"This conversation is officially over," I said, pushing myself up. "I don't even want to know why the hell you're wondering about what happens to my ass."

"It's a normal thing to wonder," Raymond said defensively. "Like, how do you even fuck? I mean I know how you do it—it's my lucky day whenever a girl wants to do anal, but—"

I interrupted him with a loud groan and hunched forward, covering my face with my hands. "Can you just go check and see if dinner is almost ready?"

"You really ain't appreciating my effort to be supportive."

"And you fail to understand that your effort to be supportive is disturbing." I shoved him off the edge of the bed. "Vete. She's been roasting that fucking pernil for, like, twenty hours, and the turkey is done."

Raymond managed to look indignant while red-eyed and squinting after marinating himself in THC. "You better keep your hands off my weed if you're sending me off to fetch dinner like a bitch."

"Why does everything have to be like a bitch? You sound like my students."

"Just don't be smoking my shit."

I refused to look at him and didn't drop my hands until I heard his footsteps tromping downstairs. He was so damn loud that I heard him halt in the archway to the living room and inquire about the game instead of going to the kitchen. He needed some Adderall like my uncle needed the stick removed from his ass.

I groaned again and looked at Nunzio. "Let's pretend we're twelve and go hide in my room. I need to recover from that plot twist."

"Fine by me."

We took the narrow staircase to the attic. Compared to Raymond's cluttered, narrow room, it was a studio apartment.

Nunzio stepped inside, and I flipped the deadbolt on the door.

"Damn, I haven't been up here for a long-ass time."

"You haven't visited the house in general since I moved back."

"Because you always come running to me."

Nunzio stood by one of the circular windows and peered out at the large snowflakes that had begun to drift around in the wind. A tiny smile appeared on his face, and I had to force myself to look away when the fondness in my chest swelled to a suspicious portion.

"Want a drink?"

"Definitely. Having your aunt and cousin grill me about my love life for two hours was pretty stressful."

Nunzio turned away from the window and plopped down on the bed. He reached over to my nightstand and poked at a messy stack of books that I'd discarded there months ago. There had been a time when I'd refused to unpack fully while I fibbed to myself about only returning to the house for a month or two to make sure everything was in order. But a month or two had turned into a year, so it was time for me to just rearrange my bookcase and quit living in a fantasy world.

"It seems like everyone in my family is obsessed with your love life." I grabbed a sleeve of plastic cups from the top of my dresser, a half-full bottle of rum, and joined Nunzio on the bed. "I had my dad and uncle practically accusing me of fucking you."

"They're pretty perceptive about gay sex for some drunk old guys. They never showed this much interest in your love life before."

"Yeah, well," I said, measuring out the amber liquid like it was life blood. "Just because Raymond is cool with it doesn't mean they will be, and I'm not planning to have the conversation tonight."

I handed Nunzio one of the cups. We toasted, and I muttered a salud. I'd intended to nurse it, but a baby sip turned into a continuous swallow. Nunzio kept his head tilted back, ever competitive, but failed out before me and set his cup to the side.

"What did Clive think about you being in the closet with your folks?"

The empty cup crinkled in my hand when I started to refill it. "He thought I was a coward and a big baby, and made sure to tell me in detail about his own dramatic coming-out adventure and the harrowing tale of striving for acceptance."

"How did you deal with that guy for two years? He talked so much bullshit I was tempted to wipe his mouth anytime I was forced to be around him."

I turned sideways, not hiding my wry smile. "He thought the same thing about you."

"Me?" Nunzio stared at me, disbelieving. "That guy was saying shit about me and you never told me nothing?"

"Yeah, because you would have started something."

"Oh, because I'm that immature?"

"Yup." This time, I nursed the drink. "He thought you were this loud, ghetto guido, and tried too hard to prove yourself."

"What the fuck is that supposed to mean?"

"Clive just liked to make a lot of assumptions because he was insecure. I told him you came from the same neighborhood as me, and you didn't have to prove anything to anybody. After that, he quit criticizing you in my presence, but I'm pretty sure he just found it annoying that you knew my whole family when he never got to meet anyone." I tipped my head back, regarding him. "He also claimed you would brag about it to him every chance you got."

There was not even the thinnest veneer of shame when Nunzio replied. "Yeah, just like he made sure to brag about how hard he tapped your ass every chance *he* got."

"What the hell? Did you two sit around trying to one-up each other about me?"

"Pretty much."

I hadn't spared Clive a thought in the past several months. A relationship that had once seemed so steadfast and imperative had ended with an unchecked breakup that I hadn't even mourned. A lot had happened since then, but maybe that was just an excuse and I was as capricious with my lovers as I always accused Nunzio of being with his.

Nunzio drained his cup, and I took another chaste sip from my own. The addition of more rum to my bloodstream was starting to make me woozy.

"What was the point of you trying to make Clive jealous?"

"Why the hell was he trying to get *me* jealous?"

I licked the traces of rum from my mouth. "Because he was intimidated by you."

Nunzio brightened. "Yeah?"

"Yes. He swore you wanted to fuck me, and that's why you convinced me to go out and drink with you so much. But I don't think any normal person would be cool with the number of times we got wasted and passed out in your apartment. What isn't normal is the two of you sitting around bullshitting each other like immature-ass kids."

"Hey, he started it. Always telling me how hard he made you come, and wondering why you never gave me the time of day. He loved flaunting that he had you and I would never get you."

There was no use in feeling mortified about something that had happened months ago, but it still hit me like a truck.

"Come again?"

"Oh, forget it. It don't matter."

"Uh-huh."

I wasn't sold on the idea of it not mattering, but I let the conversation come to a full stop and drained my second cup.

I scooted back to lean against the wall but followed my body's command and lay down instead. I looked out the window, tracing the swirls of snowflakes and wondered whether it would stick. The little kid in me wanted to see snow on the ground, but the adult who trudged from Queens to Brooklyn every morning wasn't thrilled about an added complication to that commute.

With my nerves pacified by over-the-liquor-counter sedatives, the combination of snow, the smell of Thanksgiving dinner, and the muffled cacophony of salsa, football, and loud voices, I found a grain of comfort and eased into the lull.

I was vaguely aware of Nunzio rummaging around beside the bed, and was only a little caught off guard when he exclaimed, "Holy shit, you have an arsenal of sex toys in here."

My head lolled to the side. Nunzio was pawing through my nightstand. He looked half-scandalized, half-intrigued, and I didn't even have to ask what he was seeing. The drawer was filled with enough condoms, lube, and sex toys to keep the entire staff of the Moonlite Bunny Ranch entertained. A couple of vibrators, cock rings, three different Fleshlights....

Nunzio lifted a curved, black prostate massager. "You use all of this stuff on yourself?"

"Yeah, why the hell else would I have it?"

"Obviously but—shit man, I never knew your alone time was this exciting. I just get busy with some lotion and a tight grip."

"And when exactly would that come up in conversation?" I asked, grinning at Nunzio's shocked expression. With his tan gone and his complexion back to its typical sandy hue, the rosy flush stealing over Nunzio's skin was easy to notice. He wet his lips and tore his gaze away from the device to look up at me.

"You don't want to know what I'm imagining right now."

"Try me."

Nunzio rose from his kneeling position and reached down to adjust the crotch of his pants. I knew he was hard. He threw off pheromones like a beast. His lust was so intense I could practically smell it, and my own dick stiffened in response.

"I want to watch."

I slid down on the mattress until my hips and the small of my back were mostly flat against it. Nunzio's gaze darted down to my stomach when my shirt skewed up, and then slid down to my dick.

"What do you want to watch?"

"I wanna watch you fuck yourself." Nunzio held up the prostate massager, rapt expression tipping toward the kind of filthy leer that made me pant. "And then I want to see you fuck one of those Fleshlights."

"Now? Here?"

"Where and when else?"

I swallowed. "You have to be insane. My whole family is downstairs."

"You have a dead bolt on your door."

"Oh, that's not suspicious at all."

The mattress sank beneath Nunzio's weight when he knelt at the edge of it. "Don't hold out on me, Mikey. I need to see."

"Need?" The question came out breathless when Nunzio slid the rounded tip of the massager along my erection. The pressure wasn't enough, but I still canted my hips up with a hint of desperation. "You don't need it."

"I do. For when I'm having my own alone time." Nunzio dragged the massager up, digging into my torso and then the hollow of my throat. "Come on. I bet you put on a show for Clive."

"Nope."

He inched the toy up to my chin, but I turned my head before he could touch it to my mouth.

"Good old Clive didn't want to watch his baby," Nunzio drawled, always having hated when Clive called me that, "fuck himself like a slut?"

"He wondered why I needed all of that." I was overly conscious of how fast I was breathing and how difficult it was to keep my hand away from my crotch. "He was insecure."

"I'm not." Nunzio dragged my lower lip down with the tip of the vibrator. "Suck it."

"No."

"Please." His voice was velvet and sex, somehow commanding and pleading at once. "I love to watch those lips work a dick."

I groaned and reached down to grab myself through my jeans, losing all self-control and opening my mouth so he could plunder it with the vibrator. I didn't know what he got out of it, how he could possibly be so turned on by watching me blow the curved silicone until it became slick with my saliva, but Nunzio's eyes were glued to the spectacle and dilated until the blue was just a thin ring around his pupil.

"Yeah," he whispered, fucking my mouth with it faster. "You love sucking dick, don't you?"

My answer came in the form of a sloppy humming sound. I could do nothing else as I undid my belt one-handed and stared at him from beneath my lashes. When he dragged the vibrator from between my lips and slid his own tongue along the length of it, molten lava filled my belly and tightened my nuts.

"Now get your clothes off and put it in your ass."

You would have thought it would take more convincing, given the possible outcomes. A couple of months ago, the most physical we'd gotten was lying next to each other during a *Breaking Bad* marathon and eating off the same plate, but it took roughly ninety seconds for Nunzio to convince me to strip, lie on my back with my thighs spread wide, and screw myself while he watched. A few minutes later, he had taken over and was stabbing my prostate with the device set to full blast as I pumped my dick with the Fleshlight.

Covered in sweat and a boneless sack of trembling limbs, I surrendered to the violent urge lancing through me. I had to bite the knuckles on my free hand to keep quiet.

Nunzio hunched over me, fully clothed and panting. "Fuck it faster."

I obeyed, sliding the lube-filled device over my cock, and bit my fist harder to muffle the groan that followed.

"Let me fucking hear you."

I shook my head, nearly delirious from the constant buzz against my sweet spot, but did nothing to evade when he knocked my fist away from my mouth. The sounds I made could only be described as desperate, and far too loud considering the number of people downstairs, but I was far beyond caring.

Welling pressure and tingling in my balls struck me so suddenly that I yanked the Fleshlight off my dick with a wet sucking sound, and clamped my fist around the base of my shaft. "Wait. Fuck, fuck—*wait.*"

Nunzio's hand stilled. He switched the device off and pulled it out, slow and gentle.

"Shit." I bit my lip and shut my eyes. I didn't want to come yet, but I was sure I'd bust as soon as I removed my fingers. After a long moment of guttered breathing, the oncoming orgasm receded.

I wrenched my eyes open and found Nunzio naked and clutching the thick column of his cock. It took only my heavy-lidded stare and a tiny smirk for him to get the message and shove his dick home.

No care was given to the sound of skin slapping skin, and with a buffer of two floors, music, and football, I decided it was acceptable to not even attempt muffling my hoarse groans. I couldn't contain it and didn't want to—if Nunzio wanted to watch and hear me be a slut, I'd give him enough material to jerk off to for the next six months.

And there was no denying that I wanted it. That I *needed* it. The feel of his sweat-slick body sliding against mine, and him stretching me open with an agonizing burn, triggered the part of me that wanted to be fucked until I couldn't take it anymore.

I thought he would give it to me that way; pound me hard and fast until he filled me up with hot spurts of come that I craved with every nasty fiber of my being, but Nunzio slowed his movements when things got too frantic.

He dropped messy kisses on my stubble-covered cheek. "Shh," he murmured. "Slow the hell down."

I started to bare my teeth at him, but he grabbed a fistful of my hair and drew my mouth up to meet his. Nunzio said my name when he kissed me, a faint hint of syllables as I swallowed each of his breaths. It was too sweet, too gentle, and my heart stuttered in response.

I reached around to palm one of his asscheeks, urging him on, wanting the hard usage he'd given me moments ago, not the delicate brush of his lips.

"Nunzio, come on."

"I wanna make it last," he said.

He slid a hand between us to squeeze my sac, and laughed quietly against my sweaty face. Everything Nunzio did was so smooth, so deliberate and practiced, that I felt shameless and out of control in comparison. He could draw this out all night, and all I wanted was to be screwed until I was sobbing into the mattress and aching from the violation.

"Just come in me," I said in a voice that Clive had never gotten to hear. "And then fuck me again later."

Nunzio laughed again, his voice thick and low. "I love that you want my dick this bad."

"Do it." I clenched up around his cock, working it until his laughter was replaced by labored breathing.

"Shit," Nunzio said and grabbed my throat with one hand while shoving my knee sideways with the other. He fucked me so hard I just clung to him and enjoyed the ride. When he came, it was abrupt and explosive, and the raw cry that tore out of his mouth was so loud that he had to press his face into my sweaty neck. But he kept pumping his hips and sliding his still-swollen dick in and out of me with decreasing speed.

"Jesus," I whispered. "I want to come."

Other words tried to formulate in my brain, but none had the chance before Nunzio pulled out and flipped me over. My ass was in the air, and the smooth, cool length of the massager was reinserted into my hole.

"Oh fuck, yes."

I rode back on it like I'd been waiting for another dick all along. He jammed it into me hard, and by the time he activated the highest power, I was shaking. My mouth dropped open, but no sound came out. Between the repeated strokes of the vibrator against my prostate, and Nunzio reaching around to pump my straining cock, I blew my load with a blinding intensity that drained my balls of every drop of semen.

I collapsed. My lungs burned from the lack of oxygen.

Nunzio said something to me but it was an incomprehensible whisper. I was only aware of him stretching out beside me and pulling me close. He kissed the side of my neck, then my cheek, but my daze prevented me from reciprocating.

I was too destroyed to attempt to be anything other than dick addled in front my family, but even with that in mind, I made no effort to crawl out of the bed, or to ignore the ache in my abs and the throb of my abused ass.

If anyone walked in now, it would be a wrap. The room stank of sex, we were both naked and drenched in sweat, and parts of my body were reddened from Nunzio's gripping hands. But I stayed wrapped up in his muscular arms because I didn't care about family or holidays or anyone's opinion anymore. I only cared about the warm contentment pooling inside me as Nunzio stroked my back.

"Spend the rest of the weekend with me," he murmured.

There was no hesitation before I nodded.

Chapter Twelve

December

"I'LL FUCKING kill you, you gay piece of shit!"

My head jerked up so quickly that something popped. I searched the classroom for the perpetrator. Shawn was the usual suspect, but he had his headphones on despite my repeated demands for him to put them away. He was in his own world, ignoring his group and drawing in his notebook. So much for him catching up.

"Oh my God, relax."

I turned from Shawn to Mac—the gay piece of shit in question—and Alex, the biggest asshole in all of my tenth grade classes. Besides Mac.

Putting them in the same group had been a strategic move; force them to make a bomb-ass presentation with their superior critical thinking skills and get over the bullshit that kept them at each other's throats. It had gone well until now.

Walking around the kids who were not even pretending to be focused on preparing their presentations, I approached the cluster of tables where Mac and Alex were facing off. Mac was grinning at Alex, both palms planted on the desk, and leaning down. Their faces were inches apart.

Alex was crimson, and his eyes were so wide I could see the whites around them. Alarmed, I shouted, "Mackenzie!"

Alex's nostrils flared. "Get this faggot away from me before I break his nose."

"Do it," Mac challenged. "Do it, pussy."

I put a hand on Mac's shoulder and pulled him back just as Alex leapt out of his seat. Next to him, his best friend Eric seemed torn between helping and going back to his project.

"Alex, take a walk. Mac, move away. Now."

"Keep him away from me, or I'll wreck him."

Alex was breathing hard, his body tense and coiled for a fight. I had seen him in action before and had zero desire for him to flip out in my classroom. Especially when Mac was just as capable of getting crazy. He'd been responsible for instigating the "Ninth Grade Riot of the Gays" as Nunzio and I had dubbed it—a massive brawl between a dozen of the most out-and-proud gay boys in the middle of the hallway last year. It had been the worst fight in the school's history and had ended with cops called and blood smeared all over the floors, with Mac at the center of it all, throwing punches and laughing like a hyena.

I shot Eric an impatient look. "Take your friend to get some water."

"Uh...."

"Go!"

Eric stood up and hauled Alex to the door.

Shawn had glanced up to observe the confrontation and looked utterly unimpressed. The other kids whispered to each other until I gave them a sharp reminder that this was their final period to work on their presentations and there was only ten minutes left. I don't know if it was the time constraint or my tone that got them to stop bullshitting, but they fell silent.

I brought Mac to the back of the room.

"What was that about?"

Mac smoothed a hand through his hair, lifting one shoulder in a move too elegant for a fifteen-year-old sociopath. "He's just a little sensitive, okay?"

"Yeah, I got that part, but did you have to keep antagonizing him?"

"Mr. R...." Mac flashed a condescending smile. "I need to get back to my project."

"No, you need to explain to me what the hell the problem is with you and Alex before I write up the both of you."

"Me?" Mac held up a hand in protest. "Seriously? Did you *not* hear him calling me gay slurs?"

"I heard him, and believe me, he will be dealt with, but you can't keep picking fights with him. At some point, it will happen while one of your teachers isn't around to get in the middle, and then what are you going to do?"

"Get his ass kicked," Shawn muttered loud enough for his deep voice to be heard across the room.

Mac flipped Shawn off and puckered his lips. "Shut your sexy ass up. Don't even pretend you don't love me."

Shawn just shook his head and went back to his doodling. Mac continued to grin at him, not caring that we were in the middle of a tense conversation.

I clapped my hands to reclaim his attention. A little more contempt and the look he speared me with would have actually killed me.

"Oh my God, fine. I started telling Eric and Rosemarie that Alex came over my house to finish the project. That's it, and it's a free country so I can basically say whatever I want without being threatened."

The pieces came together and my annoyance heightened. He had essentially disrupted class just to start some Alex-is-gay-for-me rumor. It was inevitable that Mac would end up in a world of trouble someday, but at least we had avoided it this time.

"You need to control your mouth, kid."

"Oh please, Mister. My mouth has plenty of control. Just ask Shawn."

I held out a hand to ward him away, wanting his leering face to be gone from my sight. "Go away. Please."

"You're welcome for the visual!"

I continued to hold out my hand, cringing in horror and trying to mentally bleach my brain. The bell rang before Mac could say any other horrifying things, and the sound just added to my growing headache.

I was so disgusted that I forgot to assign their homework before they ran out of the room. I had never understood why kids acted like their next period class was an exciting destination. Maybe they were just that thrilled to be out of history class.

Collapsing into a chair, I looked around but couldn't muster the energy to put away their strewn supplies. It was the week before Christmas break, and I'd deliberately planned a long project complete with two days of presentations, but the kids were still more unruly than usual. I didn't know why holidays turned the students into little monsters, but it happened every year without fail.

I sat there zoning out and staring at still-open laptops and folders of research lying on the cluster of desks until Nunzio walked into the room holding two paper cups. I jerked my chin at the door, and he shut it behind him.

"'Sup, boo."

"Please never call me that again."

"Why not?"

Nunzio crossed the room and handed me a cup. I took a sip and smiled. Hot chocolate.

"Thanks."

"Not a problem. It's an excuse to see your morose face. I'm having a horrific day, and my grade team leader is riding my fucking ass. I think she knows I'm keeping track of reasons to quit, and she wants to push me over the edge."

"Maria is just an asshole to everyone. Pay her no mind."

"Easy for you to say. Your team leader is a piece of ass who is terrified of you. I get told I'm a shitty SpEd teacher because I'm not nurturing enough."

"Damn. I'm sorry, niño."

"It's whatever at this point." Nunzio sat on the edge of a desk and removed his own cup from the carton.

The sound of shouting teenagers, ineffective commands from the deans, and running footsteps filtered through the door. Sometimes it seemed like I worked at an elementary school instead of a high school for all the self-control they had. I tried to tune it out and studied Nunzio. He was the only person I knew who could look edible in a pair of jeans and a black sweater.

"I haven't seen you much lately," he said.

"You see me every day."

"Yeah, here, but we haven't hung out besides work for a while."

I rotated the cup in my hands, dragging my thumbs against the sides. Examining the lid was preferable to starting the conversation I'd been running through my head for the past several weeks. Since I'd spent Thanksgiving weekend locked up in his apartment being turned out six ways to the 22nd century. Four days of nonstop sex, nonstop kissing, touching, and playing house, and I'd felt myself falling so quickly down the rabbit hole that panic had swept in to dampen the constant burn of lust.

By the end of the weekend, there had been a shift so sharp that I didn't know where we stood anymore. There had been too many half-said comments, aborted sentences, and lingering touches that had nothing to do with getting off and seeing what we could do to each other and for how long. Something was building between us, something that took my breath away from anticipation, but also created anxiety about how little I could handle the possibility of it all going wrong.

"Did you have a fucking stroke?" There was a glimmer of irritation in his eyes. "What's wrong with you?"

After another moment of hesitation, I worked up the courage to speak.

"I just think things are getting a little intense. Maybe we should calm it down for a while."

"Oh, holy shit." Nunzio set his cup down with enough force for some of it to slop out of the cover. "How have things been getting *a little intense?*"

"Just cool out. Don't start getting mad."

"Who the fuck is mad?"

I unfolded myself from the student desk and moved to the side of the room where I was out of view of the thin slice of window in my door. After a second of silent brooding, Nunzio followed.

"Don't take it the wrong way and start cursing at me. I'm just trying to tell you what I've been thinking about."

Nunzio inclined his head in a curt nod and half turned to the door. "Whatever, Michael. I gotta go write some IEPs."

"Nunzio, are you kidding me right now? You can't just listen?"

He shrugged, still refusing to meet my gaze. This was going worse than I had expected. I'd anticipated disagreement about the situation potentially becoming a problem, but I'd thought he would reassure me with a coy grin and cajoling comments, not stand there with hunched shoulders while brimming with anger.

I struggled with my explanation, but there was no way I was going to let the conversation trail off. It needed to happen, and we needed to be on the same page.

"I'm just saying," I started again, "that things have been getting way more intense than we talked about. It was supposed to be some casual once-in-a-while type of thing, something that happened when we were drunk and wanted to party without having to go out to a club, but I think it's becoming way more than that."

I took a step closer and put my hand on his arm, digging my fingers into the soft fabric of his sweater.

"You know it's true, Nunzio. Thanksgiving was…."

He shoved my hand away. "Was what?"

"It was the best time I've had in years. I'm not trying to deny that we have crazy sexual chemistry, niño. I'm just saying I can feel it heading in a direction that might make our friendship more complicated than I can handle. ¿Oíste?"

"Yeah, okay. I feel you." Nunzio took a step backward. "Look, I really got to go get some work done."

I followed him. "You're not understanding me."

"No, I understand just fine."

"Then why the hell are you getting so upset? I just—" I reached up to touch his face, but he evaded. "You're the only person who makes me happy. I won't ruin what we've had for twenty years because the sex is good."

He pushed my hand away again when I tried to touch him. "Stop."

"Why are you being like this?"

Nunzio gave me a brief once-over before turning away with a low scoff. I could feel his anger charging the space between us and had to fight the urge to crowd him, to press my chest to the taut stretch of his back, and bury my face in his hair.

I could usually calm him down with matter-of-fact explanations, logic, a hug. But now he wouldn't look at me, and the shift in our relationship, the thing that had put this fear into me, was going in a totally different direction. One that ensured Nunzio wouldn't even speak to me.

A scrabble of fear clawed at me, and I almost pulled him close, kissed him, and took back every word, but I gritted my teeth and refused to cave.

"I don't understand why you're acting this way. I just don't want to ruin what we already have. I'm not trying to upset you."

"I know you're not trying to upset me, but what do you expect, Mikey? You know I want you, and you don't want me, so what else is there to say?"

"I don't—"

"Don't say you don't know what the fuck I'm talking about." Nunzio's voice rose, getting sharper, the way it came out when his temper burned short. "The only reason we're having this conversation is because you figured out that I've been fiending for you for a long time now, and you don't want to deal with it. So fine. It's whatever. We can go back to the way shit was before, and you can go fuck David."

"Oh my fucking God, Nunzio." I slammed my hand against the whiteboard. "It always comes back to David."

"The only reason you ever looked twice at me is because he was in the middle," Nunzio shouted back. "And the only reason you looked at me after that is because he was *too drunk*, and I was a good second choice."

The fear turned into a full-on panic, and every word caught in my throat. The urge to defend myself clashed with a need to appease him, but Nunzio continued before I could go one way or the other.

"Say I'm wrong," he challenged.

I couldn't. He knew I couldn't. He was repeating my words and using them as proof of something, but I wasn't clear about what I was being accused of. That I'd never truly wanted him? That he was reduced to a backup while I waited for David? Or maybe David was just an easy target, and Nunzio was really thinking about every other guy I'd ever chosen over him?

The accusation held no truth, but I couldn't deny that the realization of him being sweeter on me than I'd ever imagined had me spooked. I knew he didn't mean to let it show, but I could taste it in his kisses, and I saw it in his face every time he gazed at me after an intense round of sex. I could feel it when he pulled me close afterward, when he'd admitted he liked sleeping next to me.

And then… I'd realized I liked that he had those feelings for me. That was when worry had taken full control of my senses.

"Good answer," he said sarcastically, and strode to the door.

"Wait—"

Nunzio was out of the room before I could protest, and I would be damned before I took the conversation out into the hall.

I was left alone with the resounding tremble of the door in its frame once he slammed it, the faint sound of Danielle teaching across the hall and wind howling outside the window.

Frustration swelled inside me. I wanted to kick over a desk, or throw the strewn supplies across the room, but I didn't. I had a class in thirty minutes and unleashing my wrath on the room would only make my mood worse since I was the one who would have to clean it.

I picked up the cup and took a sip, but it now tasted like ash.

IT FELT like the coldest day of the year when I finally stepped out of the building. I shoved my fists into the pockets of my black coat and hunched my shoulders.

I wondered if Nunzio had left yet. I'd fought the urge to track him down for over two hours before finally forcing myself to leave. Winter break was in a week, and I would have time to sort things out with him during the vacation, not when we were both stressed due to work and the looming holidays. Maybe by then I would have an explanation that would not cause him to turn away with white-knuckled fists and hurt in his eyes.

The stretch of sidewalk seemed longer and darker with the bitter cold bearing down on me from all sides. Gusts shoved me along, buffeting against me, and made the trek to the subway station feel like a journey instead of a three-minute walk. When I reached the corner, I spied a familiar form heading in the same direction.

I jogged ahead to catch up with David. "Hey, man."

David did a double take, but grinned. "Hey. I thought you already went home."

"Nah. My room was a mess."

"You should make the kids clean it up."

"Yeah. I need to get a senior intern to be on clean-up duty. I don't have time for this shit."

David's head bobbed in agreement. "I can't deal with this cold anymore," he grumbled as we headed downstairs. "It's making me bitchier than usual. I should have booked a flight to Qatar for Christmas."

"Go for midwinter recess. If my money situation wasn't so shitty, I'd go to Florida or something."

He shook his head, wide mouth curled down. "Nope. I'm making a conscious effort to pay off my student loans. I'll just suffer."

I almost made a crack about first world problems but refrained. I wanted to talk to him, not antagonize him. We bypassed a Salvation Army guy ringing a bell in front of a holiday donation bucket and swiped through the turnstile.

"So lemme ask you a question," I said once we'd settled on a bench on the Manhattan bound side of the tracks.

"I heard about Alex and Mac. They're both jerks, but I'm worried about Mac's behavior landing him in some serious hot water. He doesn't see anything he does or says as a problem, and doesn't think about the potential outcomes. Actually I've noticed that several of the gay kids in our school are like that."

I looped both my arms through the straps of my backpack. "Blame our admin. We attract so many gay kids because of our connection with the LGBT center, but the rules are so fucking lax that they run wild, and the administration is too worried about coddling them to set a standard of behavior."

David wrinkled his nose and nodded. He had come to the same conclusion within the first month of school. He was a snotty little fucker, and definitely on a mission to move up to an administrative position, but even he had deduced that our school's policy of empowerment combined with their lack of rules led to laziness and entitlement among the kids.

"In my last school, there were no out gay kids at all. I had to talk in my man-voice so they wouldn't catch on."

I released a bark of laughter, and David looked up at me with a pleased smile.

"Your man-voice?"

"Yeah, like this," he said, deepening his voice theatrically.

"Oh, Jesus. You sound like an idiot."

"The kids didn't know the difference. They thought I was a freak anyway."

"They had a point."

"Oh, shut up."

Behind us, a couple broke into a heated argument. Their voices carried through the tunnel, rising and falling in what sounded like a typical back-and-forth.

"But anyway," I said. "That's not what I was going to ask you. I wanted to talk to you about Nunzio."

David's eyes dropped down to the track bed where a massive rat was scurrying along the side. "Why? I don't talk to him much."

"I know, but a couple of times he mentioned something that had me wondering what's said when you do talk."

"Not much."

I thought I heard a familiar voice shouting up the platform and grimaced, hoping I wouldn't see my students out in the real world. I looked up and down, searching, and spoke again when I didn't see anyone.

"He seems to believe that you and I are fooling around. I know he saw us talking a couple of times and we were looking all cozy, but we both know it wasn't the way he's making it sound."

David chewed his lower lip, and appeared to consider the statement. He looked a lot younger with his nose and cheeks red from the cold and a knit cap smashing his white-blond hair against his cheeks. "Are the two of you involved now?"

"No," I said, too fast.

"That wasn't believable at all, just so you know."

"It's complic—" At his triumphant smile, I stopped myself from using the phrase. "Oh God. Just let me finish."

"Fine, fine, go ahead."

I rubbed my hands together and blew on them. "If I confide in you, can you swear not to repeat it to anyone?"

"I swear."

The oath wasn't exactly a binding contract, but I had the equivalent of verbal diarrhea anyway.

"We've messed around a few times since the summer. You started something that I couldn't put a lid on too easily and when I tried, he got mad and started ranting about me and you."

"Michael, he always talks shit about me and you. He's jealous."

"Why?" I wished Nunzio was around so I could shake sense into him. "I could deal with him thinking I put a stop to things because I don't feel the same way, or because I'm just an asshole that used him on the rebound—he'd get over that. He and his ego wouldn't get over me cutting him off for another guy. Especially the guy who replaced him on the team and is, like, twelve fucking years old."

"The age jokes are getting a little stale, don't you think?" David leaned over to peer into the darkness of the tunnel for our train. "And I don't know why he thinks that way, but whenever we're alone by some off chance, he makes a comment or joke about us. It's obvious that he's jealous."

"There's no reason to be jealous."

"Well, Michael, tell him that. I'm fully aware that you have zero interest in me."

"That's not true. I had interest in fucking you until I found out that you had boyfriend problems."

"Oh brother. Can we just get off this topic? I don't have any insight into your insane friend's attitude problem."

The edge in David's tone whenever he talked about Nunzio bugged me, but I couldn't defend my friend when I didn't know what kind of lip he gave David when they were alone. The idea of Nunzio picking on David bugged me, and I wondered: if Nunzio was this possessive when things were casual, how would it escalate if we got serious?

My stomach bottomed out at the idea of him believing I was rejecting him for someone else. How could he even consider the possibility that I would choose anyone over him?

"Man, I screwed this all up."

David nodded his agreement, and I rolled my eyes. "Thanks for the support, colleague."

"You are very welcome. But honestly, I'm the last person to ask about relationships. I'm clearly an epic failure at handling my own. My boyfriend dumped me after he found me jacking off in the bathroom while on the phone with a guy from Grindr."

Yikes.

I tried not to laugh, but the strain was obvious. He sneered, and our train arrived before we could say anything more on the topic. Even so, his confession rallied me, and I resolved to clear things up with Nunzio as soon as possible.

He needed to understand there was nothing wrong with him. He was gorgeous, funny, and amazing in bed, and I was just a punk who was too afraid to keep screwing around for fear of losing my only friend.

David got off the train in SoHo, and I sat down and zoned out until the train arrived in Queens. By the time I was back in Jamaica, it was a little before six o'clock but already pitch-black.

A familiar sense of weariness swept me, and I prayed everything at the house was calm. A couple of drinks while sitting down with a stack of ungraded papers sounded great. I envisioned the scenario as each step brought me closer to my block, head cast down and earphones blasting loud enough to drown out the world. My mood lifted just slightly at the possibility of relaxation, but the flimsy thread of hope disintegrated when a wash of red and blue lights bounced across the pavement ahead of me.

Ambulances were parked in front of my house.

The instinct to rush forward choked me, but I stopped in my tracks. I stood swathed in the shadows of a towering tree and stared at the scene playing out in front of my childhood home. Neighbors huddled on the sidewalk, a police officer was speaking to my brother in the front yard, and an ambulance with shut doors and EMTs loaded inside, ready to drive away. Dread filled my stomach.

"Ray?" I called out. No one turned or reacted, and I moved closer, tried again. "Raymond!"

Raymond looked up.

We looked at each other across the short distance, my hands still gripping the straps of my backpack and his expression becoming tighter the longer we stared. I forced myself to go to him, to be the responsible one, the big brother, but I wanted to turn and run at the sight of the ambulance.

One foot in front of the other, and the whole block was staring. I heard our neighbor crying, the woman who had babysat us as children when Mami was working two jobs. Her hand brushed my shoulder when I passed, but I didn't take my eyes off my brother.

"Pops is dead." Raymond's voice was wooden. He looked down at his feet; they were bare. "I tried to wake him up, but he wouldn't. I thought he was sleeping."

The feeling building inside my chest was more familiar than it should have been. A widening hole dark enough to swallow my heart and leave me breathless.

"I uh—"

I looked at the cop, but he was already focused on something else. The yawning hole in my chest gaped wider and sucked every feeling I had inside like a vacuum. Raymond grabbed my arm, fingers digging in.

"I—I should have called. I didn't think—I don't know—"

"It's okay. I'll take care of it, Ray. You stay here."

"No." Raymond moved closer, clutching me tighter. "No, I'm going."

I nodded, my mind going a mile a minute and words clogging in my throat. He had to put on shoes, to get dressed, to be ready, but even after Mami, I still didn't know what else to do.

I forced my gaze away from the blur of red-and-blue lights. The cop was now speaking to me, but I couldn't make out the words. Everything was a wet warble. He may as well have been under water.

Raymond pulled me close. He was trembling. I was making things worse. I wasn't reacting fast enough, being strong enough, but I couldn't. The world was full of shadows and white noise. Crumbling around me. Once again falling apart.

What did I care? I'd basically told my father this was what I'd wanted. Made sure he knew I hadn't wanted him. Made sure he knew I didn't love him. All of the words I had spit in anger, accusing and hateful and forever in his mind before his body had simply stopped.

Those moments replayed in my mind as we followed the ambulance to the hospital, my hands steady on the wheel while Raymond called Aida and John, his voice raw from unshed tears.

We got to the hospital quickly, but I missed a turn, couldn't find the right parking lot, and nearly crashed into the gate. My hands weren't steady anymore and my throat felt dry, an itch at the back that demanded something to calm me down. The need was all-encompassing, an ache in my gut, and somehow the fixation helped me focus not just on everything that was wrong, but all the ways I could make it right.

That kept me standing when Aida nearly knocked me down, clinging so tight and sobbing so hard my knees almost buckled under her weight. It gave me something to look forward to while listening to John talk about the arrangements, after he put his hand on my shoulder.

The pity in his face broke me, and I lost it in the middle of a hospital hallway with a bunch of strangers looking on.

John took a step forward, but I backed away and turned to face the wall. Tears poured down my face, unceasing and horrible, and I knew Raymond was watching. People were talking to me, but again they sounded like they were under water; as though the torrents of tears had turned into a river that was washing me away.

All I could think of were the words I'd exchanged with Joseph—what I'd said to him in front of John on Thanksgiving, the look on his face and the contempt in my voice; the way I'd shut him down each time he had tried to express a kind word, every time he had admitted to being proud of me.

The way I hadn't stopped him drinking because I'd given up so fast.

My shoulders shook, and I hid my face against the wall. I held my hands over my ears, but I still heard the words. I saw his face when I told him he was nothing, and I hated myself so much that I just wanted to be gone.

Someone touched me, but this time the hands weren't hesitant. They were strong, sure, and I knew they belonged to Nunzio.

I turned to him, seeking his warmth, and buried my face against his neck. His arms encircled me, one hand digging into the hair at my nape while the other rubbed my back. I felt people watching, but I needed him so much that I didn't care.

"I didn't hate him. He thought I hated him, but I swear I didn't. I was just so mad."

"I know, Mikey. I know."

"He didn't know." I shut my eyes, blocking out everything except for what I could see in my head. "He didn't fucking know."

Chapter Thirteen

New Year's

I DROPPED the glass on the table with too much force, and the ringing sound reverberated in my ears. If I could hear it over the excited laughter around me, it meant my face was too close to the table.

Two hours in, and I was already fading.

The bar was not large, but the New Year's Eve partygoers had invaded in droves. I'd claimed my spot at a back table after wandering Manhattan for hours in the bitter cold, and ordered Jack Daniels in a voice so low and rough the bartender had barely heard me over the crowd. Strange how a little amber liquid could spread so much warmth.

I wondered if the combination of swank suits, high heels, and fancy dresses indicated a private party. If so, no one asked me to leave. Maybe the staff could sense my festering misery despite all my attempts to remain stoic.

Two weeks after the funeral, and I could still remember exactly how my father had looked during the viewing.

Everything from the color of the suit, the hairstyle, and the type of casket had been wrong. He would have said the stripes made it look like he was wearing a zoot suit, the combed-back hair made him seem like an extra from West Side Story, and the metallic casket resembled a spaceship. He would have also hated the phonies who took turns giving speeches about his life and making outrageous claims about the impact he'd had on theirs while leaving out the fact that each one had quit speaking to him years ago.

I had never understood why people felt the need to mythologize the dead in order to justify mourning them, but funerals had a way of bringing out the worst in the living. Especially during the family gatherings that followed.

For the most part, I'd opted out. I'd stood by my brother as much as I could, trying to support him while only operating with a tiny fraction of my brain's capacity, but it hadn't taken long for Raymond to realize that I was useless this time around.

Guilt was a disease that had infected my every thought, word, and action. It became a sentient being that whispered in my ear for the duration of the planning and the services. It told me I didn't have the right to have an opinion on my father's funeral, so I shouldn't be angry that John took complete control. I didn't have the right to criticize his phony family or lowlife friends. I didn't have the right to be there. I didn't even have the right to cry.

So I avoided everyone, kept my head down, and slunk away when my silent presence made the others too awkward to continue with their maudlin platitudes, and the days passed without transition.

I couldn't remember what I'd done on Christmas beyond staying in the attic and refusing to speak to anyone. The plan for New Year's had been the same, but Raymond had forced me to promise that I would go out. I'd complied mostly because remaining locked in the house our parents had died in was starting to feel dangerous for my mental health. It was far too easy to fall face-first into a pit of despair, and just keep falling.

Left in peace to work my way through enough whiskey to rot my insides, I tried to ignore the expanding crowd. It worked until a sloppy drunk girl in a white dress nearly fell backward on my table. I stared, she and her friends laughed, and I bet they were the type to believe in resolutions and fresh starts.

The naiveté was nauseating, and I hated them all. No resolution would improve my situation and another year flipping on the calendar wasn't going to change my luck. I could brood my way through the next century and no amount of prayers, wishes, or promises to change would undo the curse of being born into the Rodriguez family.

Looking down, I straightened the list I'd begun compiling earlier in the afternoon. It was wrinkled and a little damp, but I could still read the words. The name of every person in my family who was miserable, involved in a chemical dependency, or dead. I'd taken a shot for each name on the list, and after two hours, I was a hundred dollars in the hole. A couple more and I'd black out, but self-induced amnesia was quite all right with me even if it was a temporary solution.

"Hey, can I borrow this chair?"

I stared through the too-much-Jack sheen and tried to focus on the guy looming above me. He was young, hair too long, smile too big, but eyeballing me like maybe he wouldn't mind talking about something besides a chair. I waved him off and resumed my contemplation of the list.

"Are you okay?"

"Just take the damn chair."

The guy backed off but shot me not-so-discreet glances from across the bar. I wished everyone would leave me alone. It was stupid. I'd put myself into this situation—surrounded by people, looking like hell, and so obviously unhappy that I was practically waving a *pity me* banner, but still not willing to talk to anyone.

I muttered it aloud and seemed to jinx myself because my phone vibrated. My fingers were clumsy and uncoordinated, and I nearly dropped it twice before squinting at the screen.

I brought the phone to my ear in slow motion. "Yeah?"

"Hey."

I debated hanging up on David but croaked, "What's up?"

There was a hesitation on David's side and the rise and fall of multiple voices, laughter, and loud music. Someone called out to him, and I heard David's muffled voice request for them to wait a moment so he could step outside.

My eyes scanned the room, paranoid he would pop up somewhere in the crowd.

"I was wondering if you're going to come out," he said once the background noise faded.

"I'm out."

"I mean out with us. The whole team is at Karen's party."

"I can't be around people right now."

David sighed into the receiver, the sound hitting the microphone too loud. "Nunzio's here."

The words startled me. I hadn't talked to Nunzio since the funeral, and hadn't responded to his repeated messages and calls. I couldn't deal with the possibility of him trying to make me feel better about myself and the situation even if it resulted in him being pissed. But even as miserable as I was, I craved his touch and thought about him so much that the distance was unbearable.

"Oh," I said after a beat of silence.

"Yeah.... So he's here. You could be too."

"Is he having fun?"

"I don't know. We were dancing a little bit ago. He's wasted."

I wondered if they would make out when the clock struck midnight like a couple of fucking clichés, and then go screw each other in the bathroom. It was what Nunzio did every year without fail, bringing in the New Year with a new fuck, and then vowing that the next year he'd change everything and stop messing around so much with different guys. I could practically see them crushed together, Nunzio's olive skin contrasting with David's paleness.

"You have fun with him."

"What do you mean?"

"I mean have fucking fun with him."

"Michael, I didn't mean it like—"

I hung up. I knew I was being irrational, but I turned off my phone anyway. It was a hair-trigger response, and I almost immediately turned it back on just in case Raymond called me later in the night. But it was unlikely. Raymond wasn't trying to alienate his friends. He wasn't sitting alone somewhere like a goddamned loser.

"Fuck," I whispered, covering my face with my hands. "Fuck my life."

"Are you sure you're okay?"

Jumping halfway off the chair, I dropped my hands and glared at the guy who was now sitting across from me. "Jesus fucking Christ, don't you have someone else to talk to? Do you want the chair I'm sitting on now?"

The guy grinned in response to my vitriol. Was he an idiot or did he think I was trying to be cute? Judging from the tattoo crawling up the side of his neck, the gauges and piercings, and general aura of badass, I drunkenly assumed he just got off on people with an asshole vibe. He also had big blue Nunzio eyes, which were more of a distraction than was healthy. But his hair was too light, his jaw not as defined, and his lips not as full….

I looked down at my empty glass. Fuck.

"I don't want your chair, but I've been watching you and you most definitely do not look okay."

"Look buddy, you're barking up the wrong tree if you think I'm here looking for a friend."

"So why are you here? To languish away by yourself?"

"Yes." I traced the pad of my finger on the table. "I came here to be alone and sit in a corner, so why don't you let me do that and go back to your side of the bar?"

"I want to talk to you."

I sneered. "To instill some New Year's cheer? Don't bother. I'm fine."

Laughter erupted a few feet away. The guy's eyes flicked to the side, and I hoped he'd take himself and his fucking Nunzio eyes away from me, but no such luck; he just smiled again. The guy was hot in all the wrong ways, and I wouldn't be that into him if I wasn't in such a funk, but those eyes....

"You're a bad liar. You'll never get rid of me that way."

"You know what they say. He who can't dissemble, can't fucking reign." He looked stumped so I explained with as much disdain as I could slur. "It's a Roman thing. Forget it."

"Do you normally go around quoting Romans when drunk?"

"History teacher," I grunted. It earned me another cocked-head stare of surprise, and I bit back a retort about all Latinos not being fucking construction workers. What was it that David had accused me of all those weeks ago? Projecting? Being defensive? Whatever. It was all bullshit, anyway. "All right, well this is as entertaining as it gets so feel free to mosey on."

"Maybe I don't want to mosey on." The guy picked up my empty glass. "Maybe I want to see you smile."

"Maybe you should mind your own fucking business."

He must have really been into verbal abuse because he said, "Maybe you'd be more open to conversation if I got you another drink."

"You'd literally have to get me an entire bottle."

"Consider it done."

I started to protest but stuttered out the words too slow, and he was disappearing into the crowd before I could stop him. I looked around, craving an exit, but ultimately failing because my mystery benefactor was back before I could make a decision. He was armed with a bottle of Jack Daniels. I unsuccessfully tried to smile, but I could still see his obvious want.

It did nothing for me. Not even when he ogled my biceps and dragged his tongue over his lips. He could hit me with every rehearsed move he had, and I would still be more interested in the bottle. It was a sad testament to my situation, especially since I knew full well where this little tête-à-tête was going, but I was not drunk enough to ignore key details that were hanging my sex drive out to dry. Like the unyielding desire to forget my own name while on a brain vacation to a reality that was a lot less harsh than this one.

"How much do I owe you?

"Don't worry about it."

"I don't do handouts."

"So what do you do?"

"Whatever you want." My tone was better suited for a eulogy than a come-on, but he didn't seem to mind. He was going full throttle on the eye-fucks, even though, personality-wise, I was the least impressive person in the bar. My hand twitched around the bottle, but I didn't make a move to open it. Not my money, not mine to touch.

"What's your name?" he asked, leaning closer to hear the faint rumble of my voice.

"Michael."

"I'm Noel."

"Good for you."

Noel screwed off the top of the bottle without much effort. It wasn't full, but I wasn't about to complain.

"So what's got you looking so down?"

I watched him pour. My attraction kicked in the more generous he was. Our fingers brushed when he slid the glass closer to me, and I looked away from his smoldering gaze to fill my gut with more whiskey.

"You want my sad life story?" I asked, the words coming out thick and clumsy.

"Maybe." Noel grabbed the neck of the bottle and filled his glass. "Why aren't you with anyone on New Year's?"

"Because miserable people shouldn't be around happy people."

"What can we do to make you happy?"

That was my cue. Flash a half smile, say something nasty, maybe drop some Spanish since it gave white boys such a jump start to their cocks—I'd been playing the game for long enough to have a formula for this type of thing. But a beat went by, then another, and then Noel's smile was fading like he was finally cluing in to the fact that maybe I was actually depressed. Poor bastard.

"Ask me again after a few more," I said.

The smile returned. "Will do, Mikey."

I wiped my mouth. "If you call me that again, it's a wrap."

Noel held up his hands, still smiling and clearly not taking the emotional temperature of my frozen-over expression. "You got it."

It took three more drinks to reach oblivion. Once there, I only slipped into my conscious mind for long enough to experience fragments of real life.

A flash of a graffiti-covered bathroom. The feel of lips on my neck and a hand down my pants. The sound of my breath scraping out in low gasps. Whispering Nunzio's name. Being so sure it was his wavy hair hanging in my face, his sweat that I tasted, his hand bringing me to the brink and making me hyperventilate as I tried to keep quiet. But it wasn't. And it was all wrong.

I WAS ripped out of a persistent doze by a frail hand shaking my shoulder. My eyes snapped open. Daylight. Concrete. The curb outside St. Luke's.

An elderly black woman thrust a five dollar bill in my hand with a sympathetic frown on her face.

"Here, honey."

I blinked at her, swallowing the wretched taste in my mouth, and shifted alongside the rough texture of the wall. "I'm not—" I swallowed again, nearly gagging. "I'm not homeless."

She gave me a thorough once-over and leaned on her cane. Her skepticism was warranted. I'd woken up in the ER wearing a coat two sizes too small with no wallet and a cracked phone. I hadn't bothered to look in a mirror.

"I'm just hungover and waiting for my brother," I tried again.

"Hmph. Take the money and get some coffee."

She shook her head and toddled away, muttering about grown men acting like children. I tried to stumble to my feet to return the money, but she managed to beat me in speed and was halfway across the street before I could steady myself. I watched until she disappeared into the already bustling streets of midtown Manhattan.

I wanted to check the time, to see how long it had been since I'd called Raymond, but my fingers were stiff from the cold. I tipped back my head and waited with shut eyes and a sluggishly operating brain.

Raymond showed up nearly two hours later. He double-parked on the street, barely waited for me to buckle in before peeling off again, and didn't apologize for making me wait.

A quick glimpse at his profile showed a clenched jaw and a steely gaze that would have made our father proud. With the exception of his long hair hanging loose and tangled—and him looking younger than usual—Raymond was the spitting image of Joseph Rodriguez. I wondered if he realized it or if it bothered him.

"Sorry," I muttered.

He said nothing, looked more pissed off, and I added ruining his New Year's Day to my carousel ride of regrets.

I dozed off again, but the drive to Queens was over quickly, and the nap did nothing to help my pounding head. Raymond killed the engine and exited the vehicle before kicking the door shut behind him with a resounding boom. The world trembled around me.

"Jesus."

I clutched the handle to the door. It took a full minute of convulsive swallowing and deep breaths to beat back the pain and follow him inside. I shaded my eyes to escape sunlight that was more aggressive than it had been a half hour ago and hurried into the dark interior of the house. As a kid I had always hated how gloomy the house was due to the constantly drawn shades and sparse windows, but now I was grateful for my brother following the tradition of living like vampires.

"You aiight?"

I closed the door. "Yeah."

"Yeah, right." Raymond stood in front of the staircase like a human blockade, preventing me from taking an easy way out of the confrontation. "Are you even going to tell me what the hell happened to you?"

"I don't know what happened to me," I croaked. "I woke up in the hospital. I drank too much, passed out, and someone called an ambulance. I don't know if I lost my wallet or if it got stolen."

"And your coat?"

I had no idea how I'd come to trade my Pelle jacket for a piece of shit that looked like it'd come from the bargain bin at Jimmy Jazz.

"No clue, Ray. No fucking clue."

Raymond unzipped his coat but didn't shrug it off. Beneath it, he was wearing the same outfit he'd left the house in the night before. I'd likely dragged him out of some girl's bed by calling him at seven o'clock in the morning.

"Sorry if I messed up your morning. Were you with that girl...." I wracked my brain for her name. "Crystal?"

"I don't give a shit about that. I'm worried about you."

So much for diverting the topic.

I tried to kick off my shoes and nearly lost my balance. Throwing out a hand, I supported myself against the archway. "Don't. I had some guy buying me drinks, and it got out of hand."

"What guy?"

"Just some random guy at a bar." I clumsily yanked at my laces, grimacing when my fingers came away damp and covered in grit. "I fucked up, but it won't happen again. I don't usually get that wasted in public."

"You've been fucked-up for the past two weeks, son. It don't matter if you haven't been doing it in public every time."

"Okay. What do you want me to say to that?"

"Nothing. I just want to know when you're going to snap out of it."

"Snap out of it?" I scoffed. "Sorry my grieving period hasn't been brief enough for you."

"Don't try to twist my words and start a fight." Raymond shrugged his coat off and slung it over the banister. "Do you want me to just leave you the hell alone and let you do your thing? Is that it?"

I stared up at him. "I don't want you to leave me alone."

"You sure about that?"

I was short on patience and reliable wits and wanted to end this pointless back and forth. "Ray, you're not going anywhere and neither am I."

"Hmm." Raymond seemed to relax, but he wasn't even attempting to rock his usual smart-ass indifference. All the hallmarks of worry were etched into his face. "I know you think I don't get it, but I do. You feel guilty about the way things were, but it's not your fault he died, and it's not all your fault that things were shitty before it happened. Just... stop doing this to yourself."

"It's not that easy."

"I ain't saying it's easy. I'm just saying—" Raymond gestured at me. He lost his stride and deflated. "I'm just saying... that I want you to be okay."

"And I'm saying I *will* be okay. Just give me some time to get my head together."

It was painfully apparent that Raymond didn't want to rely on my word, but he didn't have a choice. With all his ammo spent, he stepped aside and allowed me to begin the laborious climb up the stairs. By the time I was in my room, I was achy and winded like an old man.

Collapsing on my bed was easier than dealing with the fallout of the previous night.

I knew I should cancel my credit cards and see if I could replace my phone, even though it was still technically functioning, but the urgency to take action against identity theft was nil. Booting up my laptop to search for customer service numbers seemed impossible to accomplish when I couldn't even handle sitting upright, and the idea of explaining the situation to a sales rep was a nightmare.

My apathy was almost startling. I knew it. I could identify it. But making myself react to it was a different story altogether.

A lot of things needed to happen but I had no drive to get on top of any of them. For example, I knew we had to get the hell out of this house. We needed to sell it, start over, and escape the remnants of dysfunction that hung in the halls like cigarette smoke.

Whoever said home's where the heart is had not come from a home that consistently ripped out their fucking heart. For us, home was miserable, and being bombarded with visuals of my parents' belongings on a daily basis only emphasized that misery.

I was also very aware that my little brother and I were following all the wrong family traditions.

Between Raymond inheriting our father's lack of motivation and me inheriting his propensity for drinking, we were doomed. I could see so clearly where we would end up—him collecting benefits or doing odd jobs for the rest of his life, me alone and wizened from bitterness and liver disease—and it was horrifying. Enough to make me want to throw myself out of the bed, drag Raymond to the dining table, and have a serious sit-down about the state of our lives.

But I didn't. I just looked at the ceiling and thought about it, and then let another realization settle over the others like a suffocating veil.

I had to teach tomorrow.

I had to get up, prepare lessons, commute to Brooklyn, and pretend that I was a functioning adult in front of a hundred teenagers. I had to hide that I was a mess and be a role model. And I had no idea how I would accomplish that task when I couldn't even face my little brother or best friend.

So I didn't.

I thumbed out an e-mail to Price using the cracked touch screen of my phone and informed her that I would be taking some time off to handle my father's *estate* (read, debt), and for bereavement. I also reminded her that I had only taken three days off when my mother had died the previous year.

I didn't bother to check for grammar or the appropriate amount of vague information versus actual facts, and planned to count on the obscene amount of personal time I'd accrued over the years, and the union, to cover my ass.

For now, real life could wait until I was ready to confront it.

Chapter Fourteen

January

JUST PAST five o'clock on a Sunday and the craving for a smoke hit me so hard I talked myself into getting up and going to the store for cigarettes. I was ready to fork up the twelve bucks for a pack, accepting that I was about to become a smoker again with something akin to relief. Getting dressed and walking three blocks to the bodega was a task I wasn't sure I could accomplish after two weeks of existing in a daze. I wondered if Raymond would brave the arctic January wind so I wouldn't have to leave the house.

When I ventured out of my room, the floorboards were cold against my bare feet. The house had always been drafty, but this winter was phenomenally cold. Rubbing my hands together, I jogged down the stairs and called out for my brother.

As soon as I spoke, I regretted it. There were people in the kitchen, and I'd just outed myself as being awake and in their proximity.

"Michael, ven acá."

What the hell was Aida doing here?

I took a step backward, ready to flee, but I froze at the familiar rumble of a deep voice.

Nunzio.

Wariness turned into irritation. I charged into the kitchen and found them all huddled around the counter. Aida, John, Jackie, and Nunzio. My weasel of a little brother hovered in the back doorway, looking like he was ready to bolt from his own party.

"What the hell is going on?"

Nunzio took a step away from the rest of my family and looked at the floor. When Jackie had a similar reaction, my suspicions heightened.

"¿Qué está pasando aquí?" I speared Raymond with a vicious look. "Is this some kind of intervention? Are you serious, Ray?"

"No. I don't know."

"Then what the fuck are they doing here?"

"Cálmate, Michael," John said in a warning voice.

"Why are they here?" I jutted my chin at Nunzio. "And you had to drag him into this too for ultimate humiliation?"

Nunzio stopped studying his sneakers and met my accusatory glare.

"Don't get pissed at Ray," he said, tone sharp where I'd expected him to sound contrite. "He just doesn't know what to do."

"Maybe he should grow the hell up and figure it out without calling in the damn cavalry."

Raymond reddened. "I've been trying to talk to you, but you don't even be coming downstairs for a couple days at a time. For all I know, you're up there planning to fucking kill yourself." The last bit came out shaky. He crossed his arms over his chest. "If I thought you cared about my opinion, I wouldn't need no cavalry."

I didn't know if I wanted to sigh in disgust or shake him. His self-esteem had to be nonexistent if he thought I'd listen to John before him.

"You know what, Raymond? Maybe you wouldn't think that if you'd acted like an adult *before* both our parents died."

Raymond recoiled, and I cursed myself.

"Michael!"

Jackie grabbed Raymond's hand to console him, and Aida nailed me with the kind of glare that, as a child, would have had me scampering around a corner to dodge a flying chancleta. We were long past those days, but I could practically hear her powering up for a lecture.

"This is bullshit," I said. "Where was the intervention when you were all pouring the drinks while my father sautéed his liver?"

"You are not your father." Aida moved around the side of the counter. "It was too late for him—"

"Too late?" I demanded, incredulous. "He spent every year of my life sweating out alcohol. And it wasn't like he was a functioning alcoholic. You people had plenty of time to intervene. So I don't understand why that was acceptable, but you want to break my fucking balls when I'm the only one in this family who has ever made anything of themselves."

"That's why we want to help you," Jackie said, still hanging on to Raymond, even though he was clearly trying to escape. "You're so smart and ambitious—"

"Obviously not if I'm in this situation."

Jackie clammed up. Like Raymond, her face lapsed into a whipped puppy expression, but this time I felt no compassion.

"You know what? Fine." I grabbed a barstool from the counter and sat down. I waved my hand. "Empieza con la mierda."

John heaved a disgusted sigh. I wondered why he'd even come. After his initial show of compassion at the hospital, he'd wasted no time adopting his usual contempt for me.

"Mijito—"

I cut Aida off before she could go any further. "No soy tu hijito."

"Okay." Aida marched up to me and jabbed a finger into my face. "You cannot go on the way you are. The alcohol and drugs are out of control."

I nearly laughed. If that was her opening, I couldn't wait for the main argument.

"He doesn't do drugs."

"Oh?" Aida whipped around to stick her finger at Nunzio. "His brother says he takes pills."

"Yeah, for anxiety. He isn't—"

John scoffed. "Anxiety."

"Yes." Nunzio crossed his arms over his chest. "Anxiety."

They stared each other down until Aida decided their standoff had interrupted her rant enough. The woman was like a runaway freight train once she got started.

"I know your life has not been easy, Michael. You lost both parents too soon, but you can't go on like this. It's dangerous and you should set a better example—"

"Titi, stop," Jackie interrupted.

"No." John's lip was still curled, dark eyes still trained on Nunzio. "If he acts like a child, he can be treated like one."

"Cada quién sufre a su manera," Jackie insisted. "Stop being so negative!"

There was something to be said about the fact that my family couldn't get their shit together long enough to stop bickering and focus on my intervention.

Aida took a breath and tried another tactic. "Michael. My point is this: you don't need to drink. You don't need to go on like this. Tu suerte cambiará. Tienes a tu familia."

Her words sounded genuine, but I couldn't stop watching as John looked between Nunzio and me, and the ugly curl of his mouth.

"Aparte de Raymond, no tengo familia. And he's a grown man. I don't need to set any examples for him that I haven't tried and failed to set already." I raised one shoulder in a tight shrug. "I appreciate what you're trying to do, Titi, and you, Jackie, but it's not going to work right now. And all of you sitting there judging me isn't going to change anything, since I'm just keeping with the family tradition of drinking myself to death."

This time it was John who spoke. "Tu madre estaría avergonzada."

The Spanish seemed to translate for Nunzio. He winced, and out of the corner of my eye, I saw Raymond tense.

In the past I would have exploded, but this time I didn't feel the rush of anger that would normally lead to fireworks. I stood up and leaned across the counter with my best impression of a Joseph Rodriguez razorblade smile.

"Maybe. But all of you, her included, would think a lot of things about my life are shameful. Like the fact that I never bring home women because I'm gay."

Aida covered her mouth with her hand. Her expression was more startled than surprised. John, on the other hand, just smiled coldly.

"As if we didn't know?"

"Or," I added, leaning closer, "that I was sucking dick way before Nunzio. I started with your buddy Kevin the day of my junior high graduation. I swallowed his come while you were all outside grilling and dancing to salsa."

John's eyes went round, but before he could say anything, I grabbed the sides of his face and laid a sloppy kiss on his mouth. He threw himself backward with a horrified shout. Maybe he thought traces of Kevin were still on my lips.

"Maricón asqueroso," he spat, jerking his forearm across his mouth.

"That's right. I'm a disgusting faggot. Always have been, always will be. Now all of you can get the hell out of my house."

It didn't take them long. As the kitchen emptied, Aida would no longer make eye contact with me. Jackie offered a discreet wave, but her face lacked animation. It wasn't surprising, considering I'd just accosted her father. He would probably have some kind of gay-stemmed PTSD for the rest of his life.

"Is that shit true about Kevin?" Raymond demanded when we were alone in the kitchen with Nunzio.

"Yeah."

"So that dude is like a pedo?"

"I didn't realize it at the time, but yeah, I guess so. I was only fourteen."

As a teenager I'd fooled around with so many older men that I'd stopped thinking about it in terms of legality. It was a strange realization considering how protective I was of my students. If any of them behaved the way I had as a kid, I would have a fit.

Raymond shuddered. "That's disgusting."

"Yeah, no shit."

I looked between him and Nunzio, wondering why I wasn't angrier. I'd intended to ream them for setting me up, or at least not trying to talk to me alone before calling in the rest of the family, but the energy required to fuel additional outrage was already draining away.

"I'm going back to bed."

"Mikey, wait."

"Bro, stop—"

Nunzio and Raymond both moved forward simultaneously. I edged away from them with the wariness of a cornered animal.

"I just want to sleep. I understand that neither of you apparently know me well enough to have anticipated that shitshow, but I'm done talking about my failings as an adult."

"No one thinks that," Raymond said. "But you gotta look at it from my point of view. You think you're the only one who's fucked in the head right now? It's bad enough that... that every night I think about how I stood there talking to Dad, not even realizing he was dead. I was being a dick, telling him to get his lazy ass up, and he was dead."

I flinched. "I had no idea...."

"I know, because I didn't tell nobody." Raymond's voice cracked on the last syllable, but he shrugged off Nunzio's hand, turning away. "My point is that I get it. I know how you feel, but you can't fucking die on me too. It's not fair. And I don't give a shit if you think that makes me sound like a dumbass kid."

How was it possible that before this moment I had not realized how worn and frayed around the edges Raymond looked? At some point in the past few weeks he had lost weight and stopped sleeping enough for circles to darken his eyes, but I hadn't noticed.

"I would never do that to you, Ray."

"Yeah, maybe not on purpose, but you pop bars with vodka chasers. It'd be real easy for you to just not wake up one day."

"I'll be fine."

"How the hell do you know? Pops thought he was invincible too, and look how that turned out."

I had no defense for that argument.

"I'll get it together soon."

Raymond shook his head, still facing away.

"I have no choice. I go back to work in a week."

"All right, man. Whatever."

"Ray, I'm not going anywhere. I'm not going to die just because I've been on a two-week bender. I'm just...." All of a sudden it felt like I was talking through cotton. I cleared my throat and started again. "I'm done with everything. Just, everything. I tried really hard to be the good, successful son, but everything falls down around me anyway, so what's the point? No matter how responsible I try to be and no matter how hard I tried not to be like Dad, I act just like him. And even knowing that, I can't make myself stop. I don't know what it is, but I can't... care anymore. I just don't want to think, Ray. That's all. I want to stop thinking and be able to breathe, and lately that only happens when I drink."

By the time the flow of words dried up, Raymond was silent and staring at the floor while Nunzio covered his face with his hand.

I ground my teeth together, wishing I'd said nothing. Trying to explain the mechanics of misery would never end with people nodding agreeably. They would either try to talk me out of feeling miserable or feel miserable themselves. Staying alone in my room was definitely the better option.

"Look, never mind. If you go to the store, can you pick up some cigarettes for me?"

I waited for Raymond to nod before fleeing the kitchen. I expected Nunzio to stay behind, but his quiet footsteps trailed up the stairs behind me. He hesitated in the attic doorway.

"Can I come in for a while?"

"Why?"

Nunzio took a step inside and closed the door behind him. "Just to talk."

"If it's to talk about how much of an alcoholic I am, you can forget it."

I flopped on my bed, staring up at the ceiling. The sun had set in the time it had taken me to get rid of my family, and the room was dark. I welcomed it, knowing I looked like shit, but Nunzio turned on a lamp.

"I didn't know your aunt and uncle were going to be here, Mikey. C'mon. Give me a little credit."

"You didn't give me a heads-up when Raymond suggested this intervention, though."

"Oh really?" Nunzio tossed his phone on the bed next to me. "Take a look at your missed calls and messages, asshole. I've been trying to let you know all damn day, but your phone is either off or dead."

He had me there. I didn't even know where my phone was. Lost somewhere in the mounds of discarded clothing that had accrued in the past two weeks.

"I'm sorry."

"You should be sorrier for your brother. He is genuinely terrified of losing you, and you didn't have to treat him that way in front of your douche bag of an uncle."

"I'll talk to him later."

"Will you really?"

"Yes," I snapped. "I'll handle it. I didn't know...."

I didn't know Raymond was so torn up about our father, because I hadn't thought about his feelings enough to figure it out. My own drama had prevented us from having a real conversation since the funeral. Even now, I didn't want to ask. I didn't want to know. I could picture it too clearly as it was. Raymond being a smart-ass, heckling our father and trying to get him to go take out the trash or clean something up, getting impatient and then....

I bit the inside of my cheek and closed my eyes. The macabre image rotating in my head was sucking away my control, my breath, my ability to fight a welling of tears. I reached up to dash the dampness away from my cheeks.

The crying stage was supposed to be over. The sick feeling in the pit of my stomach was supposed to be numbed. Clearly I had been mistaken.

The bed sank when Nunzio sat beside me, but I didn't look at him.

"I wish I knew what to do to help you. Both of you."

I drew my forearm across my eyes and kept it there. "You can't."

"With your mom I knew what to say. I could figure out what you needed me to do." Nunzio's hand brushed my hair back from my forehead. "But now it's like you're falling apart."

"Because it's different now."

"Why? I'm not trying to belittle your father, but I don't understand. You were so much closer to your mom...." Nunzio trailed off and kept stroking my hair. "I guess I thought the situation with your dad was like the situation with me and my folks. You know? Besides the fact that I have their DNA, I don't feel anything toward them anymore."

"I thought so too." I sniffed and dropped my arm to my side. "But it's like... When you're poor and you're struggling, all you have is family. Even if your family isn't the best, that's who you have. I know you guys were just as poor, but your folks were always coldhearted. But mine?" I shook my head. "Even if we were dysfunctional and a fucking mess, deep down I always considered us a family. And my mom tried so hard to make it that way. She busted her ass working two jobs, sometimes three, just so we could live in a real house, but she died just as soon as she could cut back enough to enjoy it. Just as soon as she... she started fixing up the backyard and all that."

So strange how that detail almost broke me. My chest was constricted and again my eyes throbbed with tears that I refused to let loose.

"And even if my father could be a monster when he drank, even if he didn't help out, I never fucking hated him. I just wanted him to be better. And I know that doesn't make sense to anyone else because he hit me and I used to be scared of him, and he made me fucking miserable, but he was still my father. He was just broken and everyone always told him he was broken, so he just accepted he was no good and that was his life. I couldn't stand him because of that.... And I let him know. I made it crystal clear. But it frustrated me that he thought so low of himself, and I still wanted to help him. But I didn't."

My words jumbled together. I wasn't positive that my point was coming across clear, or if I sounded like a brainwashed battered child abuse victim, but that didn't change the things I'd always felt and never said.

"I know it sounds fucked-up. I tried to explain to Clive once, but he didn't get it."

"No, I get it," Nunzio said, voice low. "And I get that you're hurt because you never had a chance to tell him."

"Yeah." I savaged my lower lip to keep it from trembling. There was nothing I hated more than crying, but with Nunzio so close by, my body seemed to think it was safe to open the tear ducts. Like his presence made it safe to break down. "God, I hate this. Change the fucking subject."

"Are you sure?"

I wiped my face with more vigor. He stopped smoothing back my hair, and I snuck a glance at him from my peripheral vision. Like Raymond, Nunzio's face was drawn with weariness.

"I wanted to ask you about something else," he said.

"What?"

"About us. Our situation."

Four words and I wanted to skitter off and hide under the bed. "What about it?"

"Why are you avoiding me?"

"I'm not."

"You haven't returned a call or message in weeks."

The conversation would have been easier with a cigarette burning between my lips. The constant inhale-exhale would calm my nerves and give me something to do with my increasingly nervous hands.

"I've just wanted to be alone. It's not just you."

A quiet laugh followed a beat of silence. "Since when am I lumped in with the masses?"

He lay down next to me, and my heart sped up. It was incredible how my body reacted to him now. I wanted to pull him close every time his hand brushed mine, and that was part of the problem. Too much was changing too fast with things that had once been constant in my life.

"I'm sorry."

I looked at him. "For what?"

"For me. For the way I acted."

The words didn't bring clarity, so I frowned.

"You know what I mean," he said. "With me pressuring you and being so jealous and angry. It was stupid, and I'm sorry if I made things awkward between us. I'm scared I messed everything up, and it won't ever go back to normal. No matter how much I want you, nothing is worth losing you as my friend."

I pushed myself up on my elbows and stared down at him, baffled. "You're not losing me over anything. Especially that."

"You sure?" Nunzio scoured my face, inches from his own. "I know your father passed right after we got into it about everything, but... I was afraid maybe you thought you couldn't talk to me. Like I'd make you feel worse."

"I didn't want things to get complicated. It was just supposed to be fucking." When Nunzio said nothing, I sat up fully. "Was it ever just fucking, Nunzio?"

"What do you think?"

"I don't know what to think. Everything changed after that night with David."

"Mikey...." The corner of Nunzio's mouth turned up in a small smile. "I was into you way before July. Why do you think I jumped at the chance to be all up on you as soon as your boyfriend was out of the picture? I couldn't keep my hands off you that night. I didn't give two shits about David. Even he noticed. He called me on it later."

I stared down at him. His usual confidence was replaced by guardedness.

"I just thought you were all over me because you were drunk and I was single."

"Yeah, that was part of it. I never would have had the balls to put my hands on you if I was sober. I was too scared of freaking you out. But that night... you were so hot. And the way you kept looking at me gave me some hope that I had a shot." Nunzio huffed out a breath. "But I should have known better. I always knew that if I got a taste, there would be no going back, and I was right."

His voice pitched lower with every word, but I couldn't tell if he was bashful or regretful about everything that had happened.

"Anyway, it doesn't matter," he said.

"It does matter."

"Why? Who gives a damn?"

"I give a damn! Why didn't you tell me you felt that way?" I thought back to all the times we'd screwed around in front of each other, all the times I'd brought a boyfriend along when we were supposed to hang out alone, and wondered if it had bothered him. If he'd been jealous the whole time and done such a good job at masking it that I had never noticed. Never even suspected. "I wouldn't have been so—"

"Been so what?" The hushed confessional quality faded, and Nunzio was his brash, outspoken self again. "Don't get the wrong idea. I'm not saying that I've been keeping a diary about my secret gay love since we were little kids. I'm not saying I went to sleep weeping all the nights that you went to bed with someone else. I'm saying I wanted you. Ever since the summer before twelfth grade when you came back from Puerto Rico looking like a man... I couldn't help but enjoy the view, and you made quite a few appearances in my jack-off fantasies."

"Are you serious?"

He had never acted any differently toward me. The closest he'd come to showing attraction in high school had been excessive tackling while playing football in PE.

"You remember that party we went to for graduation?"

I nodded. "That kid Kenny threw it at his grandmother's house by Baisely Park because she was out of town."

"Yeah. It was the first time we got completely shit-faced because people finally came through with something other than beer and wine coolers. By the end of the night I was wasted, and you'd gone off with Deante and Anthony." Nunzio tilted back his head, his hair spreading across the white sheet in dark whorls. "I went to look for you later and walked in on them balling you. Taking turns."

My mouth went dry. "You watched?"

"Yeah."

"The whole time?"

"Long enough to realize what a slut you turn into when you want dick. Before that, we'd always talked about it, and I saw you making out with guys sometimes, but I'd never seen you beg to be pounded like that. I'd never heard your voice when you moaned or saw your face when you came. I started wondering if you'd ever be that way with me. I thought about it a lot."

The idea of Nunzio watching me get railed by two guys, and the mental image of him possibly jerking off while watching, had me semihard. I dropped my hands into my lap, hoping to hide it, and looked away from his predatory stare.

"Did I live up to your expectations?" It wasn't the question I'd meant to ask, but it came out anyway.

"Exceeded them."

A slice of heat went through me, warring with the pitiful darkness that wanted to keep me anchored to the ground. I wanted to grasp on to that flame, but it flickered and blew out.

"Why didn't you tell me?"

"Because you didn't see me that way. I could tell. And after college you almost always had a man. And it was always some guy who was everything I wasn't and nothing I'd ever want to be."

"Like Clive?"

A measured silence went by, but he didn't drop his eyes. It occurred to me that I'd said the wrong thing, or asked the wrong question, too late. A muscle in his cheek ticked, and he shrugged.

"Yeah. And he rubbed it in my face every chance he got, because he knew I wanted you. He sniffed me out right away."

"But I never noticed anything."

"Because you were so used to the way I acted that you thought it was normal. And it's not like I was pining every night, but he saw the way I would look at you sometimes. He noticed how I got uptight when he slobbered on you and called you baby, and all of that corny shit. And he knew I hated the idea of you ever moving in with him. That was what did it—the day that conversation came up." Nunzio snorted softly. "You'd gone to the store and left me alone with his stupid ass, and he brought it up. I must have looked like someone had just ripped off my nuts, and from then on he had my number."

"That shit was never going to happen."

"True. But you were still serious with him. I'd been jealous in the past because of other guys, but it was always a sex thing. They could touch you, and I couldn't. With Clive.... For a while it seemed permanent. It was just different."

Staying quiet was better than saying the wrong thing again, so I didn't reply. I could almost hear the building tension in his shoulders, so I squeezed his hand. It was supposed to be a brief touch, but I brought it to my mouth. I kissed the backside of his palm and the corner of his wrist. I felt his pulse against my lips. The rolling wave of lust licked at me again.

"I didn't tell you that so you could give me a pity fuck."

"It's not—" I cleared my throat. "It's not pity."

Nunzio pushed himself up on his elbows. "Then tell me what it is."

We were so close. Close enough for me to feel the heat of his body and inhale his scent, and for it to be torturous to not close the space between us and lick into his mouth. To push him back on the bed and wipe that uncertain look from his gorgeous face.

"I don't know. I don't know what's real and what's me reacting in the moment like I always do, so I can't explain."

"Try."

"Nunzio, I don't know." I jerked my eyes away from his. "I can tell you that it would be so easy to kiss you right now, to beg you to make me feel anything other than what I've been feeling for the past few weeks. But that would be me using you, not me figuring out what the hell I've been feeling since we started this. And I don't know what I'm feeling. I don't know if it's real or if I'm infatuated with the sex or if I just like the idea of you wanting me."

"But what if I said I'd rather have you like that than not at all?"

I released an explosive sigh. "I can't do that to you, niño."

Nunzio dropped back on the bed. "I should have kept my fucking mouth shut."

I shoved his knee. "No. It can't be like that with us. You know it. We can't do that casual thing."

"We could try." Nunzio's intense gaze found mine again. "Maybe you don't want me here—" He brushed his fingers over my heart. "But I know when we're having sex, when I'm in you deep, you don't want anyone else. It's just you and me, and it's fucking perfect, and you're mine. That could be enough for me."

"I don't think that's true."

I knew it wasn't true, and I wasn't going to agree to anything with every thought stained by eight shades of depression. Between work, my father, and all of the drinking, I had no confidence in any decisions I'd make now, or even the ones I'd been making in the past few months. Making a wrong move and losing Nunzio was far more terrifying than not getting to taste him anytime I wanted.

Nunzio didn't respond, and we sat in silence.

It would have been easy to stretch out next to him, to burrow into his side and bury my face in the crook of his neck. To let him wrap his arms around me and fall asleep that way, warm and enveloped in the arms of someone who wanted me. Maybe loved me.

I wanted that. I wanted him. But I wasn't going to keep using him for comfort when he knew exactly what he wanted and my own reasoning was lost in a dreary abyss of confusion, self-loathing, and cynicism.

Nunzio rolled off the bed and stood. "Call me if you need me."

I knew I should speak, but he left the room before any words came to mind.

Chapter Fifteen

Regents Week

I WENT back to work during the week of the state Regents examinations. With no classroom instruction and students only in the building for a couple of hours for testing, I didn't have much to do. I wasn't on the schedule to proctor all week and my room wasn't being used, so that gave me plenty of time to throw myself back into planning.

Not that I actually planned.

After pulling down the shade over my door, I spent an hour reconfiguring the wreck of my classroom before sprawling at my desk with the newspaper. I didn't read it, though. I just drew random things in the margin and thought a lot about going home.

No one came looking for me for the entire morning, and not falling asleep was a constant struggle. I had brief bursts of activity where I would flip through my curriculum binder and puzzle out the mess the substitute had made of my Latin America unit, but it didn't last. It couldn't. Not when I kept losing focus and staring into space.

I missed being home where I could bask in lethargy without shame.

"Knock, knock."

I looked up. David's smiling blondness nearly blinded me.

"Hi."

David stepped into the classroom and shut the door behind him. He looked around with a pained expression. I bet it tore his perfectionist soul apart to see so many things out of order. I'd fixed the seating quads, but the room was still a disaster.

A mass of bottles had accrued on the top of bookshelves, and everything on my desk and at the computer station was in disarray. It wouldn't have taken more than an hour or two to get the place in shape, but I was tired just from looking at it.

It would have been nice for someone on my team to have checked on the substitute.

"How does it feel to be back?"

I turned on my laptop to give the impression that I was going to do something productive.

"There're no kids, so it isn't that big of a deal. I'm just trying to get my shit together for next Tuesday."

"Ugh. I keep forgetting we have a PD on Monday. I'd rather teach."

"Yeah." Teaching was better than nonstop meetings, especially since I never felt more developed professionally when it was over. PD day often turned into catch-up-on-blogs-and-Twitter-feed day.

I watched my computer inch along to a full start-up and avoided David's fervid stare. He seemed to be checking for signs of self-harm and mental deterioration.

"Are you sure you're okay? You don't look normal."

"How do you figure?"

"You're just...." David waved his hand to indicate my appearance. "Pale and it looks like you've lost weight. Are you sleeping okay?"

"Just fine."

"Well, it doesn't seem that way. You look tired. And sad."

I snorted, casting him a derisive glare. "I've lost both parents in less than a year. Obviously I'm sad. It's not breaking news, okay? I'm fine."

"You don't seem fine."

"Jesus, kid. What do you want me to say? I don't want to talk about it."

David winced. I thought he would scamper off like he did any time I got sharp with him, but he just opened my binder. He extracted a reading on Otto von Bismarck and wrinkled his nose. "Who the hell is that?"

"A German nationalist." When he gave me a vacant stare, I snatched the paper. "Didn't you pay attention in world history?"

"I guess not." Having the decency to look chagrined, David glanced at my binder again. He couldn't stand the idea of not knowing something. "Did the sub do anything useful? She was having a hard time with the kids. Apparently Mac terrorized her every day."

I wasn't surprised. Mac got off on bullying everyone around him. He had the sassy, judgmental queen routine down pat.

"I'm trying to figure out if I should just reteach Latin America or move on to nationalism and unification in Europe."

"Do you have time to reteach?"

If I took out the end-of-year project, I would, but it was one of my darlings, and I hated to see it go.

I clicked randomly at my laptop, wondering if it had always been so slow or if it was deliberately trying to make me look worthless in front of Captain Grade Team. He raised a brow, opening his palm and gesturing, and I realized that I had not answered his question.

"I don't know. Maybe."

"I'm sure you'll figure it out. You're an awesome teacher."

I could not resist an eye roll. "Oh God."

"What!"

"Please don't give me weird compliments."

David scowled. "How is that a weird compliment? We're in a classroom discussing pedagogy. It's not like I complimented you on your angling."

"Angling?"

"Fishing."

"You're so white."

David smirked. "Actually I got that from Sims."

The corners of my mouth twitched. I tried to stifle a bubble of laughter but failed when David's face lit up with apparent pleasure at having caused me to smile. He may have started out as a royal pain in the ass, but the kid could be endearing when he wasn't trying to supervise me.

I shoved his shoulder. "You're such a nerd."

"That's the first thing you ever said to me."

"And it's been proved time and time again since that night."

David shrugged and poked around my desk. Several ungraded and unsorted stacks of student work had accumulated over the past three weeks. I hadn't bothered looking at any of it because I knew it would make me cringe. I'd already spied a few essays that stated Simón Bolívar had liberated South Africa, and it had led to me wanting to bash my face into a wall. I had no idea how things could go so wrong when I wasn't in the classroom.

Seeming to sense my frustration, David patted my shoulder. "I wasn't kidding about you being a good teacher, you know. The kids missed you. Shawn asked about you every day. Mac too."

"That's good to hear," I said, meaning it. I'd thought about my students a lot in the rare moments of being wide-awake and lucid.

My laptop finished loading, and I opened my data cloud to go through a number of slideshow presentations. If I was going to do a two-day recap on Latin America to fix whatever inaccuracies they'd developed over the past couple of weeks, those two days would have to be notes and lecture heavy. It wasn't my usual style of teaching, but there was no time to do anything else.

What bothered me the most about that unit being nixed was that most history teachers at McCleary skipped or glossed over Latin America entirely to focus solely on Europe, even though 85 percent of the student population was from Mexico, South America, or the Caribbean.

I flipped between two different presentations, so critical of my own notes that I didn't notice David had stilled beside me. When he continued to hover at my side like a stealth helicopter, I looked up. His expression was pinched, eyes trained on a point just beyond my laptop. He was staring into my open backpack. And the bottle of vodka I'd stashed inside.

I grabbed the bag and shoved it under my desk.

"Michael…."

"It's not what you think."

"Then what it is it? What the hell are you thinking bringing a bottle to school!"

Fuck. Fuck everything. I was such an idiot.

"I haven't drunk anything."

"Then why did you bring it?"

I slammed the laptop shut, and the precious moments it had taken to boot up were flushed down the drain. I stood, pushing the chair back. David was still crowding me, so I jerked my chin at him.

"You want to give me some room?"

David backed away. "Michael, I don't know what to say. I'm so worried about you."

"I advise against that. I'm fine."

"It's obvious that you're not fine. Don't give me that bullshit! Fine is what people say when they feel like shit but don't want anyone to know. And in your case, it's so false that I would be a pathetic excuse for a friend if I left you alone. I can't just not say anything when I see what's happening."

"Nothing is happening, David. Please stop."

I sounded more defeated than forceful, and sank into a student desk.

I stared at the pockmarked floor, and he stood there with a bowed head and fidgeting hands. I was making him nervous. I could practically hear his internal struggle: leave me in peace and remain a bystander or do something constructive to guide me through my drama? He was so idealistic and helpful, never knowing when to leave well enough alone.

Although at this point, I wasn't a good judge of what *well enough* entailed.

I buried my face in my hands. What a disaster. What a goddamned embarrassment. I could say nothing to change what he'd seen. I wished I could rewind time—go back ten minutes and prevent it from happening.

The silence was more awkward the longer it lingered, and I was desperate for him to go the hell away so I could flambé myself in peace.

"I appreciate your concern, but unless you saw me drinking, there's nothing to say."

"I just want to help."

I spread my hands, laughing humorlessly. "How could you help me? Just think about it, really think about it, and then explain how the hell you could possibly improve this situation at all. You and I have nothing in common. We don't think the same, we don't feel the same, and we have totally different lives. Nothing that would work for you is going to work for me. So please. Please stop trying to make the world a better place starting with me."

My words had the desired effect.

David shrank away, crossing his arms over his chest. He looked smaller and younger, innocent and crushed by the reality of what I was saying. Or maybe just by the harshness. I didn't regret saying it, but I still felt like a monster at the sight of his scrunched-up face.

"The last thing I want," I said quietly, "is to hurt anyone else that I know, but right now I can't handle trying to make you feel better about not knowing how to help me. Especially since it isn't your responsibility."

"I understand," he said, head still bowed. "I get it."

I didn't think he did.

"Can we just pretend this didn't happen? Can you do that for me? Please?"

David shrugged, not saying whether he would or wouldn't, which essentially meant there was no way that was going to happen.

PARANOIA IS a funny thing.

For two hours after my conversation with David, I alternated between considering seeking him out to ensure he kept his mouth shut and wanting to stay locked in my room to avoid the situation. By the time the end of the day rolled around, I was in full-on panic mode and had drunk two thirds of a bottle of orange juice in order to fill the rest with vodka.

I didn't take a sip, but I felt better having it close. From time to time I picked it up, shook it and then pushed it aside. Just in case I slid over the edge, it was good to know I had myself a convenient grappling hook in a bottle.

At three o'clock, I'd already packed my stuff—not that I'd used my laptop or planner for anything productive—and finally sampled my screwdriver. The vodka was overpowering. I had never been too good with ratios.

I took another swig and screwed on the top to shake it again. Before I could give it another try, the door opened.

"What's up, Mr. R?"

Shawn barged in without knocking and walked right up to me without hesitation. I immediately replaced the lid on the bottle but fumbled and nearly dropped it before managing to get it shut.

Shawn's eyes dropped to the bottle and lingered. My paranoia inched up one distressing notch at a time.

"What are you still doing here?"

"I had a test this morning, and I get extended time or whatever."

"How do you think you did?"

Shawn quit eyeballing the bottle, but I still thought he was looking at me funny. I took a step back, overly conscious of the smell of liquor on my breath. Wanting a nice buzz for my commute home was starting to look like a bad idea even if I was officially off teacher time in twenty minutes.

Aggravated by yet another unfortunate turn of events, I ran a shaky hand through my hair.

"Mr. Rodriguez, are you good?"

I tried to smile but only managed a faint twitch of the muscles around my mouth, likely passing more for a grimace than anything else.

"I'm fine, Shawn."

He shoved his hands into the pockets of his sweatpants. A measure of discomfort crept into his posture in the way of hunched shoulders and shuffling feet.

"You know, I ain't like the other kids here. I understand things. I respect you a lot, and I know something's up. I think something bad happened, and that's why you weren't around for a couple weeks."

"I know you're more mature than a lot of kids your age, but I'm fine. Don't worry about some old-ass man."

"Oh please, you're not even old."

"If I was old enough to vote when you were born, that's old."

Shawn rocked on the balls of his feet. His fidgeting drew my eyes downward, and I noticed his sneakers were looking a little beat-up. There was a rip in the side of the canvas.

"Mr. R, you're trying to change the subject."

"No, I'm not. But I'm your teacher, and it's not my job to talk about my personal stuff."

"But I asked."

I started checking out the rest of his clothes with a more critical eye. He looked clean, but he was wearing the same thing he always wore. I wracked my brain to remember whether he ever came to school in anything else, but couldn't recall noticing a pattern before. My paranoia was making me jumpy about everything, including whether he had proper winter attire.

"How was your test?" I asked, changing the subject without even an ounce of grace.

"I bet I failed."

"What was it, Algebra?"

"Yeah. I can't do math for shit. I'm basically retarded. That's why I get extended time."

"Don't come out like that. A lot of kids get extended time and a lot of kids have IEPs. It just means you need more help in some areas than others." I snorted. "And you'd do better on a math test than me, so I must be nonfunctional if we go by that as a standard of intelligence."

"You be saying big words for no reason."

I walked to the door, subtly nudging him in that direction. "And you be getting down on yourself for no reason. If you always think you're going to fail, you're not going to get anywhere in life, because eventually you'll just quit trying to do anything at all."

"Thanks for the pep talk." Shawn's voice was flat, but he grinned and zipped up his hoodie. The coat he wore looked pretty solid, despite the state of his footwear, and that took the edge off my worry. "Take care of yourself, Mister. You're the only real motherfucker working up in here. And if something bad is going on, maybe you should just stay home for longer. Global ain't going nowhere."

The kid was throwing subliminals like a pro. I hoped he was just intuitive and my angst wasn't actually this transparent.

"Look, Shawn, my dad passed, okay?"

Shawn's head jerked back, brows shooting up. "Damn, I'm sorry. I had no idea or I wouldn't have pressed you so hard."

I looked down the hall, wanting to avoid his intense stare. He wasn't asking a million oblivious-kid questions, the kind that were way too personal and way too intrusive, which made me think he knew a thing or two about losing someone close. I wondered if I'd inadvertently triggered bad memories for him. This was why I hated discussing anything personal with the kids.

"Don't apologize. He was sick, and I should have seen it coming. Sometimes we think we and the people we love are invincible despite all evidence to the contrary."

"Yeah." Shawn bopped his head, dark eyes too old in his young face. "You're right about that. Shit."

"Stop cursing so much."

He sneered. "You suck at changing the subject."

"Indeed." I tugged at his jacket, pulling the zipper up all the way and ignoring the smart-ass smirk on his face. "Now go home. It's freezing outside, and it's supposed to snow later."

When I was done dad-ing him, Shawn pulled up his hood. It dipped low, shading his eyes. "Take care, Mr. R."

"You too, kiddo."

Shawn backed away from my door, hand in the air. Just before he jogged down the staircase, he said, "Just so you know, Butler was talking shit about you with one of the eleventh grade teachers."

What the hell?

I started to demand an explanation, but Shawn disappeared through the door too fast for me to react.

ALTHOUGH THERE were technically twenty more minutes left in the school day, the halls were deserted. Even the payroll secretary seemed to have vacated the premises. I swore under my breath and half jogged down the corridor, jerking at my lanyard before managing to unlock the door to the lounge.

David wasn't there, but Nunzio was. I hadn't seen him since the day of my family's failed intervention, and the sight of him hunched over a table with his lip caught between his teeth packed a punch.

My thoughts scattered somewhere between "fuck, I miss him" and "fuck, he's gorgeous," and I briefly failed to grasp the right neurons to make my brain operate. I took a step farther into the lounge, saw that it was empty, and released a breath.

"Have you seen David in the past few minutes?"

Nunzio didn't even look up. "Nope."

"When's the last time you saw him?"

My only answer was the click-clack of keys on Nunzio's laptop. I walked around the table and stood beside him.

"Did you talk to him at all today?"

Nunzio stopped typing. He stared at the laptop screen, shook his head, and pushed his chair back without standing. "What's the problem, Michael?"

"Allegedly one of the kids just heard him talking about me."

This time Nunzio's gaze rose. He was off in a way I couldn't easily decipher. Face pale and vacant, eyes flat and glum.

"Are you okay?" I asked, starting to touch the side of his face.

He evaded and got to his feet, ignoring the second question and gruffly responding to the first. "I'm pretty sure the only person David was talking to was me." Nunzio gave me a visual pat down that I swore had the power to expose my thoughts as well as liquid fire contraband. "He told me you were drinking in the classroom."

"I wasn't drinking. He's full of shit."

"He said he saw you with a bottle. Same difference in my opinion."

"How the hell is that the same thing?"

"Because even if you weren't throwing it back while he was in the room, you were obviously planning to get the party started earlier than is typically a good idea." Nunzio leaned in and inhaled, his lips almost brushing mine. I swallowed hard, forcing myself not to take an automatic step back, and let him smell me. I didn't try to hide it and didn't flinch when his eyes narrowed with condemnation. "And it looks like he and I were right."

"You're acting like I was smashed all day. I didn't crack it open until thirty minutes ago."

"So you can be drunk on the ride home? I don't get it."

"What's not to get? Who the hell wants to be sober on their commute?"

"Gee, I don't know, Mikey. Maybe people who don't need a drink to function in everyday activities like taking the subway."

The sarcastic tug of his mouth almost prompted me to end the discussion there, but I pushed on. "Is he going to tell someone else or what? It wouldn't hurt for you to keep me in the loop when this kid is going around and running his mouth about my business."

"There wasn't a need to keep you in the loop because I handled it. I wasn't trying to get you more stressed when you've already obviously gone off the fucking deep end."

Knowing they'd discussed the situation loud enough for a kid to overhear had me more stressed than them chatting about it over coffee with Price. I'd rather her send me to rehab than have my students knowing what a lush I was.

Again I thought of the look on Shawn's face and the way his gaze had flicked down to the bottle.

"Damn."

I saw Nunzio shake his head in my peripheral vision.

"You're going to fuck yourself over at this rate. I guarantee it."

"I know," I said. "I know, and for some reason it's still hard to care."

"Oh, so you just decided to stop giving a shit about your job?"

"Yeah, pretty much."

It came out just flip enough to enrage him, and he grabbed the collar of my shirt. "Bullshit. You love this job way more than I do." He pulled it taut and gave me a slight shake, forcing me to meet his glare yet again. "We have been best friends for almost as long as we've been alive, and this is the first time I don't know what to say to you. You sank so fast into this shitty spiral that it seems like your ass was slicked up with WD-40 from the start. I've accepted the part where you have decided to shut me out while you're walking around under this permanent dark cloud, but I can't handle this defeated, bullshit attitude."

I put my hands on his, intending to disentangle them from my collar, but didn't follow through with the motion.

"The only thing I'm giving up on is my desire to be lucid most of the day. I thought being back to work would help, but it didn't. There was still too much time to—"

To think, to wallow, to roast slowly on the spit of my own despair. I didn't want to say any of those things. I wasn't looking for pity or sympathy, and people assumed you wanted one or the other if you spoke out loud about your problems.

"If I'd been teaching today, it wouldn't have been this way, and you know it."

"I have little confidence in that claim."

The faint pang of anger turned into a bludgeoning hammer, and I pushed Nunzio back. "I wouldn't drink around the kids. I'm not that stupid. Shawn only has a clue about what's going on because of you and your loud mouth."

Nunzio looked at me sidelong. A frustrated sound escaped his lips. "Are you—Michael, seriously? You can't even own up to the fact that you shouldn't have brought in a bottle? That maybe it's time to admit that you have a real problem?"

The issue wasn't admitting I had a problem. I was very much aware of that. The real issue was whether or not I wanted to stop. The answer was almost always no. Not at all.

"You sound like my aunt."

"Maybe because she was right."

"Maybe."

Nunzio watched me, waiting for a response, maybe one that was profound and heartening. Promises to chin up and change. When I said nothing more, he slumped.

"I can't watch you do this to yourself, Michael. I can't watch you do it to Ray."

I shrugged, my movements wooden. "So don't."

Nunzio drew back as though I had hit him, and I realized the implication of my words. I opened my mouth to reword the statement, to fix things, but I was struck silent by the flush that stole over his face, and the sudden dampness of his eyes.

"I wish I didn't love your stupid ass so much."

My stomach dropped.

"Nunzio, I didn't mean it that way."

"Just leave me alone," he said, voice thick. "And next time someone comes running to me out of concern for you, I'll tell them to piss off, and I'll mind my own business."

"But that's not what I meant." This time it was me who grabbed his arm, fingers digging in, even as he shoved me away with way more force than I'd used on him. "Can you please just calm down?"

"No, I'm not going to fucking calm down. You're a dick, and I'm tired of running after you and begging you to give a damn. I'm tired of trying." Nunzio grabbed his laptop and tucked it under his arm. "Just go home. Everyone else is gone, anyway."

I wanted to follow, but an invisible force kept me in place and prevented me from taking the three strides needed to stop him from leaving, and he stormed out of the lounge.

My stupidity and failure to act was becoming the stuff of legends.

I returned to my classroom to get my things, and popped a Xanax bar to ease the constant pang of foreboding about the state of my job and the state of my relationship with the scant people who mattered. The fragile mental walls that had kept me upright for the majority of the day were crumbling. It was imperative that I get my ass home before I fell apart in public.

I fled the building, and the cut of the wind forced me into lucidness, but that was a big problem while Nunzio's words were still on blast in my ears.

I went over the conversation multiple times on my way home, but the analysis brought no clarity. He was right, I was wrong, he was sick of me, and I deserved it. Simple investigation, case closed.

My overspiked orange juice was finished by the time the E train made it into Queens. I could smell my own breath and sweat, and in my mind, the people around me knew I was drunk. Instead of NYC indifference, I read judgment on their faces. When the combination of booze and benzos hit me, the phantoms of my paranoia grew more opaque. I churned out make-believe headlines that would be plastered across the Post if I keeled over in the middle of the subway.

High School Teacher Hit by Train After Schooltime Binge.

They would work in the gay angle somehow, and then a conservative Republican from Staten Island would notice my last name and start ranting about immigration even though Puerto Rico was a fucking territory.

Gay High School Teacher Hit by Train After Schooltime Binge— Citizenship Status in Question.

That was more like it.

The sudden need to get the hell out of the packed subway car was nauseating. I tried to breathe evenly, to stop feeling overheated and amped up, ready to pick a fight just so I could be mad at someone other than myself, but it didn't work.

When the train jerked to a stop at Sutphin Boulevard, my head was spinning. I was fully marinated in vodka, the feeling intensified by the Xanax, and I took slow, stumbling strides to my block.

Raymond's car was gone, and the house was dark. I crawled to my room, the walls and stairs shifting like shadows through my blurry eyes, but I was still not disoriented enough to forget about David and Nunzio and the look on Shawn's face.

Everything collided like tumbling dominoes, and the unavoidable reality of my life falling apart bit by bit had me on a gangplank leading to some ominous abyss. Needs and wants wove together until I couldn't tell what was imperative and what was arbitrary, especially when I knew I would never get any of it anyway. Especially not a way to escape this cycle of failure and regret that dragged me below the surface with insistent waves.

I polished off the dregs of a bottle of whisky, and when the clawing anxiety wouldn't subside, I gobbled down another bar. A voice tickled the back of my head, reminding me that I'd already taken some, but I forgot the warning almost as soon as it crossed my mind.

The pressure in my chest and the endless machinations of my fucked-up brain built until I knew, without question, that I was losing my mind, and that my life was a cosmic joke. It set me off like a pin yanked from a grenade.

I broke into great, heaving sobs that wouldn't cease no matter how many breaths I sucked in, no matter how many times I tried to count to ten and find a sense of calm. It didn't come, and I took it out on my room. Punching walls, throwing things, ripping books from shelves, and kicking over furniture—destroying everything in my path until the pills kicked in and exhaustion caused my knees to buckle, and I sank to the floor.

Time stuttered to a stop, and I fell backward into the nothingness I craved.

Chapter Sixteen

At the age of eighteen, I'd known with absolute certainty that I would never end up like my father. The clarity had come to me one day after seeing him with his lifelong friends—street corner cowboys with methadone twitches—and realizing that I was ashamed of him. Not because he was an alcoholic, and at the time, a methadone abuser, but because he hadn't cared about us enough to try to be something other than his addiction.

I'd said that to my mother every time she let him back into the house. She'd told me it wasn't as easy as I made it sound, and I'd called her weak.

Now, fifteen years later, when I awoke to beeping machines and an IV snaking into my arm, I wondered if I finally understood her point of view. On the other hand, maybe I was just looking for a convenient excuse.

I didn't remember what had happened to land me in the hospital, but I had no doubts it was due to something I'd done to myself. The events of the previous night—assuming it had only been one day—replayed in my mind like grainy footage recorded with an unsteady camera.

Large sections of the night were missing, but I recalled at least two instances of myself downing pills when things had begun to feel too real. It had been easy to forget about half-life once my vision had regressed to scattered pixels.

Years of after-school specials and acute intoxication awareness campaigns had clearly done nothing to prevent this embarrassment. The worst part was that it had likely been Raymond to find me in some stupor. It had likely been him, once again, dialing 911.

I stared up at the half-drained bag of fluid hanging near my bed.

Each drip was a second of my life confined to a hospital room instead of being at work, and one more step toward screwing myself in a way that was so complete things would soon be out of my control.

I closed my eyes. It felt like I'd swallowed broken glass, and my entire body was sore, fatigued, as though someone had kicked me in the head several times. Everything was wrong, and I couldn't remember why.

Hospital ambiance filled what should have been an endless silence. The hush of voices, the louder tones of a nurse, footsteps, something rolling across tile—all of it combined to make a return to unconsciousness impossible.

I was acutely aware of where I was and of the situation. Had Raymond called for me? What had he said? Where was he, anyway? Had he finally given up on me and gone home to pack his shit to get away from the steadily sinking ship that was his older brother? Also, did Nunzio know? The possibility was enough to make a sickening sensation curdle my stomach.

I had spent the last few weeks living with a continuous low-grade sense of guilt accompanied by a thousand what-ifs, and had forgotten what real regret felt like. Now, it hit me with jarring awareness. The resounding disappointment came ashore with such totality that I was left dismayed by a flickering montage of all of the wrong moves I'd made since New Year's.

What had I done?

I sat up and threw my legs over the side of the bed. The floor was cold beneath my feet, and I cringed but stood anyway. My head swam, causing me to stagger back and sit for a moment longer before making another attempt.

Gathering the thin hospital gown around myself, I dragged the IV stand to the door and peered out. A person was pushing a food cart around, two little kids were racing in and out of a room at the end of the hall, and a nurse stood by the station on the opposite side.

The urge to inquire about the details of my admission to the hospital, and to leave, won over human decency and fear of flashing the kids due to the skimpy gown. I dragged the IV stand with one hand, clutched the hem of the gown with the other, and shuffled along like an old man.

I was halfway down the hall when Raymond's exasperated voice sounded behind me.

"Ven acá, pendejo. Nadie quiere ver tu culo."

Raymond hustled me back to my room and shut the door. He tossed a bag at me and stood with his back to the door. "I got you some clothes. You were in your fucking underwear when they brought you in."

I gripped the bag but didn't open it. I tried to meet his gaze as he looked at everything but my face.

"Ray, I'm sorry."

"You should be. I thought you were dead."

I winced. "Would you mind telling me what happened? The last thing I remember is digging through a bunch of picture albums and crying into a bottle of vodka."

"Oh, so you don't remember the parts where you wrecked your room and then passed out in the bathroom?"

"No."

Raymond shook his head, still refusing to look at me. "I came home and your music was blasting. I went to turn it off and found your ass unconscious on the bathroom floor. I couldn't wake you up at all, so I freaked and called an ambulance. You were barely breathing."

"Jesus."

"Yeah, you fucking idiot. Maybe if I'd have stayed out or not gone to turn off your damn music, you'd have died because you're too much of an asshole not to do the exact same shit I'd just warned you about."

"I'm so—" I stopped myself from repeating the utterly pointless words, but he was already nodding in agreement.

"Yeah, you are sorry. You're a sorry-ass bitch."

His anger was so complete that it filled the bleak little room. I held up a hand to thwart any further insults.

"Okay, bear with me for a minute. What exactly was wrong with me?"

"Gee, I don't know, bro. Maybe your point four blood alcohol level and all the benzos you'd swallowed. They had to shove a tube down your throat and give you oxygen before they even took you to the damn hospital. You had a fucking tube up your nose for half the night."

"Why?"

"The nurse lady said it was absorbing the chemicals in your stomach or something. I have no idea, bro. I was freaked out and crying the whole time. I hate your guts."

Even though his voice was low with fury, Raymond looked close to crying even now. I tugged him forward, and after brief resistance, he allowed me to enclose him in my arms. My eyes stung at the sound of his ragged sigh. I distantly remembered that we hadn't hugged this way for years. Not even when our parents died. Not even when we had taken turns falling apart.

I hugged him tighter.

"I'm sorry I didn't listen to you. I'm an asshole." He nodded and tried to back away, but I held him in place until the tension drained from his frame. He eventually returned my embrace, and the knot in my chest unwound a bit. "I'm sorry for everything. For being so hard on you and for being so goddamned selfish. I don't know what's wrong with me, Ray. I really don't."

"You're an alcoholic, Michael," Raymond said, voice muffled. He sniffed and pulled away, face smoothed of emotion even though his eyes were bloodshot. "It's not rocket science. Unless that was actually a suicide attempt and not an OD like I told them."

"No." I sat on the edge of the bed, pressing my hands against the thin, uncomfortable mattress. "I made this colossal fucking mistake at work and had a meltdown. I just don't cope well."

"You never have."

His agreement shouldn't have twisted my guts, but it did.

I'd always lorded it over him and my mother about how I was the one who had it together. The one who was ambitious. And I'd complained that they didn't appreciate having one reliable family member. But Raymond had apparently known I was more fragile than I looked. Even Nunzio had subtly pointed it out over the years.

I should have listened instead of viewing my drinking as a juggling act. I'd always thought that if I became too aware of the precarious balance I maintained, everything would fall.

"I need to get out of here."

"Nah. You gotta wait for the doctor to discharge you. And the social worker."

"What social worker?"

"The one that's gonna talk to you."

"Thank you, Raymond. Can you give me a real answer now?"

"I guess." He picked up the bag and set it on one of the turquoise chairs. "They said a social worker talks to everyone that comes in here after an overdose. To talk about rehab and whatnot."

I blinked. "Rehab."

"Yeah. Rehab." Raymond unzipped the bag but didn't take anything out. "I know I ain't the smartest guy, but I do know a thing or two about addiction, and I'd say you could use some rehab. Nearly dying of your own stupidity is what I like to call a red flag."

My hands fisted in the folds of the coarse white blanket. "I don't need rehab. That's for people who don't realize they have a problem."

"No, it's for people who don't know when to stop even when they know they have a problem." Raymond tossed me a clean pair of boxers and a black undershirt. "Can you really tell me that if you went home now, all depressed and feeling sorry for yourself like I know you are, you wouldn't be tempted to start popping pills and drinking again?"

"Maybe not, but I won't end up in the damn hospital again. I've learned my lesson, okay? I'm a big boy, and I'll handle it." I stood up and yanked the boxers up beneath the gown, then shed the gown once everything imperative was contained and covered. "I have a job. I can't just dedicate my time to some group therapy session for a bunch of drug addicts."

"I already told your job."

Everything came to a screeching halt.

"What?"

Raymond scrubbed his hands across his face, bouncing from foot to foot—a nervous gesture he'd inherited from my father and displayed when he was cornered with no way to lie.

"I talked to Nunzio, and he told me what to say. He said—"

"You told Nunzio what happened? *Why?*"

"Because I was freaked out and he's the only normal person who's like family to us!" Raymond snapped. "Should I have called Titi or Tío?"

What a laugh that would have been.

"Yeah, right. What did he say?"

"He just told me what to tell your boss. He said you'd already gotten into some shit yesterday, and I needed to cover your ass. He also said since you have tenure, you can take a medical leave of absence with no trouble. So I told your principal you got really sick last night, and that you been dealing with some major issues after the death of our parents and would be gone for a few weeks while in therapy. She got all concerned and said for you to contact her as soon as you can, and to call the DOE to handle all the paperwork."

"Jesus Christ."

I lay back on the bed and covered my face with my hands. The tape from the IV pulled at my skin, and I felt the tube twisting with the abrupt motion. I bit back the urge to unleash a tirade that would send Raymond storming out of the room.

"Who the hell," I managed to grit through my hands, "gave you two the right to interfere in my life?"

"What, you wanted them to just wonder where the hell you were?"

"I'd have liked you to not make decisions for me, like implying that I tried to commit suicide or something!"

Raymond slammed his hand on top of the rickety table, sending a stack of plastic cups falling to the floor. "I didn't imply that. I just left it open for you to say whatever you want. I was trying to help you out."

"Helping me?" I dropped my hands. "How the hell is making a decision like that helpful to me?"

"Because if I'd left it up to you, you'd have told the woman you'd be back tomorrow!"

"And that's my choice."

"It shouldn't be," Raymond shouted. "You were so far gone last night that you couldn't even stop yourself from shoving pills down your throat. You don't think that's gonna happen again? You've been blackout drunk multiple times a week in the past month. It's gonna happen again, I guaran-fucking-tee it."

I sat up and steadied myself with the bed's railing.

"It's my life. Do you get that? It's my life and my decision to make."

"You sound like a broken record. *It's my life*," he mimicked. "Let me tell you something, pendejo. Maybe you think I'm a piece of shit and worthless and a bum, but I'm still your brother, and you're all I got left, and if you wanna kill yourself, I'm not going to be the one to sit around and find you dead."

"I already told you—"

"I know what you're telling me, but what you fail to understand is that you're not as in control as you think you are!"

"Is everything okay in here?"

We looked at the nurse simultaneously, identical glares on our faces.

"Yes."

"What do you want?"

"Raymond!" I shot him a dirty look before forcing an apologetic smile at the woman in the doorway. She didn't look particularly ruffled by his reaction. "Sorry. Can you tell me when I'll be able to sign myself out?"

"Dr. Weiss is making his rounds, and the social worker will be here to talk to you shortly."

"Wonderful." I speared Raymond with another lethal stare as she retreated from the room.

I grabbed the bag and disappeared into the bathroom, awkwardly dragging the IV beside me. I changed, but fresh clothing didn't help. My skin was grimy beneath the clean clothes, but the idea of trying to shower with a needle jammed in my wrist nearly put me over the edge.

Cursing quietly, I turned to the sink and used the hard soap to wash. The inside of my mouth tasted horrible, and the cotton-filled sensation wouldn't go away no matter how many times I rinsed. Despite my best efforts, I was still uncomfortable and wretched.

I wanted to go home.

A thought followed that one with an immediacy that gave me pause.

I wanted to go home, shower, and then kill my hangover with a drink. I wanted to do that so bad I could taste it. I could almost feel the relief, the ache in my head dissipating, and the tension in my body easing away. Rejecting the idea worked for thirty seconds before I told myself one drink wouldn't hurt. It was just to get my head right. Just to help me relax and kick the hangover. But would one drink do the trick? My tolerance was so high it would have to be strong....

With my body flushed of toxins, well-rested for the first time in weeks, and the fluorescent light beaming down on me, I was far too clearheaded to ignore the way each thought aligned closely to Raymond's accusations.

Fuck.

Bile rose in my throat. Whether it was the hangover or disgust with myself, I couldn't tell, but either way the world swayed. I counted to ten, then twenty, then thirty, until I could stand up straight without the urge to puke. Not that my reflection was helpful in that matter....

The bruises under my eyes and the dull sheen in them reminded me too much of my father. Except the sickly tinge of yellow wasn't there.

Yet.

When the hell had this metamorphosis begun? The summer? After I'd gone back to work? It must have taken longer than a few weeks to start looking this wrung-out and used-up, but I couldn't pinpoint when things had gotten this bad.

The nausea rose again.

"You okay in there?"

"Yeah. Gimme a minute."

Trying to avoid looking at my reflection again, I splashed water on my face one last time. I used a paper towel to dry off, and dragged my IV through the door.

Raymond was standing in the same position I'd left him in, chewing on the corner of his thumb.

"Are you really pissed at me?"

"No."

He nodded, still gnawing on his nail.

"So does that mean you'll give the rehab thing a shot? It's not just me who thinks it's a good idea, you know. Nunzio agrees."

Resuming my sprawl on the bed, I sighed. Why did he have to keep bringing up Nunzio? The situation with my best friend was the last thing I wanted to think about now that I'd just discovered I resembled a Sutphin Boulevard derelict.

"And you think because Nunzio says it, I'll jump to do it?"

"Yes," Raymond said without hesitation. "I know he's all you give a damn about. Everyone knows it. That's how Tío and Pops started suspecting you was gay. Do you know how many times they grilled me about you two?"

I was too tired to even be surprised.

"Again, why didn't you ever tell me?"

"There wasn't nothing to tell. You obviously didn't want me to know. Neither of you did."

My brow creased. "What are you talking about? Nunzio never hid that he was gay."

"That's not what I'm talking about, stupid. I've known forever that you two wanted to fuck around."

This time, surprise wormed its way through my weary layer of defeat. "Just because we're gay doesn't mean we want to screw each other."

Raymond snorted. "Yeah, aiight."

"What are you, a gay matchmaking psychic all of a sudden?"

His snort turned into a dry laugh.

"It don't got nothing to do with being a psychic. When we went to Atlantic City for my twenty-first birthday, you creeps got wasted and humped each other for like fifty hours while I was trying to sleep in the next bed. It was embarrassing as fuck, but at least y'all passed out before anyone got fully naked. I thought I was going to have to camp out in the damn hallway so you could get it in."

Well, that was humiliating. And news to me.

My face burned. "That was—that was like four years ago."

"I know," Raymond said with a smirk. When I stared in horror, he laughed, clearly smug and proud of his ability to stun his asshole of a big brother into silence.

"Are you messing with me?"

"Nope. Neither of you remembered. I didn't bring it up before because you nearly had a heart attack when I told you I'd already figured out you're gay."

"For fuck's sake."

I wanted to believe he was just having fun at my expense, but now many things about that trip made sense. Even years later, I remembered waking up wrapped around Nunzio with my clothes askew, and Raymond making weird, joking comments for weeks after.

"You're such a dick."

"It runs in the family."

"Facts."

Raymond smiled, but it faded quickly. "I'm gonna go give them your insurance card. I didn't bring it last night, and next thing you know they'll be claiming you owe them thousands of dollars for shoving a tube up your nose."

"You don't have to do that, Ray. Seriously, you've done enough for me."

"Nah, I'll do it. You just wait here, okay?"

I wondered if he planned to stall in order to ensure that I was trapped in the hospital long enough to not duck out on the social worker. A tingle of resentment wanted to work its way up my spine at the notion, but this time it lacked conviction.

"What a fucking mess."

It seemed impossible that Raymond was sitting here giving me life tips, but I had never imagined a situation that would lead to me winding up in the hospital twice in less than a month because of drinking.

Would my insurance reject the claim just on the basis of me costing them money by bringing problems on myself? I imagined some clerk behind a desk, frowning at the hospital bills and sending me an automated letter about rehab.

Any social worker would take one look at my file and recommend I join a program, probably at some government-sponsored shithole with a bunch of heroin addicts and crackheads. I didn't think my situation was comparable to theirs, but then again, they were mandated to an inpatient program because they'd pawned some stolen jewelry; I was the one who had nearly killed myself.

I groaned softly.

Even with Raymond trying his best to put me back together, the part of me that craved Nunzio felt very lonely. And there was something about being sick and alone that was more dangerous than a game of Russian roulette. Every ache and pain, every whisper of fatigue, and every hopeless thought was magnified to an immeasurable scale.

There was no question that, even as shameful as my situation was, I needed him here with me so badly that my insides felt hollow. And the ache in my chest was anything but platonic.

I cast a longing look at the hospital phone, wanting to call him just so I could hear his voice. It would be easy to dial his number—the only number I had memorized—but I knew I shouldn't. I'd repeatedly pulled him in and shoved him away since the summer, and it wasn't fair to keep doing this to him. He couldn't be the crutch I held on to only when I felt unsteady.

The weight of a hundred dismissive comments and oblivious actions settled on my heart until it grew so heavy I thought it might rip out of my chest.

Why did I keep pushing everything that was happening between us—that had been happening for months—aside? What was the point of packing away reality when I could think back to the last time we'd been together—his body crushing mine to the bed, our fingers twined together while we stayed locked in a languid kiss—and see so clearly that there was more between us than being best friends who had good sex? Yet... I'd given him the impression that there *wasn't* more between us or that if he thought there was, it was all in his head.

I dialed his number before I could change my mind, my pulse jumping with each ring. By the fifth time, I knew he wouldn't be picking up, but I was still unprepared when the recording started.

Hey, this is Nunzio. Leave a message and I'll get back to you.

I'd heard the message hundreds of times over the years, but the sound of his voice cracked a wall inside me. My eyes burned, and I convulsively swallowed as the piercing beep filled my ear.

"Hey," I croaked out. I cleared my throat. "I uh… I'm not really sure when this all got so fucked-up. When I got so fucked-up. It's like I don't even know who I am anymore. I'm just—"

Low voices drifted into my room from the hallway.

"I'm so sorry, Nunzio. For being so caught up in my own head that I… really fucked things up with you. Got us to this point. I never meant to hurt you—to hurt us. To drive you away and say things that… that we both know had zero fucking basis in reality. God, I was lying to myself and lying to you, and now I'm terrified that I've lost you. I was just so scared of wrecking our friendship that I acted like an idiot and now—"

I heard Raymond talking from the other side of the door. My fingers tightened around the phone's receiver.

"Please just wait for me," I said, speaking lower. "Just give me time. Let me fix things. Fix myself. Please. You mean everything to me."

I hung up and thudded my head back onto the bed. I wondered where he was and why he hadn't answered. If he would even check his voice mail. Whether it was too late. At this point, I wouldn't blame him for saying *fuck it* and walking away.

Stupid. I was so stupid and careless.

I'd been careless with my father, with Nunzio and Raymond, and with myself just so I could wallow in the self-pity that had only led to me repeating the same missteps again and again. And even knowing that, I still just wanted to lose myself until I didn't have to think about my failings anymore. But that was starting to not seem like an option.

Rehab.

Therapy.

Talking about my feelings with strangers when normally I didn't like talking to people at all. Could I do it? Dumb question. I knew I could do it. And even if I didn't want to do it, I could fake it.

A little voice whispered that maybe I'd see a psychiatrist inside, and maybe that psychiatrist could give me a script for some Xanax or Klonopin. Maybe he or she would see that I was clearly drug seeking, but would also identify that I was decaying from self-contempt that flayed my insides every time I thought about the last few months.

And then I could stop dropping six bucks a bar when I copped Xanax on the street.

The irony of going to rehab for easier access to benzos was not lost on me. I was utterly pathetic.

With resistance becoming less substantive, I lay in bed and waited.

THE SOCIAL worker arranged for a thirty-day program at a clinic that was connected through OASAS. She'd made the arrangements with the diligence of someone who handled this type of thing every day, and she had called me a cab to the facility in Queens Village less than forty-eight hours after entering my hospital room.

The place was a dump. When the social worker had described the privacy and in-depth treatment I'd receive at the center, she'd failed to mention it was located on the same property as an abandoned mental hospital. But then again, New York State sponsored it, so I'd been naive to expect anything more glamorous. This wasn't rehab for celebrities and Upper East Side geriatrics.

Slinging my backpack over one shoulder, I nodded at the cab driver. He didn't seem particularly interested in whatever plight had landed me here, and it was anticlimactic when he sped off and left me standing on the curb.

Raymond had heeded the social worker's advice and stayed behind. No one was there to see me off. No hugs and teary good-byes, and no fist bumps of pride because I was doing the right thing. This was not panning out like a scene from the movies. Apparently, in the real world, no one threw you a party when you finally decided to get your shit together and be a grown-up.

I approached the long brick building, looking for signs of life. I could hear the distant sound of a television and laughter. At least someone was having a good time even if the place looked like an old folks' home from the '70s.

Weeds shot out through cracked concrete and bits of broken glass crunched under my boots when I ascended the steps. All of a sudden I could think of twenty-five things I should have done before making this commitment, and told myself to come back later. I could walk home from here. It would take me two hours, but it would be two hours of freedom.

Tempting. So very tempting. But I'd sworn to myself, to Raymond, and to Nunzio, that I would try. There was no going back.

The intake process took longer than I'd imagined, yet not long enough. They combed through my bag, gave me a piss test, and had me fill out a couple of surveys and questionnaires before assigning me a tentative program schedule and a roommate all before the sun went down.

The staff was nice enough, and the inside of the facility was cleaner and more modern than I'd expected, but I still felt like I'd been dropped off on another planet where everyone spoke a language I just happened to understand. Without my phone, the ability to leave when I wanted—unless I decided to check myself out—and the knowledge that visitors were only allowed once a month, I had been cut off from the outside world in a handful of hours.

Reality, and the sense of being trapped, set in. I stared at the daily schedule, but it only made the creeping dread inch along faster until I was cringing and crinkling the paper in my hand—breakfast, individual counseling, group counseling, lunch, another group session, and an appointment with a psychiatrist later on. What did these people think was wrong with me that I needed this much therapy? Did they actually believe I'd intended to off myself? Was this the standard procedure for every drunk and junkie who walked through the door?

A sharp knock on the door broke the silence, and I jumped. One of the counselors I'd met at intake, an older light-skinned Puerto Rican guy named Jones, stood at the door next to a wiry white kid with spiky black hair. He couldn't be any older than twenty or twenty-one.

"How're you finding everything?" Jones asked.

"Well enough."

"How's the schedule looking?"

"Fine."

The kid nailed Jones with a nasty stare. "This is who you thought would be a good match for me?"

"Yeah, he is." Jones nodded, light eyes fixed on me. "Michael is a teacher. He'll have thicker skin than the others."

I raised my brows at the authority in his voice, but he only smiled in response.

"Yeaaaah. No." The kid crossed his arms over his chest.

"What are you talking about?" I asked tiredly. "Thicker skin for what?"

"Michael, this is Drew. He's going to be your roommate for a while."

Jones looked down at Drew. He was lolling his head against the doorjamb but took the cue and released a long-suffering sigh.

"Sometimes I don't... mesh with the other inmates."

"Inmates? Come on, Drew."

Drew sighed again and crossed the room to flop onto the bed next to mine. "Patients... fuckups... crackheads. Take your pick."

Great. My roommate was a royal pain in the ass. Just what I needed.

I resumed my stare out the window. "I'm sure we will be fine."

"You will be." Jones rapped his knuckles on the side of the door again. "I'll see you both tomorrow in group."

When he was gone, Drew rolled over on his bed with a squeak of springs. I sensed him scrutinizing me and returned the stare.

"I got used to having the room to myself."

I resisted the urge to scoff. "Sorry, I guess."

"No problem," he said, oblivious to the sarcasm in my voice. "I'm sure it's not like you're dying to be here or something." He surveyed my meager belongings. "You didn't bring much."

"I pack light."

"You in for a fourteen-day run or something?"

"Thirty."

"Not a big talker, huh?"

"Not really."

"Good. Me neither."

It didn't seem that way, but commenting on the obvious would have just extended the conversation. I concentrated on my beautiful view of the abandoned hospital looming in the distance. It was the type of place Nunzio would have pushed me to explore when we were kids.

"So what are you in for?"

This time I sighed. "Similar to you, I'm sure."

"Doubt it."

The kid sounded so smug that I spared him another glance. He was sitting on the edge of his bed, swinging his leg, and flashing his shiny white teeth and his dimples at me. He reminded me of Mac.

"Well," he drawled. "Just so you know, I'm so desperate for a smoke that I'd give my ass away for free."

Christ Almighty.

"Just so *you* know," I said, "if you're selling your ass for cigarettes, it's not for free."

"Touché."

I thudded my head against the wall. This couldn't be my life.

Chapter Seventeen

Week One

"HOW ARE you feeling?"

"I'm okay."

The lie was so automatic there was no conceivable way of stopping it. "I'm fine" and "I'm okay" had become my standard reply to any question.

I cradled the phone between my chin and shoulder to turn sideways on the couch. I was alone in the office, but it still wasn't very private. Windows extended along one wall, and a smaller office was attached via a short corridor. I heard faint voices in that direction.

I'd sneaked in to make the call without half a dozen people listening. They did it with exactly zero attempts at discretion. Maybe they were monitoring calls to ensure patients weren't arranging for kilos of coke to be smuggled in.

All I wanted to do was talk to my boss without an audience.

"Listen, Ms. Price, I'm sorry about the way things have been." I picked at a loose thread in the slumping tweed couch. "I know you had reservations about me when the year first started, and I validated every one of them."

"My reservations had nothing to do with the situation you're in now." There was a pause, and I heard someone talking to Price in the background. "I know you're worried about your job, but this conversation doesn't have to revolve around you apologizing to me."

"But I left you high and dry."

"You're not on vacation."

"I know, but I still feel guilty." I tugged the spiral wire, twirling it around my finger. "The kids have been without a real teacher for over a month. I hate it when students are put in this position. Like when that guy quit in the middle of the semester last year."

"And I'll say it again, this situation is not about you choosing to walk off the job." Frustration seeped into her tone. I was sure it had more to do with me disagreeing with her than her desire to ease my conscience. "Did you get the paperwork I faxed to the facility?"

"Yeah. I sent everything to the DOE."

"Then don't worry. Your position is secure, Michael. When you get out of treatment, it will be here waiting for you. The students will be here waiting for you." This time there was a longer pause. "Unless you don't think you're coming back."

I pulled the wire, watching it straighten and curve around my finger again.

"Do you not think you're coming back?" she pressed.

"I want to come back."

"But do you think you will?"

Through the window along the wall, I watched my fellow patients moving from the cafeteria and splitting in separate directions as the next set of activities began. Four days in, and I still wasn't used to the routine—or the nightmare of group therapy.

"Michael?"

"Sorry. Someone was talking to me." I uncurled myself from the couch. "I plan to come back," I said with forced conviction. "And I want to thank you for supporting me."

"We've been working together for five years now. What else would I do?"

"You'd be surprised. My former principal would have hung me out to dry." My former principal had also possessed a Napoleon complex that had sent dozens of teachers fleeing the school in a mass exodus. "So thanks again. I'll call you when I'm closer to the completion of the program."

I hung up but didn't let go of the handset. I wanted to call Nunzio again.

I'd dreamt of him the night before, and I'd woken up with the taste of blood and ashes in my mouth. The details of the nightmare were unclear, but it had left me exhausted and heartbroken, and now I was desperate to know if he would wait for me. If he still loved me.

I replayed the message I'd left him every day, and I wondered whether it had been enough to convince him to give me another chance. Not knowing was killing me, but I didn't make the call. I'd promised myself to make a real effort with rehab and that meant playing along.

My one-on-one therapist had advised against reaching out to people in the first week. He thought my friends and family had become triggers that sent me plummeting into binges when things didn't go my way.

He was right, but it didn't lessen my yearning to talk to Nunzio.

I returned the phone to the desk and headed to my group therapy session.

It was the typical cliché—a circle of chairs, everyone introducing themselves and citing their addiction at the start of each session, and a counselor who led the meetings with different themes or topics every day. Typically Jones used questionnaires and worksheets to spark up a deep sharefest of emotions and epiphanies. It just left me wanting to jump out a window.

The second daily meeting wasn't as bad. Those centered on the biological aspect of how having a love affair with drugs and alcohol would eventually shrivel your insides.

The demographics of the groupings had no rhyme or reason. We all had different addictions, different problems, and different reasons for either checking ourselves into the treatment center or for being mandated by a court. The biggest commonality was that there were very few people above forty, and at least half of the patients were under twenty-five.

Their presence was disquieting in ways that were hard to ignore. Group sessions with a bunch of nineteen-year-olds felt too much like sitting in advisory and listening to Shawn talk about the horror story of his family life, but multiplied by six.

Jones gave me a stern look when I took my usual spot by the window.

"I'm only two minutes late."

"You're still late," Drew sang out. Over the past few days, he had continued to miss the fact that his sass was the least adorable thing on the planet. "Calling your woman?"

"Calling my boss."

"Ohhh, excuse me. I forgot you're a big-time fancy teacher."

Jones opened his mouth to thwart the conversation, but another patient piped up. It was Tracy, one of the few women in the program. "You're an idiot," she sniped at Drew. "Teachers are fucking broke."

I'd noticed her during the first session because she was the only one who didn't show any interest in my existence, which made her infinitely more likable than everyone else. She was a tough-looking girl, and the scar that twisted from her mouth to her ear only emphasized that.

"Okay, let's pause this conversation."

Jones held up both hands, face masked in the calm lines of neutrality. I could see through it, though. Even if it was the cliché setup of a group therapy session, the counselors were anything but the peace-and-love type. I could tell the kids in the group didn't take Jones seriously because of his shaggy hippie hair, and a daily uniform of chinos and flannel, but I didn't miss the track marks running up his arms. The man had a past.

"We have four new members to the group today, and this isn't the way we want to represent ourselves."

Drew shrugged and crossed his legs, once again swinging one like a go-go boy.

"Let's get started."

Everyone began dutifully introducing themselves and saying their substance of choice. Most of the younger kids, Drew included, were in for a love affair with Oxy while the older crowd was split between alcohol and heroin.

"My name is Carina." The new girl wiped an arm across her forehead. "I'm an alcoholic, and uh, I smoke a lot of weed."

"Oh please."

Carina faltered when Drew interrupted. She shot a slightly panicked look at Jones.

The counselor was giving Drew the side-eye. "Do you want to elaborate on your comment?"

Carina looked horrified by the idea.

Drew looked down his nose at her and leaned forward. He balanced precariously on the edge of his seat with his legs still crossed. "Look, weed is not even a real drug. That's all I'm saying. You look like a nice, young blonde thing, but I'm going to tell you right now—it gets way harder than that. Smoking bud was the *least* of my worries when I was your age."

"First of all, you don't know how old I am. And you don't know about my worries, so you have no way to judge them," Carina replied.

"So enlighten us," Drew said in a challenging tone. "What brought you here?"

"Like I'm going to say anything now that you're putting me on the spot?"

"This place is all about being put on the spot, sweetheart," Tracy threw in. "There isn't a comfort zone here."

"Maybe not," Jones interrupted. "But the most important part of these sessions is to respect each other. We're all here—myself included—for different reasons, but we all have something in common."

It was hard not to roll my eyes. The kumbaya, we're-all-in-it-together attitude was starting to get on my nerves. Nothing was more absurd than expecting a bunch of cranky-ass drunks or addicts to become best friends because we were all drying out together. Trying to teach Marxism to my most difficult cohort of students was preferable to this.

Right on cue, Jones spewed the same tired line he repeated at nearly every meeting. "We all have substance abuse problems, even if the substances are different, and even if some people consider their addictions to be more extreme, others have still not accepted that they have a problem at all."

The guy was definitely throwing subs.

"So why don't we continue going around the circle, and then *everyone* will have the opportunity to share. But keep in mind, there's no opting out of the conversation."

He turned to Tracy. She raised her hand in a limp wave.

"I'm Tracy. I'm an alcoholic, and I used to do meth."

Everyone looked at me.

"Michael." When they kept looking, I added, "Alcohol. And benzos."

"Thank you, Michael."

Jones always thanked me and not anyone else. I was starting to think it was counselor-style passive aggression. Once we went through the entire absurd ritual, he held up a sheaf of papers.

"Drew, you actually started us off on the right path with your earlier comments," Jones said. "Today we're going to focus on defense mechanisms."

A couple of people laughed, and Drew made a face, although a smile tugged at his lips. "Super funny, Jonesie."

Jones passed the papers around, and I skimmed my copy.

Below the title was a list of ten words and descriptions.

"We all have them," Jones said. "Even people who don't abuse illegal or harmful substances have them. If you've ever heard someone claim that being on social media nonstop throughout the day is okay because everyone does it, that's a defense mechanism."

"It's also true. Times have changed, Jonesie. It's not 1976 anymore. iPhones are the thing."

"As an Android user," Jones replied, smiling at Drew. "I beg to differ."

A collective chuckle went around the circle as I read each description on the sheet. For all that the actual people in the group annoyed me, some of the paperwork they handed out at each session tended to hit close to home. When Jones gave out golf pencils and told us to check off the mechanisms we could identify as using, it was yet another case in point. Out of the ten, I checked off five. All they needed to add was *be a total douche bag to friends and family*, and I would be set.

"I don't get why this is specific to us," Tracy said. She held up the paper, indicating that she, too, had checked off nearly half the options. "Everyone does this shit. The world does this shit. It has nothing to do with being addicted to meth or an iPhone. It's normal."

"I kind of agree," Kenan, a guy with a foot-long beard, said. He braced one colorfully tattooed forearm against his knees. "It's human nature."

"That doesn't mean it's a good thing."

Everyone looked at me, and I cursed myself for speaking aloud. Jones practically jumped on the opportunity to press me further.

"Why not, Michael?"

I hesitated but didn't stand a chance with Jones and Drew now fixated and clearly intending to hang on every word. Jones was probably thinking he was getting through to me, and Drew would undoubtedly find a way to twist or pick at whatever I said. And if I refused, the commentary and jeering would be even more of a headache.

"It's a problem for everyone," I said at last. "Even kids and their addiction to social media and smartphones. They use it so much to communicate, their verbal skills suffer, and it's a constant distraction, but they rationalize it by saying it's a cultural thing. Everyone does it."

When the rest of the group remained silent, I shifted on the chair, uncomfortable due to their expectant stares. Were they waiting for an entire lecture or what?

"But people with substance abuse problems rationalize that everyone gets high or drinks three or four beers a day, and they will end up falling into a more serious hole while the kid with the iPhone may just end up failing history."

"Well said." I'd expected an approving grin, but Jones kept giving me his usual intense stare. "Does any of it resonate with you?"

"Look, maybe someone else wants to talk now."

"I'm curious too," Kenan said. He twirled his beard. "What did you identify with?"

I glanced at Drew, hoping he would want to steal the spotlight. He winked, thrilled by my discomfort.

"Fine." I looked at the paper again. "I do a lot of blaming and minimizing."

"Can you give everyone an example?"

I shot Jones a dirty look and rested my ankle on the opposite knee, bouncing it slightly.

"I blame other things for my behavior, even when I know my behavior is wrong. I don't necessarily blame people, but I blame circumstances. I get wasted because I'm depressed and stressed out. I pop pills because the alcohol just makes me more depressed. I do both because without it, I have to deal with the rest of the world. And then I tell myself that it's not a serious situation because I'm aware of it, and I can stop when I want."

"And now you know that's not true."

"I have no idea if it's true or not because I came here before giving it a shot."

"If you think you can handle it on your own, why did you come?"

The question came from Carina, so I softened the defensive edge that had started to sharpen in my tone. "My brother wanted me to."

"That's the only reason?" Drew didn't look convinced. "It's not gonna work if you don't want it, sweetie."

I wanted to throat punch people who called me *sweetie*. Maybe I would inform Drew of that later.

"Half of you are here because it's court ordered. Not everyone runs to rehab with stars in their eyes, believing this is going to fix everything. Could I benefit from a month to dry out? Yeah. Things were getting critical. But that doesn't mean I'm thrilled to be here."

"So you think it won't help at all?"

Carina was digging in good.

I shrugged. "At the very least, it will give me time to figure things out."

I could see it in their faces—they wanted me to go deeper, show all my cards, and turn myself inside out for full disclosure. But it wasn't going to happen. I set my jaw and stared down at the handout again. A moment passed, then two, and Kenan broke the awkward silence.

"I can relate to that."

Most of the group turned to him and his beard, but Jones was still eyeballing me. The guy was seriously deluded if he thought I was going to be his project of the month. Removing myself from the toxic situation that had caused me to spin out of control was one thing. Buying into this sharing-is-caring propaganda was another story entirely.

THE BORGATA Hotel looked different in my dream.

The glass elevator reflected the flashing lights of Atlantic City down below. I leaned on the cool surface of the wall and stared down at the stretch of ocean and nightclubs. Nunzio's weight against my back felt secure. Comforting. I shuddered at the feel of his lips ghosting along my skin.

"Having fun?"

He turned me so I could face him and the view shifted in a dizzying arc. I dragged my fingers down the dark stubble shadowing his jaw. We stood eye-to-eye, but he looked bigger as he pushed me back.

"You still okay to share the bed?"

All I could do was look at him, drink in his intense gaze—the soft black hair, his broad smile—and pull him closer. Where else would I want to sleep? Who else would I want to sleep with?

I nodded.

Nunzio tilted his head and brushed his lips to mine. I licked them, wanting inside. He acquiesced and let me taste the inside of his mouth. A groan bounced off the glass walls. I couldn't be sure which one of us had made the sound, but it was clear that we both wanted so much more.

More came with a suddenness that ripped me out of the dream.

My eyes slit open, and I was aware only of the darkness surrounding me, the dampness of sweat on my T-shirt, and a hand stimulating my dick. It made no sense, but I arched into the grip. The feeling intensified, the pressure increased, and the sound of my own moan woke me up fully.

"What—"

"Shhh. I got you."

Drew.

He was sitting on the edge of my narrow bed and gazing down at me. His hand moved faster.

"Oh fuck."

My eyes shut again, and my hands balled up in the sheet. It felt good. I wanted it. Wanted him to sink between my thighs and tug my cock until I busted all over his face, but I shook my head.

"Stop."

"Want me to suck it?"

"I said stop."

"I'll swallow."

I grabbed his wrist. "Get the fuck away from me."

Drew snatched his hand back. His breathing was almost as fast as mine, and his pajama pants were tented.

"You don't even know me, you stupid fucking kid."

"Oh, like you've never blown someone on a one-night stand?" Drew didn't move from the bed. He sat there, glaring.

"That's not the point. Go back to your bed, and don't put your hands on me again, or I'll break them."

"Fine."

He leapt to his feet and crossed the small space between our beds with loud footsteps.

"Me cago en diez…." I hunched forward, scrubbing my face with my hands. I was caught somewhere between sexually frustrated and wanting to lecture him. "Why would you ever think that was a good idea? Have I looked at you twice?"

"You don't have to be an asshole."

"You don't need to be groping people in their sleep. I don't give a shit what you did with your other roommates. I'm not them."

"You think I just suck off every guy in here?" Drew asked shrilly.

"I met you seven days ago. I don't know what the hell you get up to, but between this and your cigarettes for sex comment, you're not exactly making a good impression. Also, you're practically a child to me."

"I'm twenty."

"Whatever, kid."

I expected one of Drew's now infamous retorts, but all I got was stony silence.

I lay down and adjusted my dick. I had no idea how I'd given myself away as gay. Apparently I was a massive fail at being halfway in the closet.

"Can you not make a big thing of this?" he asked after a stretch of silence.

"How would I do that?"

"Like make a complaint. You might be leaving in a couple of weeks, but I'm stuck here for months. I don't want everyone thinking I'm the center cum-dump, okay?"

"Then don't act like one. Is this why you had problems with roommates in the past?"

"No. It's not like I wave my flaming gay banner for everyone. I didn't think you would freak out over a hand job."

I raised my arm to look at his side of the room. Drew's eyes were luminous in the darkness, open wide. That combined with the sight of his slender body swathed in sheets chipped away at my annoyance.

"Look, it's not that big a deal. If I gave you the wrong idea at some point, I'm sorry. But I'm not interested."

"I just thought maybe you were lonely too."

"Why would you think that?"

Drew continued to stare at the ceiling. "You look down a lot, so when I heard you making noise in your sleep, I figured maybe we could have a good time."

My brow furrowed. "Making noise?"

"Moaning. Saying some guy's name."

"Jesus fucking Christ." Heat rose to my face.

"Are you embarrassed?"

"Hell yes, I'm embarrassed."

"Good."

"I appreciate the gesture," I said dryly. "But my hard-on was meant for someone else."

"That's adorbs, but my mouth is here and his isn't."

If he expected me to spill the details on Nunzio, I wasn't going to rise to the bait.

I watched him fidget with his sheet. It was a drastic change from his usual sass monster tactics—deliberately offending everyone in the room and eating up every drop of attention that followed.

"Why are you here for so long, Drew?"

"I got into some trouble."

I waited, hesitating to push when I was so unwilling to share. It took half a second for him to crack.

"I had a boyfriend who... helped me get into a lot of trouble. We got caught up in a bad situation, and I ended up in here as part of a plea bargain."

"Where did he end up?"

"Jail."

"Sounds serious."

"Yeah. He deserved it." Drew twisted back an arm, propping his head on it. "I still miss him, though. I don't have that much family or friends anymore. When you're alone, even shitty people start to look like saviors."

I nodded, but I couldn't relate. The people in my life weren't toxic to me. It was the reverse.

"Is he doing a lot of time?"

"Yeah. I met him when I was in high school and I was living at a group home. I was already into Oxy, but he helped me get it faster."

"Was he older?"

"Yeah, he was around thirty."

I cringed. "Sounds like a real winner."

"I was seventeen, not twelve. Or let me guess, perfect teacher over there never messed with an older guy either?"

"I didn't say that, but when you speak, all my mandated reporter instincts kick in."

"What the hell does that mean?"

I shook my head. "Never mind."

"Hmph." Drew turned his head. "Do you want to hear the rest of my sob story or what?"

I smiled. "Go ahead."

"*Anyway*, he had these friends, and they'd go upstate to, like, New Rochelle and Yonkers to rob pharmacies for painkillers and benzos. I think mostly they sold it, but Rob was in it just to get free shit. I started going with them."

"And got caught?"

"No. Not with the group." Drew curled onto his side. "A few months ago, he got it into his head that we should try to do it here in the city, just me and him. He wanted to rob this twenty-four-hour Walgreens in Staten Island, and I fucking knew we would get caught, but I went anyway so he wouldn't do something stupid. Turned out he didn't listen to me when he was desperate, so... he shot the girl in the pharmacy."

"Did she die?" Now that he was talking about it, I vaguely remembered hearing the story on the news.

"No, thank God. But I testified against him and got probation and a few months in here."

"You're lucky, then."

"Yeah...."

"Any risk of retaliation from his friends?"

"I don't think so, because I could have turned them in about all the other stuff too and didn't. And they like me."

I cringed at the lilt in his voice. I didn't want to know what them liking him entailed. Instead of asking, I wondered about my students. In a lot of ways, Drew reminded me of Mackenzie. In other ways, he reminded me of Shawn. Drew was a combination of their worst flaws and all of the horror-movie scenarios that played out in my head every time Mackenzie alluded to how many guys he'd blown since he'd hit puberty, and all of the shady things I suspected Shawn of doing to get by.

"Damn," I whispered.

Drew looked at me again. "What?"

"I miss my job."

"What about that guy you were dreaming about?"

I closed my eyes again. "I miss him too."

Chapter Eighteen

Week Two

THE SOUND of a flipped chair yanked me out of my silent contemplation of an unappetizing lunch.

In the time it took me to look up from my tray, the dreary cafeteria erupted with chaos. Drew was screaming at Tracy, and she was being restrained by Kenan and a member of the staff. Some of the other patients circled around them to help, but most watched from their seats.

"What the hell?" I muttered, pushing away from my own table.

They went back and forth, Drew's shouting growing louder and Tracy's voice booming in return. Between lack of sleep and their high-pitched yelling, any chance of peacefully choking down my rubbery chicken seemed impossible. I had little interest in their argument; Drew getting into screaming matches with one person or another was almost a daily occurrence.

I stood, dumped my tray, and left the cafeteria. Bypassing the indoor common areas, I grabbed my hoody from my room and headed to the small fenced-in courtyard at the back of the building. It was almost always deserted because of the subzero temperature but was preferable to the constantly bustling facility.

My breath fogged in front of me the moment I stepped outside, and I pulled the hood over my head. I walked toward a group of benches partially blocked by a tree, but paused when I caught sight of Jones sitting there with a cigarette dangling from the side of his mouth.

"You're not supposed to smoke on the property," I blurted.

Jones snorted. "I'm not a patient."

I walked closer, zeroing in on the burning white cylinder between his fingers.

"Can I bum one?"

"Nope."

Shaking my head, I scanned the area. "Does anyone else catch you out here?"

"Not so much in the winter, but I usually sit in my car."

"Oh." There was nothing else for me to say to him, and my desire to sit down was gone. "I guess I'll go back inside."

"Why?"

"I don't want to intrude."

"You're not intruding." His eyes fixed on me like they did when he tried to figure me out. I retreated a step, then another, but then he extended his arm and offered me the still-burning cigarette. "Kill it."

My hesitation vanished. I sat next to him and brought the cigarette to my lips. I wasn't even that much of a smoker, but just the taste of one of my vices loosened some of my tension.

"Thanks," I muttered.

"You don't strike me as a smoker. Usually they're biting their nails off and starting trouble right off the bat."

"I don't smoke much, but being in here has me craving it."

"Makes sense."

I exhaled slowly and nodded at a metal rack next to the gate. "What is that thing?"

"A bike rack. Apparently the state had high hopes of us being good little bicyclists."

I snorted. "I bet Kenan rides a bike everywhere."

Jones was trying to suppress a smile and failing. "He seems the type."

I closed my eyes and concentrated on the calming effect smoking had on my nerves. It would have been even better with a drink. Vodka—no, something smoky and dark that would warm me up. Scotch. Neat.

I could practically smell and taste the spices from a mouthful of Johnnie Walker.

"You got it bad, my man."

Blinking away my fantasy, I glanced at Jones. "Got what?"

"You're jonesing bad."

"Did you just make a pun?" I sucked on the cigarette again, watching with regret as the distance between the cherry and the filter lessened. I should have drawn it out more.

"Heh. Kind of." Jones put his hands in the pockets of his down jacket. "My real name is Carlos. My friends used to call me Jones because I always had that look on my face. The same look you just had—like you'd rather be doing something other than what you're doing right now."

"Huh." Carlos fit him better than Jones, but I kept that information to myself. "What did you jones for?"

"Heroin. It took me thirty years to get clean."

"Damn."

Jones inclined his head. "It's not easy. Anyone who says otherwise is a liar."

My eyes dropped to his arms, but the track marks were covered by the sleeves of his jacket. He couldn't be older than his early fifties, and I wondered how and why he'd started using.

"When are you going to start opening up in therapy?" He switched gears so quickly I was caught off guard.

"I really didn't come out here for this."

"I know, but it's a good opportunity for us to talk one-on-one."

I killed the rest of the cigarette and flicked the butt over the fence. "You're not my one-on-one counselor."

"That doesn't mean anything. You're good with people individually. I noticed it right away with Drew and Carina, but it makes me wonder why you don't work better with your own therapist."

"Because I'm not sold on this whole process."

"Is that so?"

My comment was probably offensive to a person who was dedicating their time to trying to make us all better, but I couldn't bring myself to take it back.

"The problems I have are deeper than me jonesing for a glass of scotch. I don't think thirty days of feel-good sessions and positive vibes is going to change the direction my shitty life is going in."

"It won't with that attitude."

"Jones, not for nothing, but you don't know much about me."

"Maybe not, but I knew your father."

I stared at him, trying to find something that would set off my bullshit meter, but it didn't even flicker. The guy just looked back at me, his expression placid. Maybe he was waiting for me to remember him or put two and two together, but my father had introduced me to so many of his Sutphin Boulevard buddies as a kid that they'd all blurred together after a while. I could vaguely summon a memory of a tall, white-looking guy who spoke Spanish—the only reason he'd stuck out to me at the time.

"Did he call you Carlito?"

Jones smiled. "Yes. He was the only one who did. We met when we were kids. Both lived in the Baisely Park projects before I was jonesing all the time. He didn't care for my nickname."

I shouldn't be this freaked out. My father had known a lot of people, and they both had heroin, and likely methadone, in common.

"Why didn't you tell me before?"

"Didn't see a reason to and couldn't figure out a good time to do it."

"Were you at his funeral?"

"Yeah. You were so out of it that I left you alone. I spoke to your brother. That fucking kid looks just like Joe. It was eerie."

"Imagine living with that resemblance."

"Must be hard."

I shrugged. I wondered about a lot, but I couldn't verbalize any of it without inviting a slew of questions. How close had they been when my father died? Did they see each other often? Had he known my dad was sick? And most of all, I wondered if my father had ever talked about me and Raymond during those great expanses of nothingness and radio silence. The times when it had seemed as though I didn't have a father at all.

"How's Ray doing, anyway?"

"Same as usual."

"Getting by?"

"He's holding it together better than me," I admitted. "But his ascension to adulthood is a little delayed."

"Huh." Jones slid his hands out of his pockets and toyed with his lighter. "Your father talked about you both sometimes. He thought Raymond would turn out like him."

Wasn't irony just lovely?

"Raymond is a big baby because our parents set it up that way."

"How?"

"Low expectations, coddling…." When Jones frowned, I hastened to add on to the harshness of my statement. "But I think that's starting to change. He's not a bad kid."

"Does he have a girlfriend?"

I shrugged. "Not a serious one. He doesn't date much. Just fucks around."

"Good friends?"

Raymond's friends were just like him or worse, and the ones who weren't tended to lose interest after a while. I didn't particularly want to say all that, so I stayed quiet and made a vague gesture with my hand. Jones seemed to get my drift.

"Let me ask you a question." He went on without waiting for encouragement. "Before your parents died, had the drinking ever gotten out of hand?"

"No."

"So if you didn't need a drink permanently fixed in your hand before, why are you telling yourself you need it now?"

"I don't tell myself that."

"Don't you?"

I wanted to escape the conversation, but it would be pointless. I was stuck with him for the next two weeks, and there was no way he was going to let up. Not now that I knew he had a vested interest in my sobriety. And how ridiculous was it that someone genuinely giving a shit bothered me?

"I know you think I'm being harsh, but I'm trying to have a real talk instead of that scripted bullshit we do in group. I know your family, I knew your father, and I know you have the need to drink in your blood like I have the craving for that hard shit imprinted in my brain, but you have to try. You have potential to be so much better and you're going to waste it."

"Why does everyone say that?" I wondered aloud. "I have potential for *what*? And how does me drinking take it away?"

An impatient look stole over Jones's features. "Tell me something, kid—why do you drink?"

"Because I like it."

"I'm not talking about doing shots on a Friday night," Jones growled out, poking my arm. "I mean why do you like to get so wasted that you end up in a place like this? What happens to make you throw back that first drink?"

I had reflected on that question multiple times since stepping foot inside the facility.

"When things snowball…." I paused, trying to put into words the thoughts that ran through my mind every day. It was difficult, and that was a big reason why I stayed quiet during therapy. "When something happens that I can't fix or control, I get so stressed out that I need to make myself shut down. My mind goes and goes and goes." I twirled my finger near my ear. "I can't sleep, so I stay up and think, and then I'm fucking exhausted all day, which makes things worse. Everything compounds until I'm ready to explode, and all I can do is replay those same shitty thoughts again and again. So what it comes down to is me wanting that to end, and it doesn't until I can stop being me and step outside myself. Outside my problems. Outside of everything."

"And drinking gets you there?"

"It does."

Jones nodded in understanding. "So you prefer a blackout to being you?"

"Sometimes, yes. And I know how it sounds."

"It sounds like you want a black hole, not real life. A big gap where a memory used to be. And when people tell me that, I wonder how long it will be until they start wanting to get to that point indefinitely."

"I don't want to die," I snapped. "I don't know why everyone takes it to that level."

Jones huffed out a laugh. "You don't want to die, but you don't want to be conscious. At that point, what's the difference?"

I started to dispute his claim but faltered when a rebuff didn't immediately come to mind. *Was* there a difference between death and a nice, extended blackout? With the blackout, I would inevitably come to my senses, but these days I woke up only to start drinking my way to oblivion again. And either way, my actions, my thoughts, and the things happening around me were blanked out and forgotten until there were no memories left to have.

Jones leapt on the pause and continued.

"Can you function when you're in that state? Can you talk to your brother, your friends, your students, or a woman? Can you dance or laugh or fuck? No. You're not living when you spend life in a void." He leaned closer, intense and foreboding, and daring me to disagree. "Am I wrong?"

"No," I said. The word came out hollow. "You're not wrong."

"So then…. Dime."

"No sé."

Jones tilted his head to the side.

"Look, I don't know what you want me to say," I said. "Drinking has always been my go-to when planet Earth gets too stressful. It's just that lately my need to get the hell out of Dodge has become overwhelming. I know I'm messing up. Believe me, I am well fucking aware. And that's why I'm here. I just don't know what to do about it. I could stop, but that doesn't mean inside"—I tapped my chest—"the need is going to go away."

"It doesn't go away. I said that before. But you have to be strong enough to understand that and deal with it, and try to find other ways to handle this fucked-up life when your thoughts start spinning in the wrong direction."

The sound of a door shutting caused me to jump, but nobody appeared in the courtyard. Jones pulled out another cigarette.

"There has to be something that made you happy before all of this happened."

"Maybe."

Jones flicked his Zippo, the lick of the flame extending high. "Think about it. Now."

I quit staring at his cigarette with envy and looked at the distant shape of the abandoned hospital. My mind returned to the previous winter. Before I'd lost my mother to cancer, before Clive dumped me, before the doomed trip to Italy, and before everything happened with my father, what had made me happy?

Teaching, for certain. I loved my job even if I didn't love my administration. Going to work and seeing the results of my efforts gave me pride. I loved working with my students, and going to work had never been a chore.

Had I been happy with Clive? I scraped my jagged nail alongside the bench and pondered the relationship that had ended with zero fanfare.

I hadn't even missed Clive over the summer. I'd been too busy worrying about my father and thinking about Nunzio. The new developments with my best friend had managed to overshadow that I was single again, but this time, at thirty-two. I'd expected a frantic, quarter-life crisis but that moment of "what the hell am I doing wrong?" had never come. My thoughts had rerouted to an option I'd never even considered before: my best friend, my one-and-only, my fucking soul mate. Nunzio.

Nunzio, without a question, made me happy. He always had. I wondered how much different the past month would have played out if I'd allowed myself to find solace in him rather than ducking and dodging the reality of our evolving relationship because I was afraid it would end up in the same pile of failures as my previous attempts.

I had no delusions that being with Nunzio would have been a magical cure-all for my problems, but maybe I wouldn't have been so dependent on drink after drink if I'd been with him, instead of isolated and slowly going insane in my room.

"Christ." I scrubbed at my face, feeling weary and subdued. "Why does it take hitting rock bottom for me to have a goddamned epiphany?"

"Because it's easy to ignore things before you reach that point."

That was for damn sure.

Chapter Nineteen

Week Three

TIME PASSED in uneven lurches.

At certain points the days sped by at a rate that surprised me. The sun rose, signaling breakfast, and by the time I was departing the second group session of the day, it had set below the horizon. With nothing to do but follow my daily schedule, I became keenly aware of how few hours of daylight there were in February.

I took my vitamins, tried to cooperate with my counselors, and developed a rapport with most of the other patients during group sessions. My grudging comments became known as the moments when "Michael dropped knowledge," and Jones made sure to call me out at least twice a session. The days went by quicker once I stopped watching the clock, but at night, time staggered along once again.

I hadn't talked to Nunzio since that day in the teachers' lounge, and he hadn't returned my call. Raymond claimed Nunzio asked after me almost every day, but it wasn't the same as hearing his voice.

I couldn't stop wondering whether the message I'd left him had been good enough. Or whether I had said the wrong thing while blurting out my feelings in a rush.

I spent hours replaying our last conversation in my head. In turn, I was furious with him and myself. How could he have taken me seriously? Did he really believe I could so casually advise him to walk out of my life? It seemed stupid for him to have taken my words to heart. I wanted to sneak into the office, call him, and force him to listen to me. Force him to respond, and hope that he would give me another chance. That he hadn't already given up on me.

I didn't, but when I woke up from yet another dream about his hands and mouth and gorgeous eyes focused on me (or sometimes, someone else), I was tempted.

No amount of group therapy, of discussions about family and self-expression and triggers could ease my frustration. And every day that went by, I wondered if he would get used to my absence. The idea was terrifying.

It ratcheted up several notches when my one visitation day arrived. I knew he wouldn't show up, but I found myself obsessively primping in front of the mirror regardless. I wanted to look decent if I saw him—wanted him to see that I wasn't as much of a mess as I had been last time we spoke.

Drew watched me fuss with my hair, smirking.

"Is your man coming?"

"I don't have a man."

He rolled onto his back, watching me upside down from the bed. "Is the guy you have sexy dreams about coming?"

"I doubt it. I haven't talked to him since I came here."

"Why not?"

"Because—" Because I was a dickhead. "I don't know. Just because."

"Man, you're all agitated and wound up, aren't you?" Drew rolled over again. I could feel his critical gaze wandering over my outfit. "I would love to see you in something other than sweatpants and T-shirts. Your body is sick."

I snorted and looked over my shoulder. He was giving me a comic leer. "Shut up, Drew. Why don't you get out of bed and do something constructive?"

"Like what?"

"Go find Carina and look at those GED papers I had Marg print out for you guys."

"Oh my God, you're obsessed."

I turned away from the mirror. "You should be obsessed too. I don't know what you think you're going to do without even a GED. Let me put it to you like this—"

"And here we go...." Drew covered his ears.

I kept talking, raising my voice. "If Starbucks and Barnes and Noble are full of kids with college degrees because those poor suckers are having trouble finding anything else, where do you think someone without a high school diploma will end up?"

"I *know*! You've told me like thirty thousand times, Mr. Rodriguez."

"So stop dicking around and go look at the paperwork."

Drew stuck out his tongue. "I'll do it later. I'll need a distraction, anyway."

He didn't say the last part until I was halfway through the door, but I still paused to look back. I wanted to say something uplifting about his lack of visitors, but I failed at compassion, and Drew wrinkled his nose when he caught me staring. He made a run-along gesture as if sensing my pity and wanting none of it.

The staff had cleaned the cafeteria, pulled the tables apart, and decorated each one with a single, crappy flower. I sought out Raymond and did a double take. David was sitting next to him. My disappointment and bitterness momentarily flitted away.

In his black hoodie and with his long hair hidden beneath a fitted Yankees cap, Raymond was a total contrast to David's golden hair, navy pea coat, and tight khakis. They were a seriously odd couple.

I grinned after taking a seat across from them.

"How did this happen?"

"He—" Raymond started to say.

"I found him on Facebook," David interrupted. He looked proud of himself. "And made him tell me where you were and how I could come see you."

"You didn't make me do anything. I just told you."

"I still found out."

"It's not like it was rocket science. It's Facebook."

David rolled his eyes. "You're just as grumpy as Michael."

Raymond shook his head. "This dude is annoying."

"You're rude and should take your hat off."

I looked between them, unable to wipe the grin off my face. "Should I leave you two alone?"

David smirked. Raymond just sneered.

"You look good, Michael," David said. "I'm not just saying that, either. The last time I saw you—"

"I was doing shots in my classroom?"

"Wow, son. You're mad retarded."

David whipped his head around and pinned my brother with a lethal glare. "Don't say that word."

"Sorry." Raymond kept staring at me. "You're mad special ed."

David scoffed, and I burst out laughing.

The combination of the PC police and my offensive little brother was too hilarious to stifle a good chuckle. A couple of the other patients glanced over at us, and I wondered if I was interrupting some tearful reunions with my obnoxious guffaws. I swallowed the sound, but it felt good to laugh.

"Thanks for coming. I know it's only been a few weeks, but it's weird being cut off from everyone."

"It's weird being in the house alone," Raymond admitted. "It fucks my head up after everything that happened. I try to avoid being there."

"I took him out for lunch the other day," David said. "After my amazing Facebook detective work."

"Maybe I really should leave you two alone."

Raymond kicked me under the table. "Stop throwing your gay subs."

"Yeah, Raymond made sure to inform me that I'm not his type." David unbuttoned his coat. "I told him every hetero boy says that at first."

"Anyways...," Raymond said in a droll tone. "I thought you might wanna know that I got a job."

My eyebrows shot up. "Really? Where?"

Raymond glanced at David from under the brim of his hat. I could read his hesitation and reached over to clap him on the shoulder.

"Don't hold out on me, Ray. I know you been looking for a job for a long time."

It was a total lie, but he relaxed. He took off his hat and smoothed back hair that had escaped from the ragged knot he'd tied it in. "My friend's pop got me a job as a casual dock worker over in Red Hook. It ain't nothing special—" Raymond peered at David again. "But, you know, it pays like almost thirty Gs a year if I put in enough time."

"Cripes." David screwed up his face. "Maybe I should have become a longshoreman. I wouldn't have a stupid master's to be paying off. I'd trade my forty thousand in debt for a job that pays ten thousand less."

"So who told you to go to a private school to become a teacher?" I asked. "State school would have had the same outcome."

"Yeah, that was pretty stupid," Raymond agreed.

"Oh, thank God I chose to look to you guys for sympathy."

"That was stupid too."

David scowled at Raymond, and I cracked up again.

"Where's the bathroom?" Raymond stood up. "I gotta take a leak."

I gestured over my shoulder. "Out those doors and to the left. I know you get lost easily, so ask someone if you need to."

Raymond flipped me off and walked away. When he was gone, I made a face at David. "Can you stop flirting with my brother?"

"He's cute."

"You have a sort of boyfriend."

"Nope. We broke up for good after the Grindr incident."

I'd forgotten about that. "Raymond is straight."

"How do you know?" David grinned. "He didn't protest too hard when I asked him out to lunch, and he doesn't freak out when I flirt with him."

"Oh my God, can you not creep on my brother? What's with you and grouchy *boricuas*?"

"I can't help it. You have good genes." David's smile was broad and unapologetic.

A rosy flush had risen to his face, and I wondered if he was joking. I was more surprised at Raymond's willingness to hang out with David than I was with David's alleged attraction. Raymond was more open-minded than I had ever given him credit for. But if he'd stayed in the room while Nunzio and I had drunkenly tried to get it on, he had to be.

"Seriously, though." David folded his hands between us on the table. "How are you doing? You really do look better."

"It's easy to look better if you're rising up from the gutter, but thanks."

"Is it just on the surface, then?" David's face was wide open and imploring. He didn't realize how much pressure his hope could put on someone.

I shrugged, looking around the cafeteria again. Unsurprisingly I didn't see Drew anywhere in the room, but Carina and Kenan were present. It wasn't a completely gloomy scene, but no one seemed that thrilled to be there, either. The blank indifference and discontent on their faces caused a swell of affection to rise inside my chest for David and my brother.

"Michael?"

I looked back at David. "I don't know. It's not like I suddenly want to go straight edge, but being here has given me a lot of time to think and get my priorities straight. Also, hearing about what some of these people have been through has given me a shitload of perspective. There's kids in here not too much older than some of our students."

David winced. "I noticed that."

"Yeah. So—perspective. I really have no right to act like the world ended. Some of these kids have been through crap their whole lives."

"Yeah, but don't fall into the trap of thinking they have it worse, so you can't be depressed. Everyone has their own stuff, and you're entitled to feel what you feel."

I nudged his knee with my own. "You sound like one of the people who run my meetings. Maybe you should get another fifty-thousand-dollar master's and become a guidance counselor."

"Shut up."

I laughed just as Raymond returned to the table. He dropped into the seat next to David and put his hat back on.

"Did you tell him about Nunzio?"

My heart stopped.

"No." David wrinkled his nose at Raymond. "I didn't just come here to gossip."

I looked between them. The spit had dried in my throat. "Gossip about what? What's wrong with Nunzio?"

"Nothing's wrong with him." David toyed with the wilting flower in the spindly vase. "He put in his thirty days with the DOE last Friday. He mentioned it at happy hour."

"*What*?" My gaze drilled into Raymond. "*¿Por qué no me lo dijiste?*"

"I didn't say anything because I didn't know!" Raymond held up his hands, sitting back in the chair. "He didn't tell me, and I text that fucker, like, every day. David told me on the way over here. He was all worried about breaking the news to you."

David reddened again. "That's not what I said. I just wondered if you knew. To be fair, I think it was an impulsive move. He was telling Karen that he'd applied for a teaching position at some LGBT center in SoHo a while back, and a position opened up last week."

"If Nunzio quit the DOE, it wasn't just a random decision."

All traces of my good mood evaporated. I rubbed my temples. Bitterness scorched through me, settling on my shoulders and dragging the sides of my mouth down in a deep scowl. Nunzio and I had done everything together since junior high. Him making a major life decision without talking to me about it was the sharpest knife of rejection. Maybe he was really over me.

"He must have been wanting to leave since the beginning of the year," David said quietly. "After they replaced him with me."

"You?" Raymond's tone was thick with incredulity. "Man, I'd be pissed too."

"It wasn't just that." I dropped my hands. "It was building up from other things."

"Like what?" David asked. "He always looks fine when I see him."

"Yeah, because he's professional. He can hide his discontent. Unlike me." But apparently Nunzio had hidden his desire to leave even from me. The only time it had come up was in September when Price had first switched his position, and even then, he'd deflated quickly. He had not once mentioned applying to another job. Never once expressed his desire to up and leave before the end of the year. "I can't believe he didn't tell me."

"I can."

I gave Raymond a sharp look.

"You been in your own little world since Dad died. You wasn't trying to hear anything anyone had to say."

David wrung his hands and stayed quiet.

As angry as I wanted to be, I had no legitimate defense. I thought about all the times I'd interacted with Nunzio at work since winter and the anxiety in his voice as he'd talked about the job. Had I ever showed a real interest in what was up with him, or had I just brushed it off as the typical work annoyance? I couldn't remember.

"Damn."

"Sorry, Michael. But you know it's true."

"Yes, I know that, Raymond. Thank you." I bounced my knee up and down. "Anything else I should know? Did he get engaged in the past three weeks? I would have missed the invitation since my ass is stuck in here."

"You're taking this way too personally."

"Yeah, I fucking know that too, Raymond. Thanks again."

Raymond didn't look very charitable, but David put his hand on my arm.

"Listen, don't get upset. He just didn't want to put his problems on you when you were already going through a lot."

"He should have. He's always around for me, and I was oblivious to the fact that things were so bad off at work that he wanted to quit."

"I still think it was a last-minute thing," David insisted.

I shook my head. I wanted a cigarette so bad I could taste it. "Is he fucking anyone?"

"Uh...."

"Just tell me."

They both looked reluctant to respond, but I wasn't about to explain why I was so desperate to know. Discussing my reoccurring nightmare of leaving the program only to find that Nunzio was in a committed relationship with someone who didn't choke on their own vomit after drowning their sorrows in booze was pretty much my idea of complete humiliation.

"He hasn't mentioned anyone, but you know Zio. He's always messing around." Raymond looked nonplussed. "What does that have to do with his job?"

"Nothing. Forget it."

"O-kay...."

David shot my brother a dark look. "You're cute but phenomenally dense."

Raymond started to retort, and I forced myself to not tune out their semiflirtatious banter. I was no longer amused, but I wasn't about to ruin the visit when they'd made the effort to come to see me.

I swallowed my unhappiness and changed the subject. I asked about Raymond's new job and then the goings-on at McCleary.

David filled me in on the kids, my substitute, and the newest teacher drama. Some of my spirits lifted when David told me that Shawn had passed his Algebra Regents. The kid had actually asked Nunzio to tell me.

"I'm so ready to go back to work."

"Good! Price keeps asking me if I know whether you're definitely coming back," David said. "Believe it or not, everyone misses you."

"Yeah, well, I miss you too, asshole." Raymond jerked his thumb at the window and in the direction of our neighborhood. "I'm starving to death at home. I tried to make rice the other day, and it was a disaster."

David tilted his head. "Just follow the directions on the box."

The look of disgust that Raymond aimed at David dragged an unexpected laugh out of me. David looked between us in confusion, and Raymond shook his head.

"White people."

They succeeded in distracting me by being endearing and ridiculous, but after they were gone, my brain went right back to obsessing over Nunzio.

Once visiting hours ended, I made my way to the evening group session.

"How has everyone's day been?" Jones asked, looking around the circle. "I know for some, this is the best day of the month, but for others, it may be the worst."

I noticed Kenan nodding out of the corner of my eye, his expression drawn. He twisted his wedding ring idly.

"Just in case anyone is curious, no one visited me again!" Drew grinned, nodding at the patients who had been in the program with him for longer than a month.

"Not even your parents?" Carina asked.

"Girl, I don't have no parents. I grew up in a group home in Staten Island, and no fosters wanted to keep my rotten ass."

"Damn. I'm sorry."

"Why?" Drew began to swing his leg, rolling his narrow shoulders. "I don't give a shit."

No one looked convinced, but more than half the group was as tense and upset as me.

Jones held up his usual stack of papers. "I want to talk about setting boundaries today. Like I said, seeing loved ones can be uplifting or it can be a trigger for relapse, and part of that is because of issues maintaining healthy boundaries."

I wasn't in the mood to talk about healthy relationships, but I began reading anyway.

Connected: You are able to engage in balanced relationships with others and maintain them over time. As conflicts arise, you are able to work them out.

What a joke. I was the antithesis of that statement.

I wondered if Jones had planted a little microphone under my table during visiting hours in order to dig this deep in the right direction. I was being narcissistic, but yet again, the guy had targeted something I was feeling in just the right way.

I read the section about boundaries being too close and too distant, and could see Nunzio in the *too close* column. He was too giving and had difficulty saying no. I was in the *too distant* column. I isolated and distrusted people, and pulled back without explaining why.

"My relationship with my wife is so unbalanced," Kenan said, breaking the silence. "It was really obvious today."

"Did it not go well with her?" Jones asked.

Kenan kept twisting his ring. "She's going through a rough time while I'm in here, but it's like she's starting to fall out of love with me, you know?"

"That's a pretty extreme assessment," I said.

"Yeah, but it's true. I don't see anything in her eyes when she looks at me. There's just nothing there anymore." Kenan dropped his hands. "I expect her to act like everything is the same, but it makes no sense. Things have changed."

I nodded, processing the words and churning them out into something that looked like my situation.

Expecting too much, but in my case, also giving too little. I still wasn't sure if any of it was related to my drinking or just my bullshit behavior once I was sunk so thoroughly in misery. I'd shut everyone out, focused only on my own needs, and I had sat around feeling slighted when people adapted their behavior accordingly. Like Nunzio had done.

The direction of the conversation was making me antsy, and I wanted out. The craving for nicotine and a shot reared up with a blinding intensity. I visualized the minibar in my room at home, but knowing Raymond, he'd have dumped it all already.

"What do you think, Michael?"

I gave Jones a wild look. For a startling moment, I thought he could somehow see the craving in my face.

"I don't know."

My default answer was getting less impressive every day.

"Do you not think boundary issues affect your situation?"

"Uh. I don't know." I sounded like an idiot. Wincing, I looked down at the handout again. The words had transformed into meaningless symbols. "To be honest, I'm really not in a good mood right now and really want to get wasted."

"Amen to that," Drew muttered. A couple of people laughed, but not Jones.

"What's happening, Michael?" he asked.

"Can I just—" I stood and put the paper on my chair. "Look, I'm sorry, I just need some air."

Jones didn't stop me when I hurried from the room, but I heard him ordering someone to give me some space. I appreciated it, but space wasn't what I wanted. I wanted a drink and 4mg of Xanax. I wanted to put a stop to the incessant merry-go-round of regretful thoughts in my brain.

Speed-walking through the common area and past the office, I shoved open the back door and stepped out onto the courtyard. The wind hit me like a sledgehammer in the chest, but everything slowed down and reset, my anxiety dialing back now that I could suck in breaths without worrying about trying to appear calm.

After several moments, I hunkered down and forced myself to reflect.

Had I freaked out because I needed to drink? No. But I wanted to drink because I'd freaked out. And I'd freaked out because my future with Nunzio looked bleak. And while stuck in the confines of the center, I couldn't do a damn thing about it.

Chapter Twenty

February

BEFORE LEAVING the center, I exchanged contact information with Jones. He offered to be my unofficial sponsor, and that didn't sound like a terrible idea, especially since he continued to show interest in Raymond. It would be nice for him to have more support.

I returned to a house that looked cleaner than it had in months, and a room that Raymond had emptied of all pills and alcohol.

I walked from room to room and tried to figure out why things were so different. The biggest alterations were the absence of our mother's porcelain saints and Jesus pictures, and the cleared out master bedroom. Raymond had removed the bed, and he'd lugged up workout equipment from the basement.

I'd avoided the room for the past year because it had reminded me too much of my mother, and then because it was where my father had died. Now the same heaviness didn't swallow me up when I stepped over the threshold. It felt new.

"Nunzio helped me," Raymond said. He stood in the middle of the room, looking around. "I told him it was driving me crazy, feeling like this room was off-limits, and it was spooking me nonstop, so we made some changes. You're not pissed, are you?"

"No. Of course not." I hadn't even remembered that we had so much equipment downstairs. I'd been paying hundreds of dollars a year for a gym membership for no reason. "The house looks great, Ray. You're turning out to be pretty useful."

Raymond sat on the weight bench. "I know, right? Who'd have thought? Maybe soon I'll get a real girlfriend and everything."

"Or a boyfriend."

"Shut up with that! Damn." He flushed and became fascinated with a screw in the side of the bench. "You're annoying."

"What's the big deal? You apparently watched me and Nunzio dry hump for *fifty hours*—"

"First off—it wasn't that dry. Second—I did not watch."

"And you went on a date with David...."

"Yo, if the dude wanted to buy me Italian food, who am I to say no?"

"Also," I said, enjoying this more than I had any right to, "now that I think about it, you used to follow Nunzio around quite a bit."

"Because he was like my brother!"

I laughed, the sound too loud in the quiet house, and only cracked up more when his ears turned bright red.

"I'm sorry, I'll stop."

"Uh-huh." Raymond scowled. "I should have made your sorry ass walk from Queens Village."

I tried to stop grinning and failed. "I swear, I'll stop."

Raymond swept his hand over the leather bench. "I feel funny not telling him you're home."

My smile wilted. "Don't. Besides, it's Friday night. He's probably out partying."

"True, but still. He was really worried about you. I don't know what the deal is between you two, but you're both getting on my nerves. I'm tired of running between y'all like a fucking messenger service."

"You won't have to anymore. I'm going to go see him myself in the morning."

"Good. Your drama is stressing me out."

"Oh, pobrecito." I turned away from the transformed room. "Come downstairs and I'll teach you how to make a damn pot of rice."

It was the first time I'd spent an entire evening with my brother without getting annoyed or aggravated, and I listened with rapt interest when he talked about his new job. I wasn't sure if it had been my father passing or my own downward spiral that had triggered Raymond's change, but I was proud of him.

When I went to bed in my room for the first time in a month, I felt optimistic, but it didn't last.

My thoughts turned to Nunzio and all the things I wanted to say. Trying to figure out the right words kept me up for more than half the night, and I got out of bed before sunrise.

I couldn't wait anymore. I needed to know where we stood.

IT WAS six o'clock on a Saturday, which meant the likelihood of Nunzio being awake was nil. I tapped a light rhythm on his door and waited. Several seconds went by without a hint of noise inside the apartment.

I wondered if someone else was inside with him—wrapped up in those long, strong arms and crushed against his chest. If so, I didn't want to see it. I didn't even want to know. Or worse, maybe he wasn't home. Maybe he was dating someone and he was sleeping at their house, a rare occurrence that usually meant it was going in a direction that was uncommon for Nunzio.

I knocked again, louder this time, and clenched my teeth until I heard the rustle of footsteps on the other side of the door. There was a slight pause before the locks unbolted, and then, for the first time in weeks, Nunzio was in front of me, wearing nothing but a pair of briefs.

My heart swelled at the sight of him, but I stopped myself from striding forward and yanking him into an embrace. I stopped myself from saying anything at all. I just took in his sleepy, tousled form, the heavy-lidded eyes and the slight purse of his mouth, the line between his brows, and wondered if he would ask me to leave.

"Why didn't you tell me you were out?" he asked, not moving from the center of the door.

"I wanted to surprise you."

Nunzio's eyes raked over my body before settling on my face. His inscrutable expression didn't shift.

"Look, if you're not alone—"

"I am."

"Okay…." Relief flooded me, but it didn't wash away my uncertainty. "Did you get the message I left you?"

"Yeah. I did."

I almost asked why he'd never called me, but I bit down on the question. He didn't owe me answers. He'd stood by me without inserting himself. Watching out for Raymond, asking about me, and helping to take care of the house. I was the one who needed to explain.

"I know you're pissed at me," I said after a beat of tense silence. "And I deserve it. I was a dick to you and made dick moves."

Nunzio's mouth twitched.

"But if you would just talk to me—if you'd give me a chance—"

"Mikey, it's too early to be having this conversation. I went to bed less than two hours ago. Can we do this later?"

The jumbled apology clogged in my throat, and I took an automatic step back. He grabbed the front of my coat.

"You can come in, but we can talk later if you want to wait."

"Yes. Of course."

Some of the tension melted from my body, and I followed him inside. He detoured to his bedroom, and there was an immediate sound of bedsprings creaking. I didn't go in, and he didn't invite me, so I slunk to the living room and sat on the couch with a head full of questions and doubts.

He'd only gotten in a couple of hours ago? Where had he been? Partying with friends? Or had he been fucking someone else? Him being alone this morning didn't mean he'd been celibate for the past month.

I told myself to sleep while he slept, and to rest my racing thoughts so I wasn't high-strung and on edge when he woke, but it was a lost cause. I paced his apartment as the sun came up and felt like an intruder because it had been so long.

The sun barely managed to stream through the heavy curtains to illuminate the tidy living room and kitchen, but I still looked for clues to what he had been up to for the past couple of months.

I found none.

After an hour, I dropped onto the couch and shut my eyes. With willpower alone, I managed to doze for a few minutes and woke up a while later to the same stillness and quiet. Unable to stop myself any longer, I crossed the distance to his bedroom and moved silently toward his bed.

I had intended to merely wake him, but I wound up toeing off my shoes and slipping into the bed beside him. We weren't touching, but he was near enough for me to absorb the warmth of his body and to inhale his scent. I let the comfort of his closeness lure me into a doze.

When I awoke for the second time, it could not have been more than an hour later. Nunzio had rolled onto his stomach beside me. A single ray of sunlight had broken through the curtains and streamed down to his lean back like a beacon.

I couldn't stop drinking him in and wanted so badly to touch him that my body ached for it. The comforter was caught at the small of his back and exposing enough flesh to make my hands twitch. The golden streak of sunlight highlighted a splash of freckles across his shoulders and a faded scar on the back of his neck from a badly aimed Roman candle on a Fourth of July nearly twenty years ago. I remembered the day like it was yesterday, and the way I'd clung to him after, apologetic and teary-eyed for accidentally hurting my best friend.

Our lives had been intertwined for so long that I'd begun to take for granted just how much I needed him. I'd never acknowledged the quiet relief I'd felt each time he refused to settle down in a steady relationship, or the times I had absently compared myself to his lovers to see if they measured up.

Now I could think back, without denial, and identify how frequently I'd gravitated to him for comfort or affection. Like the weekend before school started when I'd stood over his sleeping form and had stopped pretending I didn't want him even if I'd still been ignoring how deep my feelings ran.

But I was done fighting it.

If he didn't want me, he would tell me, but for now I couldn't deny my body's need to be close.

I stretched out alongside him, and pressed a palm to his back, sliding it up in one glide. He stirred, inhaling deeper, and rolled onto his side facing the window. I closed my fingers around his shoulder and shook lightly, but he had already fallen back asleep, his breathing deep and rhythmic.

I slid beneath the comforter and aligned the full length of my front with his hard back. My body was already reacting to the feel of him, dick semihard in my sweatpants, but I only wanted to be next to him, to refamiliarize myself with this gorgeous man who was my best friend, my family, and sometime lover. I matched my breathing to his, the knots and tangles of my nerves evening out.

My fingers glided through the silky darkness of his hair, moving it away from his neck. I looked at the scar again, the evidence of another time when I'd been too careless with him, and kissed it. The combination of his taste and the feel of his warm skin unfurled desire within me, and I plastered myself to him.

I dragged the rough flat of my tongue over his neck and sealed my lips around the mark. I sucked a bruise into it with enough pressure to elicit a soft moan from Nunzio. Again he stirred, but this time the curve of his ass ground back on my cock with perfect precision. I grasped his hip and slid my hand around to fan out my fingers over his abdomen, guiding him back with gentle motions. He began rocking, still asleep but falling into the rhythm.

I dragged my teeth along the new mark and bit lightly.

The sound it drew out of him was louder, huskier, and followed by a softly moaned, "Mikey...."

My heart hammered my ribcage. I stopped holding back.

I kissed down, attached my mouth to the junction between his neck and shoulder, and sucked. I rocked harder and slid my hand down and between his muscular thighs. His dick was like an iron rod in my hand. I pumped it through the thin material, and he awoke with a groan mingled with a confused exhalation that sounded a lot like my name.

Nunzio twisted his arm back to clutch a handful of my hair, wrenching my mouth away from his shoulder. I panted, feeling caught and desperate. When he turned his face toward me, I attacked his mouth without waiting to see if he wanted it. For a flicker of a moment he didn't respond, enough of a pause for me to notice the tension in his body, but then his hand clenched in my hair and his tongue slicked against mine. Hot, wet, sloppy—I was a man starved and begging for more through breathless gasps and wordless pleas.

He pulled away only long enough to roll over, pinning me to the bed with his full weight and tonguing me so thoroughly I short-circuited. My brain filled with white noise. I was a clean slate filled with a base desire to be touched, kissed, and fucked by Nunzio.

I arched into him, letting him feel how hard I was, how much I wanted him, but his mouth ripped away again. I knew he was still angry with me; I could feel it in the violent grip of his hands and see it in the glitter of his vivid blue eyes when they opened.

Even if he later told me we couldn't be together, I wanted him one last time.

Nunzio sat up on his knees and dragged me with him, hand twisting in my collar. I nearly choked when he pulled, almost ripping it, before tossing my shirt to the side. I hadn't fully recovered when he yanked me in for another searing kiss. His hand at the back of my neck gripped hard, as did the one sliding down my baggy sweatpants to squeeze one of my asscheeks. He clutched it, dragging the blunt edge of his fingernails along the soft flesh, and then swatted it hard enough for me to flinch.

I gasped, lips parting while he continued to lick at me. Nunzio smacked my ass again and saliva skewed down my chin. I hissed, but the sensation went firmly to my engorged cock.

I pressed my forehead to his, and I knew he could read every message I was sending. *Be as rough as you want, but don't stop.*

Nunzio's breath gusted out in a whoosh. His eyes shut briefly, and then he ripped down my pants in a way that caused my cock to slap back against my stomach once freed. He wrapped his fingers around it, sliding his thumb along the sticky slit, and jerked twice. I moaned, a shuddering breathy sound, and convulsed when he brought his thumb to his lips and licked.

Nothing was gentle about the way Nunzio shoved me down, or the way he hunched over to fuck my mouth. I took what he gave me, relaxing my throat muscles so he could go in balls deep.

"Yeah...."

He humped my face with intent and only pulled back when I gagged. The head of his dick bumped my lips, smearing the salty taste of his precome all over them.

Nunzio breathed raggedly, manhandling me into the position he wanted, and shoved me facedown on the bed. His lips brushed the back of my neck, his tongue licking down between my shoulder blades before he nibbled along the ridges of my spine. By the time Nunzio's teeth sank into one of the likely reddened globes of my ass, I was undulating on the bed, the desire to get off a primal instinct that removed any sense of shame.

The wet tip of Nunzio's tongue dragged down and he pulled my asscheeks apart. I felt damp pressure against my hole. I groaned, the sound muffled by a pillow, and I dipped my chest lower to the bed. There was something so inherently dirty about his saliva sliding down my crack to pool on the sheet, and his tongue driving into me, that I was on the brink of shooting by the time he stopped.

"Nunzio, please."

"Please what?"

"Fuck me."

He shoved two fingers into my saliva-slicked hole, and I cried out, instinctively riding back on them. "God, yes."

Nunzio's voice was a low growl. "Tell me exactly what you want." His fingers jabbed deep, and I trembled.

"Use me," I gritted out. "Fill me up with your fucking come."

Nunzio's fingers yanked out. He reached out to retrieve a bottle of lube from his nightstand before smearing it on my hole with the head of his dick. After teasing me, he pushed in slow and steady, and my toes curled in the sheet.

"*Shit.*"

He slid home and started thrusting with a punishing pace. His palm braced my neck, the other between my shoulder blades, and he rode my ass with such violence the sounds that left my mouth were jarred and breathless. I managed to plead for more in a jumble of unintelligible syllables.

Nunzio grabbed a fistful of my hair and jerked back my head before clasping his hand around my throat. I shouted, again caught between the need to be dominated and a sharp blossom of pain, before the pressure eased and our position shifted. He stretched across my back, pinning me to the bed instead of keeping me upraised the way I had been before. His arm encircled my throat, trapping me in place, while his free hand gripped my jaw and turned it toward him.

When Nunzio fucked into me again, I could see his face—flushed and no longer tightened with traces of anger. We moved languidly at first, but soon the bed was wrecked and sweaty, and I could feel him starting to peak.

Nunzio rolled to the side, taking me with him, and pulled up one of my thighs. Half-twisted but mostly on my back, I was able to reach down to jerk myself off while our mouths sealed together and he drilled into me.

I came first, chest hollowing, eyes watering, and sobbing against the crush of his lips. I was still clutching my shaft when he flooded my ass with a hot rush of semen.

After several long moments of breathless gasping, Nunzio pulled out with a sigh, face still twisted with the agonizing dregs of his orgasm. I kissed him again even though he was breathing too hard to respond, and tuned in to the thrum of his heart.

"Christ, Mikey." His arms loosened around me.

I nodded for lack of anything coherent to say. The room felt too hot, but I didn't want him to pull away. He didn't. His body molded to mine, fitting perfectly.

When Nunzio looked up at me, I shot him a tiny smile.

"So," he said softly, "how was rehab?"

"It wasn't exactly a good time, but I needed to be ripped out of my slump."

"Is that what you're calling it?" Nunzio's brow creased. "Your slump?"

"To put it mildly, yeah." I touched the small of his back, and I ran my fingers along the indentation above his ass. "I can't believe I got that bad. I thought I could handle myself better than that."

Nunzio's gaze dropped. A thread of tension went through his body. "I didn't know how to help you."

"How could you? I wouldn't even let you in. I needed to figure out how to help myself."

"And you're at that point now?"

"I am."

"Good." A faint smile warmed Nunzio's face. "What about work?"

"Work will be fine. I'm going back at the beginning of March."

"I'm glad. You're made for that job."

"But you'll be gone."

Pale blue eyes flashed up at me. "Yeah. I'll be at Gateway, that LGBT youth center we used to hang out at when we were kids."

I waited for him to say more but received nothing further. When we only stared at each other, I forced a tight smile. "I met a couple of kids in rehab who might be going to Gateway to get their GED. One is like a combination of Mac and Shawn."

"Oh Jesus."

"Yeah."

Nunzio unwound our limbs and sat up halfway. He stretched and a yawn nearly cracked his jaw. "I'm surprised Raymond didn't tell me you were out. I had him giving me a steady stream of Mikey updates."

"I told him not to. I wanted to talk to you myself. In person."

"Was asking me to come in your ass the conversation you planned?"

"No. That wasn't on the agenda." I propped myself up on my elbow. His body was still generating heat, but I wasn't prepared to back away. "I just wanted to talk, but you're disgustingly beautiful, so molestation happened. Sorry."

"You should apologize. It was a real hardship."

"Was that a pun?"

"An unplanned one." Nunzio cracked a smile. "You seem less miserable, but I don't think post-fuck is an accurate time to assess that type of thing."

"I'm too happy to see you for anything to be accurate. I missed you."

"Did you?"

"Yes. You have no idea."

Nunzio relaxed again.

"While I was gone...." I pulled him closer until our damp skin glided together. "Were you with anyone? I don't have the right to ask, but I want to know."

"Would it matter?"

My fingers tightened on him. "No, but I need to know how badly I fucked up."

Nunzio's gaze softened. He chuckled. "No, Mikey. There wasn't anyone else. In your message you asked me to wait for you, and I did. I've been waiting for twenty fucking years. I could hold out for a month."

I released a shaky breath. For the first time in weeks, months, the heaviness receded from my shoulders.

"You... have no idea how much I regret acting the way I did. I was trying not to drag anyone down with me but I pushed you away, and I left Raymond caught out there after having just found our father dead. I was miserable and hating myself, but I abandoned both of you, and I'm sorry. I would have understood if you'd decided not to wait."

"Damn, is this like an AA step?"

I scowled. "I'm serious, Nunzio. It has nothing to do with rehab. Yeah, I had time to dry out and get my head together, but no one gave me a script. Can you stop being a smart-ass for a minute so we can have a serious conversation?"

"Sorry." Nunzio grabbed my hand, bringing it up to his lips. He kissed it, eyes not leaving mine. "I'm nervous."

I stared, incredulous. "You? Why?"

"Because last time we had a serious conversation you advised me to walk out of your life. That's why I've been avoiding seeing you. I thought we both needed space. I wanted you to be sure that you really wanted to patch things up with me, that you really meant what you said in that message, before I came around with more expectations. For the past few months, I'd been so demanding of you that I ended up pushing you away, and I couldn't even see it at that time."

"Yeah, because I wasn't trying to talk to you about it."

Nunzio looked down. "It wasn't just on you, Mikey."

I marveled at how we'd gotten to this point. We knew everything about each other, had been side by side for over half our lives, but I could tell he was just as terrified as I was that something had irrevocably changed.

"I would never hurt you, Nunzio. That wasn't the real me. You know the real me."

"I know the real you wasn't feeling me the way I was feeling you. You said it even before everything went down with your dad."

I leaned away, trying to collect all the words I'd put together on the train ride over. Somewhere along the line, they'd scattered and I couldn't reel them in in the correct order. I had faint indications of mentioning that humid night in July, and I'd planned to confess to the way my body had reacted to every casual and affectionate touch after that night, and how the threesome had activated a desire so strong that I'd been scared of it.

All of the things I'd never thought about cohesively, all of the things I'd never said but planned to say this morning, flitted around my brain and demanded to be let out. But now that we were sitting together on the same sweat-soaked bed, his body flawless and his expression so guarded, it didn't seem good enough.

"When I was in the hospital, there was this moment," I said finally. "When I realized that... I can't be without you. And then when I was in rehab, I kept dreaming about you. Almost every night, I dreamed about us together or you with someone else, and I woke up in a panic at the idea of you moving on. It hit me that even after dating him for two years, I'd never once had those feelings for Clive. Even after he dumped me, it was done. I didn't wonder what he was doing, and I didn't dream about him. It was just a closed chapter in my life, and I was over it."

Nunzio swallowed so heavily that I could see his throat working. I scooted closer.

"But it wasn't like that with you, and I've been scared that I blew it and missed my shot." When he continued to sit there, gazing at me and tightening his fingers with mine, I pushed again. "Did I?"

"No."

Relief hit me with such intensity that my shoulders sagged. Nunzio still looked unsure, still seemed hesitant to believe what I was saying. All of his doubt mirrored what I'd been feeling only a moment ago. But it was for nothing. We were finally on the same page.

"Go on a date with me."

Nunzio stared.

"Come on, niño." I squeezed his thigh. "Go on a date with me. Please?"

He pushed my hand away. "Come on, Mikey."

"I'm serious. I swear to God." I grabbed at him again, this time catching his wrist as he started to rise from the bed. "I want to be with you, and not just to be friends with benefits. I want us to date. A real relationship. Just us."

The tension was starting to dissipate from his posture. "Like movies and dinner? Holding hands? You calling me your boyfriend? The whole cheesy deal?"

"Yes. I want the whole thing. I want every part of you, and I won't fuck up again. We can make this work. I love you, niño."

Nunzio continued to analyze my face, my body language, and was so cautious that I fought the urge to shake him. But after a moment, he flashed his brilliant Medici grin.

"Let's do it. You can start by buying me breakfast."

I kissed his forehead. "Breakfast it is."

I tried to contain the enormity of my emotions, but he could see through me. At my best and worst, Nunzio had always seen me. What I wanted, what I needed, and the fact that we belonged together. He'd known all along, and I was just catching up.

It had taken two decades but we had finally made it, and nothing would ever again keep us apart.

Coming Soon

Sunset Park

Five Boroughs: Book 2

By Santino Hassell

Raymond Rodriguez's days of shoving responsibility to the wayside are over. His older brother wants to live with his boyfriend, so Raymond has to get his act together and find a place of his own. But when out-and-proud David Butler offers to be his roommate, Raymond agrees for reasons other than needing a place to crash.

David is Raymond's opposite in almost every way—he's Connecticut prim and proper while Raymond is a sarcastic longshoreman from Queens—but their friendship is solid. Their closeness surprises everyone as does their not-so-playful flirtation since Raymond has always kept his bicurious side a secret.

Once they're under the same roof, flirting turns physical, and soon their easy camaraderie is in danger of being lost to frustrating sexual tension and the stark cultural differences that set them apart. Now Raymond not only has to commit to his new independence—he has to commit to his feelings for David or risk losing him for good.

Coming Soon to
http://www.dreamspinnerpress.com

SANTINO HASSELL was raised by a conservative family, but he was anything but traditional. He grew up to be a smart-mouthed, school-cutting grunge kid, then a transient twentysomething, and eventually transformed into the romance-writing and sarcasm-loving guy that people know him as today.

Santino is a dedicated gamer, a former anime-watcher and fanfic writer, an ASoIaF mega nerd, a Grindr enthusiast, but most of all he is a writer of queer fiction that is heavily influenced by the gritty, urban landscape of New York City, his belief that human relationships are complex and flawed, and his own life experiences.

To learn more about Santino you can follow him on:
Twitter: @santinohassell
Facebook: http://www.facebook.com/theonlysonnyhassell
Instagram: santinohassell
Goodreads: http://bit.ly/1yBeaqc

EMERGENCY CONTACT

ELLE BROWNLEE

http://www.dreamspinnerpress.com

GERRY'S LION
ashavan doyon

http://www.dreamspinnerpress.com

SECOND-STORY MAN

ROBERT P. ROWE

http://www.dreamspinnerpress.com

UNFORTUNATE
SON

Shae Connor

SONS
BOOK ONE

http://www.dreamspinnerpress.com

THE WAY
THINGS ARE

A.J. THOMAS

http://www.dreamspinnerpress.com

FOR **MORE** OF THE **BEST GAY ROMANCE**

DREAMSPINNER
PRESS
dreamspinnerpress.com

CPSIA information can be obtained
at www.ICGtesting.com
Printed in the USA
BVOW06s0040060217
475375BV00007B/130/P